Pennyroyal Academy

Pennyroyal Academy

M. A. LARSON

G. P. Putnam's Sons
An Imprint of Penguin Group (USA)

G. P. PUTNAM'S SONS
Published by the Penguin Group
Penguin Group (USA) LLC
375 Hudson Street

New York, NY 10014
USA | Canada | UK | Ireland | Australia
New Zealand | India | South Africa | China
penguin.com
A Penguin Random House Company

Library of Congress Cataloging-in-Publication Data
Larson, M. A.   Pennyroyal Academy / M. A. Larson.   pages cm
Summary: "A girl from the forest enlists at Pennyroyal Academy, where princesses and knights are trained to battle the two great menaces of the day: witches and dragons"—Provided by publisher. [1. Fantasy. 2. Military education—Fiction. 3. Schools—Fiction. 4. Princesses—Fiction. 5. Knights and knighthood—Fiction. 6. Witches—Fiction. 7. Dragons—Fiction. 8. Adventure and adventurers—Fiction.] I. Title.
PZ7.L323944Pen 2014   [Fic]—dc23   2014014516

Printed in the United States of America.
ISBN 978-0-399-16324-1
3 5 7 9 10 8 6 4

Design by Annie Ericsson.
Text set in Albertina MT Std.

For Hannah, for everything.

If I'm still in this forest by nightfall, I'll never leave it again.

The girl's eyes darted through the misty pines. The air was wet, though it wasn't exactly raining. Everywhere she turned she found dull gray shadows, and her mind put monsters in all of them. The only sound was her own frantic breath. No birdsong. No tumbling water. Nothing.

A leafy tendril snaked up from the undergrowth and began to slither around her ankle. She tore her leg free and raced into the mist, her bare feet crackling through a carpet of dead leaves and fallen needles. Towering trees swayed overhead like mossy giants, and the small patches of sky she could see were black with clouds. Night was coming. And so were the things that lurked in the fog.

As she hurdled over a rotting stump, a heart-sized dragon scale necklace bounced against her chest. A matted drape of spiders' webs covered her body, her only protection against the elements. The rest of her was streaked with mud. She had been lost in this forest for three days. Had seen and heard things that still didn't seem real—a weathered thighbone so thick and long it could only have belonged to a giant; the deafening thunder of thrumming wings and the shadow of an enormous dragonfly passing above the canopy. Three days lost and she knew, one way or another, there would not be a fourth—

CRACK! The girl jumped at the sound, then heard the popping crackle of splitting wood somewhere above. She wheeled just in time to see the hairy branch of a beech tree swooping down. It slammed into her, knocking her over the edge of a hill. She tumbled through moldy black sludge to the bottom, where she collided with a pine trunk. She eased herself up, rolling her shoulder to be sure her arm wasn't broken.

The first day, the day she had left home, she had taken a savage beating from the trees. Her father had always warned her to stay out of enchanted forests, but she was still taken aback by the trees' ferocity. She had slowly begun to learn their moods and patterns, and before long was able to anticipate their attacks. She tried to avoid beeches especially, as they seemed the most malicious.

Today it wasn't the trees that frightened her. The sun and moon and stars had all gone, along with chirping birds and skittering goblins. In their place, the clouds and mist, and the distinct feeling that something else was out there.

But what?

She listened, silent and still, though all she heard was wind shivering through leaves. As she stood, her emerald-green eyes narrowed. There, faintly visible through the dusk, was a distant pinpoint of light. The window of a cottage.

She had always been cautious, much more so than her sister, but once she saw that light, she ran for it. The cottage was small, its timbers frayed and soggy. This was the first shelter she had seen since leaving home, and yet something inside her screamed to turn back and run and then run some more.

Would I rather be out here when the sun is gone, or inside?

She ignored her instincts and edged to the window, grabbing hold of the sill. Clumps of rot crumbled off in her hands. She wiped them away, then leaned in again.

Firelight washed across her face, and her stomach roared. At the far side of the room, a thick, brown liquid bubbled over the rim of a cauldron, sizzling on the embers. She couldn't see anything else, but that was enough. Her hunger drove her to the door, but as she clutched the handle, panic swarmed up through the soles of her feet like a million wasps.

Something's not right here—

A wolf's lonesome howl echoed down from the mountains, and she knew she had no choice. She gave the door a hard shove, but it didn't budge. She threw her shoulder into it and finally it barked open.

"Hello?" she said with a small, shaking voice. There was no answer, only the soft pop of the fire. The floorboards screamed as she stepped inside and shouldered the door shut with a resonant thud.

The cottage was warm and tidy. Beneath the lone window sat a wooden table, where waterflies buzzed around a pile of blackish-red slop. Next to that were a rusted hand-crank machine and several neat stacks of multicolored candies. A chill ran down her arms.

In the corner, beyond the hearth, next to the open door of a small bedchamber, stood a large cage, oranged with rust and age. It was just the right size to hold a person. Next to it, a small pile of children's shoes spilled across the floor.

She turned to run, but the door that had just been so solidly stuck now hung open. And outside, footsteps crackled through the leaves.

She looked for another way out, but it was too late, so she dove under the table and hugged her legs to her chest. A thick drip of red slid through the slats of the table and plopped on the floor at her feet.

Oh please oh please oh please . . .

A pair of muddy riding boots clomped across the floorboards, shoved along by an old woman draped in layer upon layer of decaying black robes. The door slammed shut behind them, though no one was there to slam it.

The girl's blood ran cold. She was trapped.

The old woman, hunched and bent like a river, shoved her prisoner into the cage and rattled the latch home. He was around the girl's same age, and wore a dark gray leather doublet embroidered in burgundy. His dark hair was in knots from countless hours on horseback, and his arms were bound behind his back.

The cage was too small for him to stand, so he threw his shoulder into the door. The frail metal clanged, but held fast.

His captor went to the cauldron to stir her bubbling broth, which hissed against the flames like a chorus of angry snakes. "Now then, what have I done with my jars?" Her voice was full of contradictions, soft and sweet, but with a knife-edge of menace. "It's been so long since I had a heart to put in them. *Eh-heh-heh-heh-heh . . .*" She leaned her ladle against the stone gently, like a kindly grandmother might, then shuffled into the bedchamber.

Now! Now! NOW!

But the girl sat frozen in place, watching as the boy strained and writhed against his bonds. He leaned back to give the door a solid kick, and that's when he saw her.

"*Hey!*" he hissed, jerking his head toward the latch. Tears welled in her eyes, and she suddenly felt as though she might faint. "*I know you're scared, but open this cage and you'll leave here alive. I swear it.*"

She pulled her legs tighter, clinging to them like the last jagged stone before a waterfall. But as her tears fell and her heart thumped in her chest, she noticed something in his eyes that calmed her. He wasn't afraid. When he said he could keep her alive, he believed it.

Somehow, before her own fear could stop her, she began to scoot forward. Each creak of the floorboards made her want to scream and run for the door, but she kept her eyes fixed on his and crept closer and closer to the cage.

"Hurry!" he whispered.

Her trembling fingers reached for the latch. She tried to work it free as gently as she could, but the metal had become violently angry over the ages. It screamed open.

"What's this?"

The girl wheeled and fell back against the cage. She had never seen a witch before, but there could be little doubt that that was what stood before her now. The witch didn't move, just stared at her with milky yellow eyes and a wide, toothless grin. Her skin was the color of a worm after three days' rain, and it drooped from her bones like a melted candle.

"Open the latch!" shouted the boy, slamming his shoulder against the door.

But the witch's gaze paralyzed the girl. The hag's eyes bored straight into her own, slicing through her brain and down her throat. The girl gasped for air as the witch stared deeper, deeper, straight for her heart. She was choking on hate, anguish, fear . . . the feeling that she had already seen the sun for the last time without even realizing it. The witch was *inside* her—

"RUN!" shouted the boy as the cage door finally crashed open.

The girl snapped free of the witch's gaze. All that choking awfulness slid out of her throat and she could breathe once more. The dragon scale whipped round to her back as she sprinted for the door. She threw it open and burst out into the night. The blackness of the woods and the swirling fog made it seem like the witch was everywhere at once. Even in the open forest, the girl was trapped.

"Over here!" The boy stood next to a massive white horse that glowed in the moonlight like a ghost.

"What? On that?"

"These are her woods! We'll never make it on foot!"

She grimaced, but knew she would have to trust him. As she raced to the horse, the flickering firelight inside the cottage was suddenly extinguished. Smoky blackness, darker than the night, wafted from the door.

"*Eh-heh-heh-heh-heh-heh-heh-heh-heh* . . ." The cackle was no longer that of a feeble old lady. It had morphed into something elemental and terrifying.

The girl swung onto the horse's back. Beneath the smooth white needles of hair she could feel sweat and muscle and knew the boy was right: this was their only chance of escape. She reached down and grabbed the rope binding his arms, hauling him facedown across the horse's backside. Black smoke billowed from the door, and the cackling reverberated through the forest like it was coming from the fog itself.

"Let's go!" grunted the boy, but the girl was transfixed by the figure floating out of the cottage. The witch's body had distorted into something monstrous, long-limbed and inhuman. Her tattered robes billowed smoke. The skin around her mouth began to crack and split as her smile grew ever wider.

"Take the reins and go!"

The girl wrenched her eyes away. Straps of leather tack dangled from the horse's head and neck. She didn't know what any of it was, so she gripped the mane instead. With her other arm twisted behind her, she clutched the rope around the boy's hands.

"Ride," she whispered, and they lunged away into the night. Every muscle in her body clamped down as she felt the horse's power beneath her. Her fingers clutched the mane so tightly, the knuckles had already gone white. As the horse sailed across uneven ground, each stride threatened to break her grip.

"I can't do it!" she screamed over the thunder of hooves. "I can't!"

"Please . . ." was all the boy could muster. His midsection slammed repeatedly against the horse, forcing the air from his lungs. He couldn't draw breath.

The girl closed her eyes and ground her teeth. *I will not let go. The horse or the rope may slip free, but on my father I will not let go.* She glanced back, and what she saw made her gasp.

The witch, a billowing, spectral fiend, swooped through the trees like an enormous owl. Waves of frigid air swept up from behind as her bony fingers reached forward.

The horse leapt a fallen tree. The landing nearly ripped the mane from the girl's fingers. Her legs, pinned tightly around the horse's shoulders, felt frail and insignificant. Her entire body hurt, but the truly ferocious pain was in the fingers holding the boy's binding. It sawed deeper into her raw skin with each stride. *I can't hold on . . . It's all coming loose . . .*

"Water . . ." he croaked.

She scanned the darkness until something in the distance caught her eye. The pale reflection of moonlight on water. A river.

She jerked the mane, steering the horse toward it. The boy's weight pulled the rope to the final joints of her fingers. She was going to lose him.

Suddenly, she released the mane and grabbed the boy's vest just as the rope slipped from her fingers. Now her legs, locked around the horse's neck, were the only thing keeping them both alive. She lay twisted along the horse's back, and the headlong gallop was driving the leather saddle into her side. The boy was barely on the horse, and she had no way of knowing if he was alive or dead.

The bristles of the horse's coat scraped farther down her legs. Lower . . . lower . . . nearly to the ankles. Behind them, a wall of pure terror rose up. The witch was enormous, wraithlike, her arms extending from a cloak of swirling smoke.

Then, in an instant, the girl lost all sense of gravity. Her body soared through the air. The boy was gone. The horse was gone. And in the next moment, her lungs filled with icy water. With shocking clarity, she realized she had made it to the river. As she began to panic for breath, she found the rippling moonlight beneath her. She righted herself and kicked toward it until her head popped into the crisp night air, and she coughed until her lungs were dry.

The witch had gone, hiding no doubt in the fog at the

shoreline. On the opposite bank, where the air was clear and stars painted the sky, the white horse staggered out of the water.

She swam toward the bank until finally her feet touched the rough, slimy stones of the river bottom, then pulled herself ashore like some ancient creature, sobbing and gasping for breath.

I made it. A miracle's happened and I'm still alive.

Her legs buckled and she dropped to the pebbly shore. She forced herself onto her back, filling her lungs with the night until her panic began to recede. As she lay there, astonished to be alive, a strange thought crossed her mind. This night sky, a pale swipe of purple-white across a black field of untold numbers of stars, was the single most beautiful thing she had ever seen. Crickets chirped rhythmically from the trees. The choking mold stench was gone. Somehow, she really was alive.

"Here . . ." came a weak voice from farther down the gurgling river. She sat up. The horse stood at the waterline nuzzling a dark figure. It was the boy, arms still bound behind him, lying facedown in the sand, his legs dangling in the current. She went to him, but her fingers were too stiff and sore to grip the crude knot. She tried pulling on the rope, and it suddenly crumbled away like it was a thousand years old.

The boy, battered and weak, pushed himself over, too dazed to drag his legs free of the water. His teeth chattered, his whole body shuddering in the steady night breeze. "You must be . . . f-frozen solid . . ."

The girl, barefoot, sodden to the bone, and wearing only a thin covering of spiderwebs, said nothing.

"What . . . what's your n-name?"

Her eyes fell to the rocks. "I don't have one."

2

THE GIRL STARED, not at the fire, but above it, where orange sparks wisped into the night sky to join the stars. The soft crackle of burning wood and the comforting smell of flame reminded her of home, somewhere that now seemed like one of the distant galaxies floating in the blackness above. She had always had an affinity for fire, though she had never quite learned to make one. Her father tried to teach her, and her sister could do it easily, but the best she could manage was a faint thread of smoke. Now that the tendons in her fingers had loosened, she picked up another branch and laid it on the pile, then watched as the fire claimed it.

"Has anyone told you you're a delightful conversationalist?" said the boy, watching her through the fire with big, amused eyes. She didn't respond. "No, I expect they haven't."

In the calm of the night, far from the border of the enchanted forest, the girl noticed something about her companion. The way only half his mouth smiled, the brightness in his eyes, the sense of constant amusement about him . . . It all added up to someone who very much enjoyed being alive, and all because he had had the good fortune to be born as himself.

"You can finish with the wood now. There are bandits out there." He lifted a cast-iron skillet from the fire and slid two bubbling eggs onto a pewter plate, which he handed to her. She shoveled them into her mouth, so hungry that she didn't even mind the quick scald as the yolks broke. With a chuckle and a shake of his head, he took a few more out of a silk sack and cracked them into the pan. She had refused when he had offered her clothes, but food she could not resist.

"For your memoirs, my name is Remington. Of Brentano, in the Western Kingdoms."

She licked the yolk from her fingers. He sighed, though the grin never left his face. His attempts to draw her out thus far had all ended this way. She hadn't helped him clear brush or build the fire or even gather cordgrass for his horse. She just watched him with mild suspicion as he worked.

"Are there more like you?" she asked.

"Pardon?" he laughed. She looked to the fire in embarrassment. Her thoughts somehow seemed inferior next to the smooth polish of his words. His voice was deep and refined, and that, too, made her feel uncomfortable. "Are there more like me? Well, according to most girls I've met, no." When she didn't oblige him with a laugh, he softened his demeanor. "What were you doing out there by yourself anyway? Enchanted forests and barefoot girls don't have a particularly warm history."

She set her plate in the dirt and studied him. Could she trust him? She already had several times. And here she was, alive and filling her belly. Perhaps he had earned the right to be trusted again. She reached into her tangled mass of webs, pulled out a rain-warped parchment, and handed it to him.

"I'm looking for her."

He unfolded the parchment. It was a hand-painted notice depicting a girl in a golden dress standing before a castle in a heroic pose. In ornate script, it read:

Pennyroyal Academy
Seeking bold, courageous youths to become
tomorrow's princesses and knights
Blood restrictions lifted—Come one, come all!

"These bloody things are everywhere. They really are desperate, aren't they? It's not to say you wouldn't make a fine princess, only that they've never recruited this aggressively before."

"So you know her?"

"I . . . suppose you could say that. You're really quite lucky I came along to rescue you—"

"Hang on, *you* rescued *me*?"

He fought away a smile, but was only partly successful. "We'll ride to Marburg together. I'm headed to the Academy myself to train as a knight."

She leapt to her feet, snatching the parchment from his hands. "You're a knight?"

"No," he said, looking at his suddenly empty fingers, "which is why I'm enlisting. Look, you're not terribly gracious, are you?"

She folded the parchment, scowling at him. He shook his head and took the skillet off the fire. He plated the eggs and prepared to eat, then, with a sigh, offered this serving to her as well. Her mother had told her from her earliest memories to steer clear of knights, just as her father had warned her against witches. Remington insisted he wasn't a knight—yet—but even the mention of the word made her nervous. She kept a suspicious eye on him as she took the offered eggs and sat back down.

He stood and stretched, then walked to the tree where his horse was tied and started unclasping something from the saddle. He was tall and lean, with the effortless bearing of an athlete who trusted his body to always do what he asked. *And he intends to be a knight,* she thought. *I should have left him in that cage.*

"I'm quite happy to see someone like you enlisting," he said. "The world is far too *unsettled* to be worrying about the color of one's blood, don't you think?" He brought back a small bedroll and tossed it to the dirt next to her. "It's a bit damp, but the fire should sort that out."

He collected the empty plates and set them in front of his horse to lick clean, though she had already done a good job of that. Then he took off his doublet and lay down on the other side of the fire, bunching it up beneath his head. "We ride at first light. Try to get some sleep."

Surrounded by the steady song of crickets, she looked to the stars, confused and exhausted. Her eyes were raw. All she wanted was sleep. But now she was even less certain whether she should trust him. She glanced into the depthless black of the forest. Perhaps she should continue her journey alone . . .

"What if she finds us?" she said. She hadn't meant to actually speak the words, but there they were. Remington propped himself onto an elbow and looked over at her. "I can't do that again. Her eyes . . . It was like she was looking *inside* me."

His smile was gone. He looked as earnest as he had in the cage. "That was a wood witch. They rarely leave the enchanted forest. Once we crossed that river, we were safe. Relatively speaking." She looked away, embarrassed by what she had said, but also comforted by his words.

Within a few minutes, the crackle of the dying fire sent him to sleep and she was alone again. She found a flat sandstone boulder and perched in the dark, thinking. But every thought inevitably led straight back to that cottage. She was safe now, but didn't feel it. The fear echoed on.

She slipped the necklace over her head and studied it under the faint light of the rising moon. A coat of dried mud covered its convex side. She licked her thumb and rubbed it away. Underneath, a smear of dried black stained the scale from edge to edge. And something in that stain, a faint shimmer, caught her eye. She tilted the scale to catch the moonlight and it happened again. The stain itself seemed to be moving.

She lifted the necklace higher to catch the moon's beams and realized it wasn't just the illusion of movement. The stain was shimmering in the light like a vein of gold. And as she lowered it to her eye, it began to swirl and pulse, the blackness moving faster and faster until she could see nothing else—

Suddenly she was plunging through an endless void. She couldn't breathe, couldn't tell up from down. The disorientation was so intense she began to feel ill.

Then, at the bottom of the sickening gyre, an image came into focus. It was the shore of a vast sea, pink with low sun. Someone stood there amidst the crashing waves and scavenging birds. It was Remington. And he held her face in his hands.

"You are the one true Princess of Saudade. I would willingly give my life to see it so." He gently pulled her closer. She parted her lips . . .

Her stomach lurched and everything went black again, but the spiral quickly settled into another image. A crumbling tower in the midst of an endless forest, pelted with rain. A woman in a tunic dress of imperial violet was in great distress. Some unseen magic was forcing her to her knees, her eyes clenched in pain. The girl turned to find the source and a monstrous witch loomed behind her, face obscured beneath a cowled cloak. She stood no less than ten feet, and the sight of her filled the girl's heart with hopelessness and despair. A long, bony arm rose up, and the woman in violet screamed. The girl wanted to go to her, but found she couldn't move, could only watch as the witch forced the woman's head to the stone in a bow of forced subjugation.

The cloaked witch thrust her glaucous arms skyward and the air filled with witches. Hundreds of them, black robes flapping, dispatched to all corners of the land . . .

The girl tore the scale from her eye. Her breath came fast and shallow, a stark contrast to the boy's rhythmic snores, the peaceful thrum of the crickets. It took her a moment to realize that what she had seen wasn't real. Still, the overwhelming feeling of dread lingered. Another wolf's howl echoed in the distance, reminding her that even though she had escaped the enchanted forest, the bad things of the world lurked everywhere.

She perched on the stone all through the night, watching the fire fade from orange to red to black. She tried to force her thoughts to her family, to her home, to anything but the monstrous witch and the unseen horrors lurking beneath that hood.

Finally, the sky grayed to a dim, sleepy blue, and the girl remembered something else from her vision. Not nearly as haunting, but equally as startling. She glanced at Remington, whose arms and legs sprawled everywhere like a giant had tossed him aside. *Why on earth would I want to kiss him? A sworn knight, or soon to be.*

"What, no breakfast? No tea? What have you been doing all morning?" She jerked her eyes away. She had been staring at him, and couldn't say how long, but now he was awake. He sat up, his face slow and sleepy. She looked away again when she found her eyes resting comfortably on his lips.

Remington made quick work of camp, and they rode hard through the morning. Now that she need not worry about the trees trying to kill her, the forest became monotonous, the ride quite exhausting. She clung to his waist, struggling to fight off the sleep that hadn't come the night before.

As the sun rose behind the dim green canopy, the air grew thinner in her lungs. They had been climbing gradually throughout the morning, sometimes up long, slow inclines coated with bracken, other times along steep switchbacks of crumbling basanite or limestone. But nowhere in their journey had the pines cleared enough to give a sense of where they actually were. Finally, after a valiant fight, her eyes fell closed. She drifted for what could have been minutes or hours, never really sleeping, always aware of the crunch of leaves under the horse's hooves.

"Ah, there she is. Pretty as I left her," said Remington. The girl opened her eyes, but couldn't make sense of what lay before her.

They were in high forest country that ended abruptly at a sheer drop. Beyond that, the world fell away into a deep valley feathered with millions of pines and furs. A thin, crooked ridge formed a natural bridge to another mountain forest, splitting the valley in two. The horse stepped onto the narrow trail, but the girl didn't even notice the vertiginous cliffs on either side of her. Because there, at the far end of the ridge, an immense fortress of stone seemed to grow out of the mountain itself. Walls of bone-white limestone, forty feet tall and marred by moss and water stains, encased towering spires where brilliant purple banners danced in the wind. Every surface was topped with battlements as jagged as the ridges of a dragon's back. Beyond the majestic kingdom, another sea of black-green forest rolled away to the ends of the world.

"What is that?" she said, her voice dry and feeble.

"Marburg, jewel of the mountain kingdoms."

Eventually, they reached the end of the trail. The horse stopped at a stony ledge that fell thousands of feet to an unseen bottom. Remington waved an arm, signaling someone in the gatehouse. A tremendous crack echoed across the twin valleys and an enormous wooden bridge began to lower across the chasm. Its timbers groaned under their own weight until it slammed to the ground. *This is how a mouse must feel in the home of a giant.*

The horse clopped onto the drawbridge. Now there was nothing beneath them but open sky and, after a very long drop, a sudden end. Two massive pine doors began to creak apart, broken shafts of arrows still lodged in them from foregone wars, and a previously unknown part of the world opened up before the girl's eyes.

The kingdom, Marburg he had called it, was alive. Ragged-clothed peasants crisscrossed bustling streets. Merchants shouted prices and counteroffers. Mothers chased filthy children who chased even filthier pigs. Woodsmen hauled giant logs. Stoic guardsmen in glinting silver armor stood watch, their spears piercing high into the air. Music poured from unseen windows. And the smells! Burning wood and freshly cut grass and mud and flowers and roasted duck. White plaster structures latticed by dark brown timbers jutted up on either side of the high street, and thatched-roofed cottages squatted down near the mud.

Everywhere she looked, the girl was keenly aware she was missing a dozen other things.

"Look at them!" she cried. "They're just like me!"

They came upon a circle of peasants happily clapping along to an elderly fiddler's song. Three small girls danced in the center with carefree smiles and bare feet. Something about the innocent joy in their faces drew her attention more than anything else she had seen thus far. The fiddler kept a bulging eye on the girls as they giggled and spun one another around. Faster and faster he played, luring them into an impossible game, and soon their feet tangled and they ended up in the dirt, tears of laughter in their eyes.

"Wait," said the girl, twisting to watch as they rode past. "Couldn't we stay? Just for a bit?"

"We're late. Stay if you like, but you'll miss your chance to become a princess."

She watched the girls as long as she could, until finally they disappeared from view. Their happiness was so pure, it made her wistful, and also a bit melancholy. *I was never that carefree.*

Remington reined the horse down an alley past yet another

timber-framed cottage, and almost immediately the joyous hustle and bustle of the high street was gone. The sharp pungency of rotting things made her bury her nose in Remington's doublet as the horse clopped through brackish puddles. The farther down the twisting alley they went, the more clearly she could hear something up ahead. An ominous murmuring sound.

"What is that?"

"That, my dear, is about to be the strangest day of your life." Remington clicked his tongue and the horse cantered up a slight grade in the dirt. Finally, they emerged back into the sunlight.

Across a vast courtyard of cobbled stone there stood an imposing palace of polished black slate and mortar. Castle Marburg. It loomed nobly over a temporary marquee held aloft by three massive timbers. To the side, a line of carriage coaches waited, each hitched to a team of horses. And the sound the girl heard was the combined voice of hundreds of excited girls milling beneath the marquee.

She went numb, unconsciously clutching Remington just a bit more tightly. The girls were all of her same age, each wearing an elegant dress of such a variety of colors the girl had never seen. All different, yet somehow essentially the same. *They're just like me,* she thought. *Only nothing like me at all.*

As Remington's horse crossed the courtyard, she began to notice that they had been noticed. Faces turned to them with unusual expressions. Delight upon seeing Remington, then

22

befuddlement when their eyes landed on her. The din of voices softened. She heard whispers of his name—"Remington"—circulating through the crowd.

His mud-spattered boots hit the stone with a soft thud. "Mind your dismount. Fall on your face before these girls and they'll never let you forget it." Alone on the horse's back, she realized that nearly every eye in the courtyard was focused squarely on her, and she began to go pale. She took his callused hand and slid to the ground. "First test, beautifully passed."

She tried to hide herself behind him, but after adjusting a strap on his saddle, he swung back atop the horse and left her alone on the cobblestones. Alone in a crowd of hundreds.

"Right. I'm off to knights' enlistment."

"Wait!" she said. "What do I do?"

He pointed into the shade beneath the marquee, beyond all the colorful dresses, to several long wooden tables. "You march straight over there and enlist. You've as much right to be here as anyone."

She looked up at him with eyes full of fear. *Take me home! I don't want to be here anymore!* she thought. But no words came.

"'Bravely ventured is half won,' as my father likes to say. The only way to find the girl on your parchment is through that lot." He nodded to the crowd, not at all surprised by the attention coming his way. "Off," he said, rearing the horse onto its hind legs with a dramatic whinny. Then he rode away across the courtyard, leaving a ripple of awed gasps in his wake.

B*RAVELY VENTURED is half won.*

As she stepped forward, her head dizzy and her legs weak and trembling, Remington's words rang hollow. Still, the girl's bare feet moved ahead, one after the other, into the reluctantly parting crowd.

"Is she wearing spiderwebs?"

These girls were draped in linen and lace, silk and tulle. Adorned with straps and belts, crests and symbols of faraway families in faraway lands. Their hair was brushed and plaited and curled, none of it littered with sticks and leaves. They had smooth skin of every shade, clear of the dried mud that covered her body.

"What do you expect when you open enlistment to girls who aren't princesses of the blood?"

As she shuffled through the marquee, the girl realized something else that separated her from the rest. Something much more painful. *They've all got their parents with them.*

"How on earth does *she* know Remington?"

She could feel the hot sting of tears forming in her eyes, but refused to let them fall. *Just get to the table . . .*

"Hey! *Hey!* Over here!"

A girl with curled hair the color of sunset motioned her to one of the queues leading to the enlistment tables. She wore a dark red riding hood over a black cloak, and the kindness of her smile was the most welcome sight the girl had seen since she'd left home.

"Honestly, you'd think we were witches enlisting instead of lowborn girls," she said. "You all right?"

The girl nodded. Now that she had an ally, the others seemed to lose interest in her, and the excitement of enlistment day returned. But as she chanced a look around, something else became clear. The girls on this side of the marquee weren't wearing silks and furs like the rest; theirs were handmade clothes, patched and repaired and altogether less lustrous. These were the lowborn girls.

"Next!" shouted a rotund old woman sitting behind a stack of parchments, and the queue inched forward.

"I mean no offense, but how is it that you came to ride with Remington?" said the red-haired girl with thinly disguised excitement. "He's half the reason there are so many girls here, all pining to be his one true love—"

"Leave her be, Magdalena, she's covered in webs, for goodness' sake," said a scowling bald man picking his nose behind them. His fingernails were black and he seemed in a great hurry to be anywhere else.

"My father doesn't understand why people like to gossip about royal families, but I can't help it. I find them *fascinating*. Go on, then, you were saying how you know Remington?"

The girl was about to answer, until the witch and the cottage and the candy-making machine flashed into her mind. "I don't know, really. I only met him yesterday—"

"Next!"

"All my friends were jealous when they heard I'd be in his year," said Magdalena. "He comes from one of the most prestigious families in the Western Kingdoms. They say he killed his first dragon before age twelve. You know him better than I do, but it seems he might actually be perfect."

The girl looked across the courtyard to where she had last seen Remington. He hadn't said a word about killing a dragon, but then, she supposed she had never asked.

Suddenly, Magdalena clutched the girl's arm, her eyes wide. A tall girl with hair like spun silk and soft, beautiful features joined the queue behind them. She wore an immaculate pale blue tunic dress with intricate gold embroidery along the trim.

"Begging your pardon," said Magdalena, "but princesses of the blood queue up over there, Your Serene and Exalted Highness—"

"Don't call me that!" the blond girl said, cringing. Magdalena blanched, as though she had just made a horrible mistake.

"But . . . but you're a Blackmarsh royal—"

"Aye, and I hate that bloody address."

"Forgive me, Highness." Magdalena lowered her head and dipped a knee. Then she elbowed the girl in spiderwebs, who did the same.

"Call me Demetra. Please. And stop doing that."

"Yes, Highness." The girls straightened up. "I'm Magdalena, of Sevigny. Maggie."

"Sevigny?"

"It's in the south. Beyond the Valley of Giants. No one's heard of it."

"And you?" said Demetra, turning to the girl. "I see I'm not the only one whose parents couldn't be bothered to turn up."

"My parents don't know I'm here."

"Don't they?" said Maggie. "How scandalous!"

"Who's next?" said the old woman at the enlistment table. "Step lively, we're running behind."

"I think that's you," said Demetra.

The girl turned. Sure enough, they had reached the front of the queue. She stepped forward, then looked back to Demetra and Maggie for guidance. They gave her a smile, but were already busy chatting about something else.

"Name, please," said the old woman, her quill tip hovering over her parchment. "Go on, child, what's your name?"

"I'm sorry, I . . . I don't have one."

The old woman removed her eyeglasses and rubbed the bridge of her nose. "Siblings?"

"I have a sister."

"And I'll wager she hasn't been to the Academy, has she?" The old woman ran her weary eyes over the tangle of webs, strewn with souvenirs of the forest.

"I don't think so."

"Where are your people from?"

With rising panic, the girl glanced back to Maggie and Demetra, but they were still deep in conversation.

"Headmistress! Over here, please!" sang the old woman, waggling her thick fingers.

Slowly, with captivating elegance, a woman with a jeweled crown and a stern bearing turned to face them. The Headmistress wore a luxuriant golden dress, the graceful arc of her crown resting atop cropped white hair. She excused herself from her conversation and strode the length of the table. The sophistication and grace she exuded from afar melted away as she drew near, replaced by an inscrutable coldness.

Another woman followed the Headmistress, angular and thin and scowling, her face as lumpy as a bag of frogs. "Spiderwebs," this other woman snarled, scratching a quill across one of the parchments she kept clipped to a piece of snakewood bark.

"Terribly sorry to interrupt, Headmistress," said the old woman at the table. "It's bloody hard work trying to sort these common girls out."

"Not at all. How may Corporal Liverwort and I be of assistance?" It was a voice of authority, of lifetimes of experience.

"I reckon it'll be another memory curse, Mum. Doesn't know her name or family."

"Not royals, you can be sure of that," said Liverwort.

"That's enough, Corporal," said the Headmistress. She smiled at the girl, but it was a smile of formality rather than kindness. "My name is Princess Beatrice, and I am Headmistress General at Pennyroyal Academy. I know this must be quite strange for you, but there's nothing you need fear. The reason you're finding it so difficult to remember is that you've been cursed, most probably by a witch. There is no shame in that at all. Curses happen to even the most seasoned of princesses from time to time—"

"But there's nothing wrong with my memory."

Beatrice stared down at her, expressionless. "Very well, then. Give me your mother's name."

"Um . . ."

"'Um,' she says," said Liverwort. "She don't know what's what."

"Young lady, quite often a memory curse leaves one completely unaware that she has even been cursed. You must trust our expertise; the Academy has the finest medical staff in all the land."

The girl stood silently, memories of years past flashing through her mind like fish in a river. She could remember the first tree she had ever climbed, a gnarled old beech that her sister called "the weed." She could remember the terror in her mother's eyes when she found her standing on the highest branch, and the words she had used to assign punishment. *How could I possibly have a memory curse?* Still, standing beneath the authoritative eyes of Princess Beatrice, she didn't argue.

"Put her on the standard treatment program," said Beatrice, setting both Liverwort and the old woman to scribbling. "How many is this, Corporal?"

"This one here is . . ." said Liverwort, scrambling back through her notes. "Ten before her, Headmistress."

"Very well, she shall be known as Cadet Eleven until our medical staff uncovers her given name. Will there be anything else?"

"No, Princess," said the old woman. Beatrice gave the girl, now called Cadet Eleven, a tight nod, then walked away, Liverwort trailing behind.

"Cadet Eleven," said the old lady, writing it onto an official parchment. "And you'll be assigned to . . . Ironbone Company. That coach right there." She pointed to the line of carriage coaches off to the side. Girls were already filing onto each of them.

Cadet Eleven. I'd rather not have a name at all.

She stepped out from the marquee and looked up at the stark, black face of Castle Marburg. She tried to picture the girl on her parchment standing before it, so full of confidence and strength. That was what she had set out to find when she ran away from home. Now, surrounded by people who looked just like the girl on the parchment, she couldn't help feeling somehow disappointed. When she finally did find her, would she gossip and giggle and back away, too? Clearly this parchment held an answer, but she had never really been sure of the question. When first she had set eyes on it, the discovery had caused an unexpected pivot in her life, sending her off in a direction she had never before contemplated. Who was this girl on the parchment? And what role would she play in Eleven's life? Standing in the shadow of Castle Marburg, she was faced with the possibility that the answer might not be as satisfying as she'd wished.

I've come too far to stop now, she thought. *And besides, where else would I go?*

She realized the courtyard had emptied considerably, so she hurried to her assigned coach. With Ironbone Company about eighty girls strong, nearly every seat was already full. The coach was abuzz with enthusiastic chatter now that the enlistees had finally bid farewell to their parents. She looked down the center aisle for a place to sit and spied an opening on a bench about halfway back.

"Pardon me, would it be all right if I . . ."

The girl sitting there glanced up. Her rain-gray eyes stared back with an intensity that cowed Eleven. Her silky black hair was so dark and lustrous it went midnight blue when the sun caught it. She wore a sleek silver gown that trailed off her shoulders like stardust. There was something radiant about her, a concentrated beauty, as though the Fates had awarded her a double measure.

"I'm sure you'll find more options farther back," she said. Even her voice was controlled, just loud enough to be heard and not a bit more. "I only just got this dress, you see, and I ... well, you understand." She flicked her eyes to Eleven's spiderwebs.

One of the girls in the seat behind her snickered. The other just stared with cold eyes.

"Don't be horrid, Kelbra," said the girl with the black hair. "This is Kelbra—her father's a king. That's Sage—her father's a king as well. And I'm Malora. And my father is also a king." She stretched her legs across the empty seat. "And you are ...?"

Kelbra giggled again. Eleven's stomach began to simmer.

"Over here!" called a familiar voice from the back of the coach. It was Maggie, waving enthusiastically. Eleven glowered at Malora, who stared back with eyes like dirty ice, then went up the aisle and joined Maggie.

Demetra turned back from the bench in front of them. "Sorry about her. Some girls think being born in a tower means they're supposed to look down on people. We're not all like that."

Eleven studied Malora, laughing at a joke she had just told her friends. She was so at ease amidst all this chaos. So at ease in her own skin.

"I never got your name back there," said Demetra.

"They told me I'm called Eleven."

"*Eleven?*" said Maggie, grimacing like she'd just eaten something rotten. The coach lurched forward, causing a ripple of screams followed by laughter.

"RIGHT, ALL OF YOU, EYES FORWARD!"

The laughter faded to confused silence. The moment hung there as the horses pulled the coach across rutted ground, no one yet sure who had spoken. It was the voice of a woman, silvery and sweet and feminine. Yet it also contained hard authority, unwilling to be ignored.

"So this is what they've trotted out as Ironbone Company. My word. That should make my job easier. Most of you lot will be gone by half term and I can catch up on my reading."

And that was when Eleven saw her: a fairy, no bigger than a hummingbird, floating up the center aisle, a mist of shimmering dust falling from her wings. Maggie nudged Eleven and gave her an excited smile.

"I am your Fairy Drillsergeant, and I am your new reality. There is very little chance you'll like me and even less chance I'll care." As she flew closer, Eleven could just make out her features. Her hair flowed blond, and her nose and cheeks and ears were as dainty as lace. She almost looked like a princess herself, albeit a fraction of the size. "You," she said, stopping in front of one of the highborn girls. "Why do you want to be a princess?"

The girl's spine was straight, her hands folded neatly in her lap. Each hair on her head was perfectly in place, and polished jewels dangled from her ears. Yet with each passing moment, her composure crumbled.

"Urm . . ."

"Well? You didn't just stroll in off the street, did you? Why do you want to be a princess?" The girl wiped her brow, her hand quivering. "Come on, Cadet, this is the easiest bloody thing I'll ask you all year!"

"I suppose I'd like to meet my prince," she blurted out.

The Fairy Drillsergeant's tiny jaw tightened like a noose.

"Get out!" She turned to the coachman: "Stop the coach!" And back to the hapless girl: "GET OFF MY COACH!"

As everyone looked on in astonishment, the coachman reined his team to a stop. The girl hurried down the aisle and disappeared off the coach as fast as she could go.

"You are no longer highborn or lowborn or sidewaysborn or anything else," said the Fairy Drillsergeant as the coach jerked forward once again. "You are third-class princess cadets. And that's all most of you will ever be."

Eleven slumped a bit lower as the Fairy Drillsergeant floated by. "I am not here to make friends, ladies, I am here to make princesses. For those of you willing to work harder than you ever have in your life, I will transform you into a Princess of the Shield, sworn sister to all who have come before and all who follow . . ."

She trailed off. Cadets began to look up in confusion. She was hovering in the aisle, staring at something in the back of the coach with an expression of utter shock.

"Excuse me," she said, her voice cold and even and ready to explode. "Boy. What exactly do you think you're doing?"

Heads began to turn. A confused murmur broke out. Eleven followed the Fairy Drillsergeant's glare to the very last bench where, indeed, a boy casually tried to shield his face with his hand. He was thin and snub-nosed with floppy hair, and he was pretending to look out the window. The moment became so heavy he could no longer ignore it. He looked up from behind his hand, cheeks red as fire. "Sorry, were you talking to me?"

Her face contorted into a pained grimace, as though the universe had just disappointed her yet again. "And we haven't even left Marburg yet," she muttered to herself.

"Uh, my apologies, Fairy Drillsergeant," said the boy. "This is where they told me to go . . . Your Highness."

Muted laughter spread through the coach. Malora dangled her arms across the back of her seat, watching with amusement.

"What's your name, boy?"

"Basil. It's . . . Basil. Of Witch Head Bay, near the sea."

"Well, *Basil of Witch Head Bay near the sea*, Ironbone Company is a princess company, is it not?"

"Yes, F-fairy—"

"And you, *Basil of Witch Head Bay near the sea*, are a boy, are you not?"

"Y-yes, Fairy—"

"THEN WHAT ARE YOU, *BASIL OF WITCH HEAD BAY NEAR THE SEA*, DOING IN MY PRINCESS COMPANY?"

"My mother wanted a daughter, a princess," he stammered, the words flooding out of him now. "But she just kept having boys. Twenty-two of us. She couldn't bear to have more children, and I was the last, so here I am." The Fairy Drillsergeant floated toward him with barely contained fury. "F-f-first was

Balthazar, he's my eldest brother, then Benjamin, Bartholomew, Bannington—"

"SPARE ME YOUR FAMILY TREE, CADET!"

Basil stopped talking, but his jaw kept moving. The Fairy Drillsergeant flew right down in front of his nose and gave him a withering look. "You'd better be a cracking princess, boy," she said, her voice so low that only the last few rows could hear her. "Because I'll enjoy watching you fail. And you won't like it when I enjoy things." She turned and floated away, showering him with the dust from her wings.

Basil slumped over and clutched his head in his hands. Eleven sympathized with him, but she never wanted what had just happened to him to happen to her. She began to formulate a strategy in her mind: *Stay quiet, keep to yourself, and do not do even the slightest thing to attract her attention.*

"You will have academic and practical training with other members of Pennyroyal staff. But all of your fieldwork is with me," said the Fairy Drillsergeant. She glanced out the window as the coach rumbled through Marburg's massive curtain walls and into the great, green world beyond. The horses snorted and stomped their hooves as they pulled the coach up a steep path and into a dense, dark forest. "This is the Dortchen Wild. It is the most dangerous enchanted forest in all the land. And Pennyroyal Academy sits bang in the middle. So enjoy your last breath of freedom, ladies. Because as of now, you belong to me."

She flew out the window and joined the coachman. Inside,

silence descended like snow. The excitement of enlistment was gone. The cadets became lost in their thoughts.

Eleven stared past Maggie out the window. As the coach jostled through the forest, and the endless black-green of trees and shadows rolled past, she was overcome with an exhaustion unlike any she had felt before. And for the first time in days, she fell into a deep sleep.

YOU MUST NEVER bow to fear . . .

Through the mist of a gently falling rain, her eyes opened, deep and piercing green in a world of gray. She stood on the roof of a crumbling tower above a sea of trees.

Yours are a warrior's eyes . . .

The voice was older, and although it had the ethereal quality of a daydream, Eleven knew it was real. She turned and found a woman standing there. She had seen this woman before, but couldn't place where. Her thoughts seemed slower, dulled in a mist of their own. The woman stepped forward. She wore a simple tunic dress, a rich shade of purple with pale sleeves, and had the small bud of a lily in her hair.

Your blood is the blood of Saudade . . .

Now Eleven stepped forward. She *had* seen this woman before, in the vision in the dragon scale that night by the fire. But just as this realization came, a wave of coldness hit her, so intense it caught her breath. She wheeled. There, nearly twice her height, stood the faceless, hooded witch from that same vision.

Her sleeves fell back as she lifted her arms, and Eleven saw her skin, slick and thin as spider's silk. Black creeping things were pushing out from inside her, like caterpillars made of smoke trying to escape their cocoons . . .

Eleven startled awake. She wasn't on a tower. There was no princess, and there was no witch. There were only girls staring back at her in wary judgment.

"All right?" said Maggie. Eleven nodded, but in truth her terror remained, like the cold droplets on her skin when she had climbed out of the river. "You've been asleep all afternoon. Nothing but endless trees."

Eleven glanced around the coach. It had all *felt* so real, and yet it wasn't. How could a dream provoke such fear that it carried over into life?

"Maggie," she said. "Do you know a place called Saudade?"

Maggie faced her, puzzled. "No, I don't think so. Demetra, have you heard of Saudade?"

"I haven't, but that doesn't account for much. My knowledge of the world beyond the Blackmarsh is woeful."

Maggie and Demetra started chatting about all the places they hoped to see some day. It quickly became a discussion of where the Academy might place them should they complete the three years and earn their titles. Eleven didn't join in. She pretended to listen, but her thoughts were far away in another part of the land where the cliffs were as high as the moon and the trees were bigger than dragons. Her homeland. She thought about her father. When she had left him, he was recovering from injury. She hadn't said goodbye, and she very much regretted that now. It had only been a superficial wound, but a fluttering in her stomach was telling her that something was wrong. Minutes passed, one by one, and that feeling of dread slowly began to build into panic. *I must get off this coach. I need to go home, but . . . no . . . I can't do that. I can't do that to them.*

Suddenly, sunlight flooded through the windows as they emerged from the gloom of the forest into a vast clearing. Eleven heard gasps all around her. She blinked away the light, and once her eyes had adjusted, she gasped, too.

A rippling plain of yellow and green wildgrass stretched on for hundreds of yards, then the cliffs and valleys of the Dortchen Wild began anew. In the distance, the diamond-white glint of the Glass Mountains cut a jagged ridge in the sky. The coach veered right, tracking through worn mud ruts around a low stone wall, crumbled and ancient, that ringed the clearing like a piecrust. But what had captured everyone's attention, what brought the excitement boiling back for the first time since they'd left Marburg all those hours ago, was in the center of the meadow.

Pennyroyal Academy sat atop a grassy plateau, a kingdom unto itself. Its towers, keeps, and battlemented walls gave it the look of a jeweled crown. Every cadet on the coach leaned to Eleven's side to get a better look.

"Right, here we are, ladies," said the Fairy Drillsergeant, floating back in through the window. The cadets reluctantly returned to their seats, desperate to see their new home but unwilling to risk her ire. "Now, before we reach my beloved Academy, I'd like you all to note the wall. It is bewitched. Princess Pennyroyal herself tricked a witch into enchanting it many, many years ago, and it is utterly impenetrable. Anyone may pass freely *out*, but the only way back in is through a fairy's wand." She lifted hers, the size of a small splinter. "Nothing gains entry to the Academy unless a fairy lets it, and that includes runaways and sneakabouts. Do you understand?"

"Yes, Fairy Drillsergeant," they replied.

"Good. I don't want any trifling with that wall. There are wolves and witches and even the odd giant out there."

The coach rumbled up to a break in the wall. Two tiny fairies, visible mainly by the shimmering sparkles falling from their wings, waved their wands. A transparent, rippling sheet of magic lifted off the stone wall, and the horses pulled the coach underneath.

Demetra looked out her window, then those on the other side of the coach. "Is that it?" she said. "Where's the curtain wall? Where are the soldiers?" But the other cadets were too enchanted by the Academy to worry about security. The closer they got, the more its incredible scale came into focus. It loomed above, ancient and bursting with history, yet new to them all, waiting to be explored.

"I can't believe I'm actually here," said Maggie, her voice quiet with reverence. "Can you imagine it, Evie? The princesses of legend . . . the most storied romances . . . all the tales we've been told since we were little girls were formed *right here*."

"Evie?"

"It's better than Eleven, don't you think?" said Maggie with a smile.

"Oh, absolutely," said Demetra. "It quite suits you, actually."

While everyone else focused on the Academy, Evie settled into her new name. *Funny,* she thought, *I've never had a name before, but this one just feels . . . right. Evie.* It was as though some part of her she hadn't even known was missing had somehow been found again. For the first time in days, she smiled.

"There's the Queen's Tower!" said Maggie, pointing to a colossal crystal spear rising high above campus. It dwarfed the other towers sprinkled across the grounds, giants of cut limestone and granite and sandstone and flint. The reflected sunlight made the Queen's Tower glow from within like an icicle in spring thaw.

"I've never seen anything like it," said Evie.

"The Queen commands the whole of the Academy."

"What about Princess Beatrice?"

"Beatrice reports to the Queen. They say no one's ever seen her before, but some believe she's actually Rapunzel."

"Blimey! Rapunzel?" said Demetra. "That's brilliant."

Evie smiled politely. She wasn't familiar with the name, though she could tell by Demetra's reaction that she should be. There was another round of gasps as the coach finally crested the plateau and the campus stretched out before them. A vast marsh sat beneath the Queen's Tower surrounded by networks of roads that snaked between timber-framed buildings and giant stone structures. The Academy looked to be two or three times the size of Marburg.

"Right, ladies, listen carefully," said the Fairy Drillsergeant. "This next bit is very important. Those buildings there . . ." She pointed out Evie's side of the coach to a series of long, low structures with arched roofs. Each flew a different-colored banner. "Those are the knights' barracks. Yours are on the other side of campus. Should you choose to tour the knights' barracks, I suggest you enjoy yourself so you'll have something to think about on the ride home. Do I make myself clear?"

"Yes, Fairy Drillsergeant."

Evie regarded the knights' barracks with a frown. Although it was true she wouldn't have made it this far without Remington, and in fact, would probably be dead, she would much rather there weren't knights at the Academy at all. Would she ever truly feel comfortable knowing they were just there across the marsh? And why did no one else seem bothered by them?

"Before us is the Grennilieu Bog. It is named for the troll who brought water back to the Academy after the Seven-Years Summer. And if you go in there without permission, you will also be dismissed."

The Fairy Drillsergeant continued to point out the larger features of the Academy, but it all sounded like gibberish to Evie. So she gave up trying to understand and focused instead on what she could see. The campus was a maze of moss-covered castles; giant fortified keeps with exposed walkways and staircases; circular towers and square towers and octagonal towers and bartizans that started halfway up the wall, blooming into towers above; arrow slits and murder holes and words from long-dead languages etched in stone, nearly worn smooth by age and weather. She could *feel* the weight of the Academy's history in every brick of cut stone. It looked immense, exciting, and above all else, fun.

The coach rattled across a wooden bridge and into a court-yard. A huge stone fountain sat in the center, creating a circular reception area. Two twenty-foot statues, a knight and a princess, rose from the sparkling pool.

As the Ironbone coach rolled past the fountain and joined the others, Evie's eyes remained fixed on the statue of the princess. The heroic pose. The expression of quiet fortitude. This was the girl on her parchment. Evie had found the thing she'd been searching for since she'd left home on that terrible night.

"I want you to look round this coach," said the Fairy Drill-sergeant, spreading her minuscule arms. "These are your company-mates. These are the people with whom you will train. On whom you will rely. These are the princesses you will follow into battle." Evie's eyes shot forward. Battle? What did she mean by that? She glanced at Maggie, who didn't seem bothered. "Ironbone Company has been around since giants roamed those woods. Some of the greatest princesses ever to live were Ironbone girls. Do them proud, or get out."

The coach sagged to a stop behind the others. Outside, fairies barked orders at their scampering cadets. Huge, bearded woodsmen chased after the boys, shouting commands. It was the chaos of intensely structured order.

The girls bubbled with anticipation, but the Fairy Drill-sergeant didn't release them just yet. Evie clutched her dragon scale necklace. She was nervous, excited, scared.

"Ladies, I don't know where you've come from or who your parents are, and quite frankly I don't care. Except your mother," she said, scowling at Basil. "I wouldn't mind a word with her. The rest of you, I don't know if you've always dreamt of being a princess or if this is just a good laugh, but there is one thing of which I am absolutely certain."

Evie, heart racing, glanced at Maggie, who couldn't contain her smile.

"Your life as you know it is now over. Welcome to Pennyroyal."

The cadets filed off the coach and into chaos. Demetra dragged Evie along by the arm, but she couldn't run very fast on the cobbled stone, her ankles threatening to buckle with each stride. She caught a brief glimpse of Remington before he disappeared among the other knight cadets; the staff was funneling the girls in a different direction, toward Pennyroyal Castle, a massive structure of glazed red brick with great circular towers topped by crenellated walls. This was where the process of becoming a princess cadet, third class, would officially begin.

"Excuse me," came a gentle voice from behind. "You dropped this on the coach."

It was a small girl in a patchwork dress, lowborn, judging by her gnarled hair. She was holding the dragon scale necklace. Evie's hands shot to her own throat and found it bare. As panic coursed through her body, she took the necklace and immediately began tying a more secure knot.

"Thank you."

"It's Amaryllis," she said with a smile. "And you're welcome."

Evie's panic began to recede as she slipped the scale over her head and tugged on the knot to test its strength. Then she continued on to the castle with the rest of her company. *That must never happen again,* she promised herself.

The next few hours were a blur of queuing up, answering questions, being poked and prodded and inspected, then racing through narrow, torchlit halls into different chambers to do it all over again. Finally, exhausted and thin of nerve, Ironbone Company emerged through a stone archway into a dank, windowless room where a fire crackled in a hearth. Beyond that, more arched doorways led to other hidden parts of the castle. The cadets stood shoulder to shoulder. Evie took her place next to Sage, Malora's friend from the coach, who glanced at her spiderwebs with a sneer.

"So," came a strange voice, wet and raw. "You'd like to be princesses, would you?"

Heads turned to search for the voice, and a troll with tight, leathery skin and bulbous warts arrayed across his face emerged from the shadows. His right leg was considerably shorter than the left, giving him an ambling stride and a hump in his back, and his cane, a lumpy piece of black wood, looked as if it might disintegrate with each step. His eyebrows were thick and white, and his beard was a bundle of taut, brittle strands. He wore a luxuriant velvet suit in burgundy, shoes of polished leather, and a crème silk ascot with matching pocket square. Though he looked like he had come out of a rotting stump, his dress was undeniably fashionable.

"I am Rumpledshirtsleeves, the tailor troll, and I shall instruct you in the *dernier cri*. I am the finest tailor in all the land, a fact that lies hill and dale beyond any rational dispute."

Malora let out a skeptical cluck. Evie noticed that once again she was exceptionally casual, one arm crossed over her chest, the other running strands of silken black hair through her fingers. She seemed to have no fear of running afoul of the staff.

"Many is the girl I've encountered in my travels convinced I have nothing to offer by way of fashion. I invite you to look in their closets now and see whom they are wearing." He clapped his hands and a team of trolls half his size waddled out from an archway. They wore voguish suits that seemed out of place with their stray ear and nose hairs and protruding facial growths. The assistants moved in unison, expertly using tapes and chalks to measure the cadets.

They disappeared again, then returned to distribute knapsacks to each of the girls. Inside each knapsack was an official Ironbone Company uniform. One by one, Rumpledshirtsleeves dismissed the girls through another archway to don their new dresses. As Evie awaited her turn, one of the miniature trolls approached and held out a bulbous hand.

"Necklace."

"Sorry?"

"Necklace," he said, pointing at the dragon scale.

"But this is . . . very important to me—"

"Leave her, Rabeneau," said Rumpledshirtsleeves. He hobbled over and slid his stumpy fingers under the scale, inspecting the slash of black blood across its surface. "Kindly return the favor by tucking it into your uniform, won't you?"

"Yes, sir," she replied.

"Taking pride in your appearance is not the same as vanity," he announced, sending more girls through. "It is vitally important that you understand the difference."

Evie followed Sage through the archway and found a hall lined with small alcoves. One of the assistants pointed her toward an open one. She drew the curtain shut and took a deep breath, alone at last. She saw herself in the wall mirror and felt a surge of embarrassment. This is what she had looked like climbing down from Remington's horse, filthy and bedraggled. This is what all those girls had seen. It was a wonder Maggie and Demetra would even speak to her. She opened the knapsack and found herself strangely nervous. *What if I put it on and still don't look right?*

She pulled the linen uniform from the knapsack and held it in front of her. It was a tunic dress, the same brilliant blue of evening sky in winter, with white sleeves and trim. She peeled off her spiderwebs, then slipped the cool fabric over her head and ran her arms through the sleeves. The moment it washed down her body, something inside of her changed. She felt silly even thinking it, but the dress somehow seemed to make her more human. She slid a tiara as delicate as spun sugar into her chestnut hair, plucking out a stray twig, then tied the trimmed white belt loosely around her waist. She studied herself in the mirror. The girl staring back was a complete stranger.

Who am I?

She could happily have stared into that mirror the rest of the night, but Rumpledshirtsleeves's assistants kept the girls moving along. As she emerged from her alcove, she balled up the spiderwebs and chucked the sticky mass into a rubbish bin.

The newly outfitted Ironbone Company had finally finished processing. They were led down a circular stair, through one of the castle's rear gates, and into a small bailey where the Fairy Drillsergeant waited. She had them fall in line, then began reciting a dry list of rules and regulations. Evie's mind wandered back to that mirror. Moments ago, there had been a very real shift in the way she viewed herself. It was further confirmation that she had done well to listen to the Fates by coming here. Yet standing with the sisters of Ironbone Company—and one brother—two things cast a pall over her budding confidence.

Beyond the bailey's far wall, a punch of ominous dark clouds rolled out from behind the Glass Mountains. They may well have been thunderheads sweeping the land with much-needed rain, but something about them troubled her.

To distract herself from the clouds, she removed a small silver compact from the knapsack and rolled it in her hand. It was standard issue for all cadets. It contained a mirror and pressed powder, nothing more. But what gave Evie pause was the engraving on the lid.

There, etched into the silver, was the official Pennyroyal Academy coat of arms. Its four quadrants depicted a princess, a knight, a dragon, and a witch.

THE CADETS OF Ironbone Company followed the Fairy Drill-sergeant through the serpentine, packed dirt streets of campus as she pointed out the major structures. Evie glanced up at a series of carved granite rain heads, strange beasts leering down with wide eyes and flaring jaws. Somehow the Academy's man-made buildings had the ability to make her feel small and insignificant in a way hundred-foot trees never did. After a few minutes' walk, the soaring towers and thick walls all began to look the same. This was meant to be their orientation, but it only disoriented her further.

The Fairy Drillsergeant offered up tidbits about historic princesses who had passed through these very streets—Blackstone, Dorothea, Snow White—as well as the more famous princesses of the modern age—Mariana, Middlemiss, Torgesson. Each name made her company-mates' eyes go wide, and the mention of Dorothea nearly brought Maggie to tears, but Evie was just as oblivious to these women as she had been to

Rapunzel. Perhaps there was something to this memory curse business after all . . .

"Here we have Hansel's Green," said the Fairy Drillsergeant as they emerged from a claustrophobic alley into a wide expanse of rippling emerald grass. "And across the way are your barracks. Now, what I've showed you today is only a fraction of our campus. But I want you to understand that the names you know aren't just characters in fairy stories. They're real people. And each and every one of them trained right here at Pennyroyal Academy. If you work hard and the Fates agree, a fairy may someday tell your story as well."

Evie pondered this as the Fairy Drillsergeant led them across Hansel's Green to their barracks. She looked at Malora, who seemed so *different* from the others, taller and more confident, and it was easy to imagine parents telling children her story. Or Demetra, who so clearly belonged at the Academy. She would be an excellent person to spin tales about. But her, Evie . . . what would there be to tell?

"Isn't this exciting?" said Maggie, snaking her hand through the crook of Evie's elbow. "All the great ones here, and now us?"

Evie smiled and kept moving across the soft turf.

"Mum used to send me to sleep at night with tales of Princess Dorothea," said Maggie. "She was always one of my favorites. I keep trying to picture her here, but it doesn't seem real."

On that Evie could agree. None of this seemed real. If her own mother could see her now, she would scarcely believe her eyes . . .

Finally they reached the building with a sapphire-blue standard cracking in the wind. A woman stood outside. She was tall, wearing a blue tunic dress similar to theirs, hands clutched to her chest in anticipation. Her flowing brown hair was shot through with gray. There was a soft and warm energy about her, a powerful aura of kindness. This was a distinguished princess in the twilight of her career.

"Welcome, cadets, welcome! My name is Princess Hazelbranch, your House Princess," she said in a voice like fresh-baked bread. "This barracks is your home for the year, so please, come in and get settled. We still have a few more things to do, and we're rapidly losing our sun."

Evie glanced at the hard wall of gray drifting steadily over the mountaintops. *From the looks of those clouds, we might lose the sun for a few days.*

Inside, the Ironbone Company barracks was surprisingly cozy for such a large building. Aged spruce timbers ribbed the vaulted ceiling. Torches glowed from sconces above ornate, wood-framed bunks with small footlockers at the ends. Round-headed windows ran the length of each wall, and bearskins lined the center aisle.

As the cadets filtered in, Demetra led Evie to the latrines at the far end of the barracks. She sat her down and brushed days' worth of dirt and detritus from her hair, then scrubbed the dried mud from her face and arms.

"Sorry about this, but it's got to be done," she said, working a coarse brush under Evie's fingernails.

"It's all right."

"One of the benefits to being raised in a castle is that I've learned the value of looking after my appearance." She suddenly stopped and stepped back. "I'm sorry, I didn't mean to imply that you don't, I just . . ."

"I know I look a mess," said Evie with an apologetic smile. "I haven't had a chance to bathe since I left home."

Demetra leaned in again and used a fresh cloth to wipe Evie's face clean. "I hope you'll forgive me for saying that. I haven't had much experience with common—" She caught herself, then blurted out, "I mean, nonroyals. And quite honestly, I'd prefer to forget all about that distinction while I'm here." She stood again and looked down on Evie with a smile. "There. You look bloody gorgeous."

Evie studied herself in the mirror. How could that girl, cleaned and groomed and uniformed, be the same one who earlier that morning had torn open a termite nest with her hands, scooping the carrot-flavored insects into her mouth for breakfast while Remington slept?

"Right, let's go claim our beds before they're all taken," said Demetra, leading her out of the latrine and back through the bustling barracks.

Evie couldn't help but smile. Girls were settling in, putting their meager personal items in the footlockers, and chatting with one another about who they had been back home. None of them stared at her. None of them laughed at her. None of them even noticed her. It was bliss.

"I've held these two," said Maggie, indicating the bunks on either side of hers. "Whichever takes your fancy—"

"Blimey!" shouted the girl at the next bunk. She dropped to a knee and dipped her head. "I didn't know you was gonna be here, Your Serene and Exalted Highness!"

Demetra looked around in embarrassment, hurrying over to pull the girl to her feet. "I'm only a cadet, no different from you."

"Touched by the royal hand! Me da won't believe it!"

"That's Anisette," said Maggie with a smile. "She's a Blackmarsh girl, too."

"Are you?" said Demetra.

"Through and through, Highness—"

"Then I order you to call me Demetra." She walked past Evie and staked her claim to the bunk on the far side of Maggie's.

"Anisette," she said, shaking Evie's hand.

"Uh . . . Evie."

"Evie, pleasure."

Anisette went back to her unpacking. Evie looked at her bunk, then watched the other girls, unsure what she was supposed to be doing. She put her knapsack inside the footlocker, then sat down to listen.

"Me da's a cobbler on Blackmarsh high street," said Anisette. She was rough-edged, as was Evie, but with a loud, infectious spirit. Evie liked her immediately. "Any time you need shoes mended, Highness, you come see him. Unless you royals just throw 'em out at the first little scuff." She winked at Evie with a smile.

"Please, just call me Demetra. I can't bear that title."

"Right. Demetra. Well, you come see us. Best cobblers on the Slope. Course, I'm a good sight better than he is these days, but don't let him hear it—"

"Ah, so that would make you a princess of the sole, then," said Malora with a smirk, her friends from the coach, Kelbra and Sage, trailing behind.

Anisette looked at her with cinched eyebrows, unsure how to respond to the insult. Before she could, Malora turned to Demetra. "I've come to tell you that the kingsblood princesses are over there, if you'd like a bit of space from these street girls."

There was a moment where no one spoke, each waiting for Malora to complete what must surely be a joke. But she only looked down at Evie with a cold smile.

"Did you really come all the way over here just to insult us?" said Anisette, but the moment was cut short as Princess Hazelbranch approached, reading from a parchment.

"Cadet . . . Eleven?"

"Offer stands," said Malora to Demetra, and then she and her friends walked off.

"Is there an Eleven here?"

"That's me," said Evie, standing.

"Come along, dear."

"Where are we going?"

"To the Infirmary. Or have you already forgotten your memory curse?" She chuckled at her own joke as she walked away. Evie followed, then hesitated. She looked back at her friends.

Only moments after finally starting to feel like she belonged, she was being singled out and led away because she was different.

By the time Ironbone's cursed cadets had traversed campus and reached the Infirmary—there were quite a few more than Evie had expected, including Sage, who always looked as though she hated the sensation of being alive—the sun had nearly reached the horizon. This would be the first night in many where Evie could sleep soundly, without worrying that a goblin or wolf was creeping up through the undergrowth. She found herself actually looking forward to the night.

Light flooded the Infirmary through a glass ceiling, while nurses in white dresses moved swiftly amongst the sickbeds attending the unwell. The girls were asked to gather near a treatment area, which consisted of several tables surrounded by shelves of tiny bottles of blue and black and green and yellow potions, exotic powders, bubbling chalices, and clay pots filled with unknown substances.

Evie had been one of the first called forward. She sat before the Academy's chief caregiver, dowdy and droopy-eyed Princess Wertzheim, and answered yet another series of questions. She made one last attempt to explain that her memory wasn't faulty, but when Wertzheim started to probe further into her family history, Evie decided to abandon the cause. She hadn't told a soul about her mother and father because she felt protective of them, and would rather drink the odd potion than expose them to these strangers. So when Wertzheim mixed her a small vial of red liquid, she choked it down without complaint.

Now, as she waited for the others to finish their consultations, she started to notice strange things about the Infirmary. Statues of men and women, boys and girls, were strewn about the room. Some stood next to bunks, but most were shoved into the far corner, as though the Infirmary doubled as a royal garden's storehouse. In addition to the statuary, animals roamed the floor unchecked. Goats, ponies, and what seemed to be an entire flock of ducks trailed behind the nurses as they made their rounds. Lizards clung to walls. Pigs and swans napped together on one of the bunks.

A fox walked past on its hind legs, as though it was a person. Her eyes followed it, and found Sage standing behind her. She had a face like a pear leaf, soft and round and tapered into a sharp chin, though always darkened with hostility. Still, for Evie, it was a familiar face in an odd place. She decided to start a conversation. "Lost your memory, too, then?"

"As if it's any of your business, I've lost my sense of humor." Evie chuckled nervously, unsure if it was a jest.

"I'm happy you can laugh. I can't."

"I'm sorry, I didn't mean to . . ." Sage scoffed and turned toward the table, where a nurse was feeding a cadet a spoonful of smoking yellow liquid. But Evie missed the cue and continued talking. "Why do you reckon they keep all these animals and things in here?"

"They're not *animals*," said Sage with a huff. "They're people with curses."

A dog lying at the foot of one of the bunks scratched its ear. Evie studied it, trying to imagine how this could be a person, when, in the same bunk, the statue of a boy lifted its head. It was alive, its calcified skin pliable, trapped somewhere between stone and flesh. When she was ten years old, Evie had stumbled upon a wounded fox cub. It looked as though it had met with an owl or hawk and somehow survived, but only just. She knew it wouldn't survive much longer. She had the strangest sensation then, an intense compassion for the cub mixed with revulsion at its horrific wounds. The same sensation came over her now when she looked at the statue. Or boy. Whichever it was.

She could feel the uncomfortable tickle of someone's eyes on her, so she turned and found a squat, fat pig. It chuffed and snorted, but its eyes never left hers. It was disconcerting, a bit too intense for such a placid farm animal, so she stepped away and pretended to admire some multicolored vials on a shelf. But the pig followed.

"What do you want? Go away."

Its bristled snout twitched as it took in her scent. She looked to her fellow cadets, as much embarrassed as alarmed, but none seemed to notice what was happening. When she tried to edge away, the pig darted forward. She backed into the shelf, vials shattering on the floor.

"Help!"

The pig's snorts grew louder and more insistent. It lunged at her again, and she tripped over a green-headed mallard, falling to the floor amid a flurry of quacks.

The pig stood only feet away, its body shuddering like the injured fox cub in the forest. Several nurses approached, but kept their distance, as though it might come after them next.

"What's it doing?" called Evie.

"Stay calm!" said Wertzheim. "Don't move!"

The pig's wheezing had become quite labored, its squeals more urgent. It was clear the creature was in great distress. Hooves clacked against stone as the pig's body was wracked with violent spasms. A large brown spot on its side began to distend. The screams of the cadets rang through the Infirmary, joining the pig's panicked shrieks.

Finally, it collapsed on its side, bleating as though it were being butchered by an invisible cleaver. The needle-haired body elongated and contracted at once. Joints cracked as the legs violently speared straight. The snout began to mash in toward the rest of the face. The stricken animal squealed uncontrollably as its entire body mutated and contorted.

Evie held her breath as the creature—it could no longer be called a pig—writhed on the floor.

"Someone do something!"

Wertzheim dashed forward and threw a burlap blanket over the suffering creature.

"Move, Cadet! Now!"

Evie scrambled to her feet. The other cadets backed away from her as though she had caused whatever had just happened.

More nurses rushed to help Wertzheim. They held the beast down and spoke in comforting tones. The thing beneath the blanket began to steady, taking huge, heaving gulps of air. The shock of the violent episode lingered like an echo, broken only by the casual honk of a swan. Finally, the nurses helped the creature to sit up.

"Oh . . ." said Wertzheim. "How extraordinary . . ."

The blanket fell. Where there had once been a spotted pig, there now sat a boy. He was muscular and long with short black hair and heavy eyebrows. His muddy brown eyes looked utterly dazed, like he had just somehow survived a fall from the Queen's Tower.

"Where is she?" His voice was a dry squeak, somewhere between pig and human. He ran his squinting eyes through the crowd until they found Evie. He tried to push himself up, but his arms buckled. A hacking cough rolled up from the deepest part of his lungs. The nurses helped him to his feet. He held the blanket around his chest like a cloak as he staggered toward her. With each shuffle of his feet, more humanness returned.

"Steady, now, steady," said one of the nurses.

"It's you . . ."

More cadets backed away, leaving Evie to him. "Hello," she said with a grimace. *Why can't he just go to someone else?*

"I'm back." He rolled his neck, producing a cascade of

cracks. Then he met her eyes again and flashed a wide smile. "I'm back!"

The onlookers murmured in confusion. The tension in the room evaporated as suddenly and unexpectedly as it had come.

"I'm back!" He pulled one of the nurses into an embrace and spun her in an impromptu dance. His delirious laughter bounced off every wall of the Infirmary. He raced after a group of ducks, scattering them with a chorus of irritated quacks. "I'm back, ducklings!" Then he wheeled on Evie, charging across the floor with fresh fire in his eyes. "Where in blazes have you been?" She tried to form words, but found she suddenly didn't know any. His hand enveloped the back of her head and his lips pressed to her own, soft and warm and entirely unexpected. Thoughts exploded in her head, each dying the moment it was born. And then his lips were gone and he spun to face the others, arm raised in triumph. "I'M BACK!"

Evie stood motionless, lips still parted, still warm with the sensation of his.

"All right, young man," said one of the nurses, placing a hand on his back.

"What's this, a kiss for you as well, my dear?"

"Oh, I should think not," chuckled the nurse, ushering him away.

As she led him into one of the Infirmary's private chambers, he shouted, "Prince Forbes is back from the sty! Let it be known!"

Evie dragged her hand across her lips and straightened her

dress, though there was nothing she could do about the hot red flush in her face. She tried to act as though nothing had happened, but inside her chest, beneath the dragon scale, her heart pounded so resoundingly she thought everyone must be able to hear.

"Incredible," said Wertzheim, shaking her head in awe. "Absolutely breathtaking. That young man's father brought him to us five years ago and we've never had a bit of luck with his curse. Tell me, Cadet, how is it that you know him?"

Evie grimaced. Just as when she had arrived at Marburg with Remington, all eyes were once again on her. "I've never seen him in my life."

"Oh, I suspect you have, my dear. The cure for a witch's curse is quite often tied to its inception. Perhaps when your memory returns, you'll find him there." Her mouth curled into a smile. "I should hope so with a kiss like that."

Some of the cadets laughed, but amidst the crowd, there was one who didn't. Sage, the girl without humor, the confidante to Malora, stared coldly back. And Evie knew then that this incident wouldn't die in the Infirmary. She was new to the twin hobgoblins of rumor and gossip, yet she understood implicitly that when she sat down at the Ironbone Company table for supper that night, her kiss would be on the lips of many, many others.

EVIE DRAGGED her feet across the uneven stone of the court-yard outside Pennyroyal Castle. Her eyes were heavy and her belly was full. With starry black skies above, a tremendous distance traveled, and too many strange occurrences to remember, she could have happily stumbled into the darkness and slept. Instead, a sea of third-class princess cadets swept toward the castle, clumped together by the colors of their company uniforms.

She had been distracted all through supper. The Dining Hall was lit by candles and braziers and roaring fires, warm and sleepy, and the long company tables were piled high with feast atop clean white cloth. Joyous conversation surrounded her, girls slowly transitioning from acquaintances to new friends, but Evie's thoughts were across the hall on the black doublets of Thrushbeard Company. Remington's company. He had been sitting next to the strange pig-boy, Prince Forbes, and it made her uncomfortable for reasons she didn't understand. What were they saying? Did Remington know what had happened in the Infirmary? Why did it bother her if he did?

Now the cadets flowed beneath the spiked teeth of the castle's portcullis and into an immense rotunda. Torches in iron sconces ringed the walls, interspersed with faded oil portraits of great princesses and knights of the past. Twin staircases of polished stone swept up to the castle's higher floors; beneath them, a series of archways led to the Royal Hall. On the domed ceiling above, an elaborate mural depicted women in tattered dresses amid the ruins of ancient places. Near the dark edges of the mural, formless shadows huddled, yellow eyes burning out from the gloom. A chill ran through her. She had seen eyes like those before, but what were they doing in Pennyroyal Castle?

"They've moved on Tarburn's Keep, did you know that?" said Demetra. "My sister's already been deployed."

She and Maggie and Anisette had been talking nonstop ever since Evie found them in the Dining Hall after her treatment. Maggie had held her a place on the bench, and even dished her a plate of food, but she still hadn't managed to find a way into their conversation. They mostly spoke of places and things she knew nothing about.

"Tarburn's Keep? Bloody hell, that's right across the bay!" said Anisette.

"We haven't had any in Sevigny yet, Fates be praised," added Maggie.

Evie was still trying to puzzle out why anyone would want to paint witches' eyes on the ceiling when she heard someone making a snorting sound behind her. Malora smirked as she and her friends passed by. Kelbra laughed, and Evie's face went red. She followed the crowd through the archways at the far side of the rotunda, yet still somehow felt completely alone.

There, House Princesses directed the cadets to their assigned benches. The Royal Hall was an enormous rectangle of flint walls and stone dressings. Two immense hearths provided both light and heat. Giant purple banners bearing the Pennyroyal coat of arms rolled from the ceiling beneath sprouted pillars. In the front of the hall stood a raised dais lined with thrones. Behind the dais, a massive painting depicted war-weary princesses mounting the stairs to a ruined castle.

"Why do all the princesses look so . . . *ragged?*" said Evie with a frown as she sat on the wooden bench. But Maggie didn't hear the question. She was deep in conversation with Basil, the boy from the coach, who wore a tunic of Ironbone blue, but with white linen breeches instead of a dress.

The staff entered and sat in the thrones. Evie recognized several of them from earlier in the day, including Rumpledshirtsleeves, who was flanked by two of his miniature assistants. The center throne, the largest and most opulent, remained empty. A footman blasted a fanfare on a bannered trumpet, and there was a great swoosh of fabric as everyone in the hall rose as one.

Evie struggled to see past the girl in front of her, a lanky cadet in the scarlet red of Goosegirl Company. She managed to find a small opening at the girl's shoulder and saw Princess Beatrice sweeping across the dais in a billowing golden gown, a dramatic headpiece flaring from her white hair like the splash at the bottom of a waterfall. Her expression was severe, almost haunted.

Everyone sat, including the staff, leaving Beatrice the only one standing. The silence was remarkable. Even the fires seemed to hiss and pop just a bit more softly. She ran her eyes slowly over her cadets, and with one simple turn of the head, unnerved an entire chamber.

"We are at war."

Beatrice delivered the words with such finality that no one dared move, not a breath could be heard. Evie suddenly felt so claustrophobic that she had to glance back at the archways to be sure they hadn't been sealed shut.

"With a very dark force indeed. I have just received word that three more kingdoms have fallen to Calivigne and the Sisters. Hundschloss has been reduced to ash."

Evie's eyes flicked around the hall. She didn't understand what any of this meant, but the grim reaction of the other cadets made the walls seem just a bit closer, the bench a bit more uncomfortable.

"Who's Calivigne?" she whispered to Maggie. "What's she talking about?"

Beatrice continued. "I understand that many of you, and many of your parents, have concerns regarding the Queen's decision to admit cadets without pedigree." She glared down at them, her expression revealing nothing about her own opinion. "First, if you feel it your place to question the Queen, you may do so from the comfort of your own homes. She is our

Supreme Commander, and to question her is a treasonous act. Second, many of you no doubt have false ideas of what it means to be a Princess of the Shield. You came because you were attracted to the majesty and glamour of life with a crown and castle. You intend to serve your three years, then go forth beloved by all." The clacking of her heels echoed off the walls. "*You* will be the first ones discharged, no matter your blood."

Evie caught a glimpse of Malora, who shook her head with disgust.

"A Princess of the Shield is courageous. She is compassionate. She is kind, and she is disciplined. Without these four core values, a girl may have all the crowns and castles she wants, but she will no more be a princess than she will a dragon.

"You must prepare for battle as any soldier would, though yours are not the weapons of the soldier. Your weapons are pure hearts and steel spines. Your weapons are already inside you. And the only way to wield them is to *know yourself.* Which is precisely what we will teach you here."

A wave pulsed through Evie's brain, and she thought for a moment she was about to lose consciousness. Some deeply buried instinct had been triggered. A warning. *She's about to say something I won't be able to un-hear.*

"Three more kingdoms fell this day. Three fine and noble kingdoms full of history and culture and innocent citizens." Beatrice folded her hands behind her back, slowly patrolling the dais. "The forces of evil are on the ascent, of that there can be no doubt. We need you, ladies, to embrace your training and join the fight. *You*," she said, pausing for emphasis, "are the only thing preventing Calivigne and her army of wicked witches from spreading misery and death across all the land."

Wicked witches. Suddenly, the little clues that had been niggling at Evie since she'd first arrived clicked into place. The mural . . . the stray comments of her friends . . . the Pennyroyal coat of arms . . . All of it pointed to one simple fact: to be a princess was to battle witches.

"As the year unfolds, you will notice that our Academy bears many similarities to the training camps of the world's great armies. This is not an accident. Our distinguished founder, Princess Pennyroyal, developed this institution to engender the same precision, honor, and discipline found in any king's army. She had seen countless kings train countless soldiers to battle other countless soldiers trained by other countless kings. She despised the endless parade of death and violence, but respected the integrity those camps infused into their soldiers. It was she who discovered that only a true princess could defeat a witch. It was she who trained the very first Princesses of the Shield. It was she who grew those virtues into an army of decency and kindness. An army of princesses."

Evie stared at the red linen of the dress in front of her, trying to remain calm. She dabbed sweat from her forehead, though her skin felt cold and clammy to the touch.

"Some ask why, with the superior weaponry, training, and numbers of a king's army, those forces can't simply ride forth and rid the world of witches. There are countless fields of stone soldiers out there ready to provide the answer. We, ladies, *we princesses alone,* possess the weapons required for this fight." A log dissolved in a hiss of ash. "This fight is bigger than you. It is bigger than me. It is bigger than any princess or knight who has ever graced these hallowed halls. This fight is about them." She jutted her finger so emphatically that it encompassed every man, woman, and child in the world living in fear. "This fight is about all the innocent people across the land who will suffer without a Princess of the Shield to protect them."

Her voice reverberated into silence. She walked back to her empty throne, but didn't sit just yet.

"These are consequential times, ladies. And your war draws ever nearer."

And with that, she took her seat. She looked exhausted, like she had aged ten years during her speech. Soft whispers began to work their way through the third-class cadets.

A hand touched Evie's back, rubbing small circles between her shoulders. "All right, Evie? You look a bit pale."

"I didn't know we were meant to fight witches, Maggie," she said, her hands trembling.

"What?" Maggie's forehead creased in confusion. "But what did you think a princess—"

"Quiet, the lot of you!" sneered Liverwort. Silence returned to the hall. Beatrice gave her a slight nod, and she disappeared through the archway at the end of the dais. Evie put her head in her hands and tried to focus on Maggie's rhythmic strokes.

A moment later, Liverwort reappeared to a chorus of horrified gasps. Evie glanced up and found her helping a huddled figure in a tattered cloak onto the dais. Gossamer-thin skin slacked from the sharp bones of her face. Her lips stretched tight over a chilling grin, and time had fused shut her eyes. The fires, roaring only moments before, died to glowing ash. One of Rumpledshirtsleeves's assistants sprang to relight them as the ancient witch hobbled to the center of the dais on a cane of weathered bone.

The black stench of smoke, the pinpricks of gooseflesh . . . Evie was right back in that cottage in the woods. She was trapped. And she was certain she was about to die.

"Girls, please," said Beatrice with annoyance. "There is nothing to fear from this witch. She is a dissident, a friend of the Academy. A friend to our cause." The horrified voices muted back to silence, though an electric tension remained. "The intuitive powers of a witch can be quite useful when her motives are pure. She is here to do a reading, nothing more. This allows us to tailor our training and better prepare for the year. The only thing you must do is sit quietly and show a bit of respect."

The blind witch mouthed a silent incantation. She lifted her cane and ran it slowly from one corner of the hall to the other. Evie flinched when it pointed at her.

"I see . . ." croaked the witch, the skin near the edges of her mouth flapping loosely. "The Queen has done quite well for herself . . ."

CRACK! Her cane slammed to the floor. The cadets—and some instructors—jumped.

"She is here! The Warrior Princess is here!"

"What?" hissed Beatrice as she sprang to her feet. "Are you quite sure?"

Around her, the dais erupted with activity. Several princesses dashed from the hall. Others scanned the cadets with great urgency. Tears welled in Hazelbranch's eyes, though her expression contained more hope than fear. Rumpledshirtsleeves slumped back, his assistants fanning him.

"Indeed. She sits among them!"

"What's she on about?" said Evie.

"It's a fairy's tale," said Maggie, her face twisted in confusion. "About a highborn girl whose goodness is so powerful she rids the world of witches once and for all. But . . . it's not meant to be true."

"Heed me!" hissed the witch, training her cane on the staff. "You must instruct this class as any other. This Warrior Princess must succeed of her own merits. Should you allow the unfit to remain at your academy in an attempt to trick the Fates, the power of your Warrior Princess shall vanish, never to return again. Do not trifle with the Fates, for the Fates will trifle back!"

Princess Beatrice slumped into her throne and held her head in her hands. The witch turned her shriveled face back to the cadets with a dry cackle, then shuffled through the archway with Liverwort, leaving a stunned silence in her wake. Finally,

Beatrice looked up, her face pale, as though she had just seen her own ghost.

"Well . . . isn't this exciting news, indeed."

The staff quickly cleared the hall and escorted the girls back to their barracks, where the night's tensions evaporated into the stars. Evie seemed to be the only one still troubled by the events of the Royal Hall. Enthusiasm rippled down the rows of bunks, topics shifting like birds in flight. The freedom! The grounds! The prophecy! The knights!

Evie remained on her bunk, legs crossed, biting her fingernails. Most of the girls were energized by the witch's proclamation, the potential of one day being the Warrior Princess as fresh and untainted in each of them as new snow. But she had found the whole evening quite traumatic. She hadn't spoken to anyone since leaving Pennyroyal Castle, trailing behind the others until finally they left her alone. And once they were inside, she went straight to her bunk.

"Oi! What's all this moping?" said Anisette with a wink. "We ain't even started the hard stuff yet!"

Evie responded with the weakest of smiles, and Anisette moved off to join some other girls in song. Finally, Princess Hazelbranch entered and raised her hands to appeal for quiet.

"I understand the first day at the Academy can be quite thrilling, girls, but the time has come for lights-out."

A great communal groan went up, but the cadets started heading back to their bunks just the same. Still, nothing could squelch the excitement in the air.

73

"Why don't I just . . . leave you to it," said Basil, standing near the door looking uncomfortable. Hazelbranch had arranged a cot for him in a storehouse behind the barracks.

"If you please, Cadet Basil, there is one final order of company business. And you are very much a member of this company."

"The prettiest!" shouted Anisette, to a flurry of laughter. Basil could only shake his head ruefully, though he couldn't hide a smile.

"Now, before you can rightfully be considered . . ." Hazelbranch trailed off. Three girls from the far corner of the barracks, nearest the latrine, stepped away from their bunks as one. They huddled together, walking across the bearskins, their faces drawn and serious. "Is everything quite all right?"

"We're sorry, Princess, but we . . . we want to go home." One of the girls began to weep, burying her head in her friend's shoulder.

"Girls?"

"We don't want to be here anymore. This isn't what we thought it would be."

And suddenly the joyous atmosphere was punctured like a bubble in a bog. One cadet shouted for them to reconsider, but they had made their decision.

"Come, girls, come," said Hazelbranch, beckoning them forward. "The three of you wait outside and I'll see you to the castle."

The girls shuffled past Basil, who stared at the floor with

folded arms. Hazelbranch took a step forward and addressed the entire company. "Does anyone else wish to join them?" The Ironbone girls looked at one another, each hoping no one else would take the offer. "There is absolutely no shame in it. Some people simply aren't equipped to battle witches."

Evie ground her jaw back and forth. It was as though Hazelbranch were speaking directly to her. *Go,* she told herself. *You're only here because of some silly parchment, not to get in the middle of a war. Go. Now.*

But she didn't.

"Very well," said Hazelbranch. "For the rest of you, I will now administer the Pennyroyal Academy oath. If you'll all place your hands over your hearts, and after I've finished, say, 'I swear it so.'"

Evie's hand rose to her chest. It felt light and numb, as though it belonged to someone else. She turned to face the Pennyroyal coat of arms above the door, with its princess, knight, dragon, and witch.

"I promise to do my duty. To support and defend the free peoples of the world against all witches. I will practice Courage, Compassion, Kindness, and Discipline to the best of my ability, and will always endeavor to live a life of high moral character."

No one spoke. It was as if they all—from Maggie to Malora—wanted to give the moment the reverence it deserved. Swearing the oath was a final step and a first step all in one. The journey toward princesshood would now begin, and each of them knew it.

"I swear it so," they said in unison.

Evie, softly, and after everyone else, said, "I swear it so."

"Congratulations," said Hazelbranch with a smile. "You are now officially princess cadets, third class. You have just joined the ranks of the greatest princesses ever to live, and if that witch's prophecy is correct, at least one of your year will someday be listed among them."

The jubilant buzz slowly returned. Hazelbranch began working her way through the room, congratulating each of the girls.

Maggie turned to Evie with a smile. "We did it!"

Evie dropped to her bunk. A black cloud swirled through her head. Swearing the oath had sentenced her to face that which she had hoped to never encounter again.

Despite her overwhelming fatigue, she lay awake hours after the last torch had been snuffed. She stared outside as dull gray clouds spread from one corner of her window to another, slowly swallowing the white moonlight like a curtain being drawn.

What's this? the witch in the cottage had said, eyes wide and hungry.

What's this? speaking of Evie as though she were a piece of candy waiting to be devoured.

What's this? said the witch.

What's this?

"WHAT ARE YOU LOT STILL DOING IN BED? IT'S TIME FOR..."

In an instant, the pink sunset and crashing seawater of Evie's dream became the dull gray of the barracks. She blinked herself back to consciousness, disoriented to wake somewhere other than the woods. And that's when she saw the incensed face of the Fairy Drillsergeant looking straight at her.

"Bloody hell ..."

The swish of bedsheets and tunic dresses, the clop of shoes on stone, everything stopped at once. The cadets followed their commander's gaze across the room, where Evie squatted atop the footboard of her bunk. She scrambled to the floor, but it was too late. The Fairy Drillsergeant darted across the barracks.

"DID YOU SPEND THE ENTIRE NIGHT PERCHED UP THERE LIKE A MAGPIE?"

"I ... I'm sorry, Fairy Drillsergeant."

"Why?" said the Fairy Drillsergeant, shaking her head. "Why do *I* always get the bloody fopdoodles? I'd lay my wand there's not a single cadet in Bramblestick Company who SLEPT ON THE END OF HER BUNK!"

Evie's mouth quivered. Her eyes had begun to mist over, but she would not let herself cry. "Please, Fairy Drillsergeant . . . I didn't mean to—"

"Looks like we can abandon the hunt for the Warrior Princess, everyone!" The Fairy Drillsergeant glared at Evie, but spoke loudly enough for the whole company to hear. "When this year ends, those of you still here will participate in a day-long challenge called the Helpless Maiden. The rules are simple. You either complete the challenge, or you're not welcome back next year."

Evie stole a glance at Maggie, who gave her a sympathetic smile. But this only made her feel worse. *How much longer will she want to be friends with the company fool?*

"One of every two of you will be dismissed before we even reach the Helpless Maiden." The Fairy Drillsergeant turned, glaring at Evie with contempt. She flittered so close that Evie could hear the hum of her wings and the soft chime of sparkles. "So tell me, Cadet, how do you intend to last to the end of term when you can't even SLEEP PROPERLY?"

Evie's eyes dropped to the floor and her shoulders slumped. She knew without having to look up that every cadet in the company was staring at her. In all her life, she had never felt like such a crushing failure. Perhaps it would be best for her dismissal to come now, before she embarrassed herself any further . . .

"Well, come on! Move!" shouted the Fairy Drillsergeant, clapping her tiny hands. "All of you, get on with it!" The barracks sprang back to life. She turned to Evie and said in a soft voice, "Get it together, Cadet, or this will be a very short year."

Less than an hour later, Evie found herself knee-deep in the mud, struggling to see through the sweat pouring down her face. Alongside three others, she had been tasked with pushing a carriage without wheels up a steep, slippery hill.

"PUSH, YOU MILKSOPS, PUSH!"

Teeth grinding, Evie peered around the wooden frame. About ten feet above, the mud leveled off and became grass. The hillside behind them looked like a battlefield, the mud churned and slashed through from the progress they had already made. Their company-mates waited at the bottom, shouting encouragement.

"Let's go, ladies!" called the Fairy Drillsergeant. "I've only got one year to get you in shape! No time for idling!"

Evie let out a cry as she pushed against the metal footplate so hard that her fingers went white. The undercarriage dug into her shoulder, but she knew that adjusting her position was impossible. The whole thing would fall.

"Heave!" shouted a spindly girl on the other side called Cadet Nadele.

One of them slipped and the carriage lurched downward. Evie yelped as the thick wooden frame pressed into her shoulder, but she somehow maintained position.

"Hold! Hold!" shouted another girl, whose name Evie couldn't remember.

But the slight displacement had altered the carriage's momentum. Now the team found themselves struggling, not up the hill, but to avoid going back down. Evie's feet plowed trenches in the mud. She centered all her weight into her toes to try to find purchase.

"It's going!" she called. "It's—"

One of her legs suddenly slipped out. She dropped awkwardly, one leg pointing up the hill, the other down. Screams came from everywhere as the carriage pitched toward her. She threw her body to the side and her face plunged into the mud. She couldn't breathe. She couldn't see, either, but she could hear the frantic shouts of her company-mates. She spit sloppy grit from her mouth and pulled glops of it from her eyes. There, at the bottom of the hill, the carriage sat atop a huge curl of black mud.

"Bloody hell, is that really your best?"

Evie's three teammates pulled themselves free from the mud, and all were looking at her.

"I asked you a question, Cadet!"

"I'm sorry, Fairy Drillsergeant, my foot—"

"Your foot is not my concern! My concern is that carriage at the bottom of my hill!"

"Yes, Fairy Drillsergeant, I'm sorry—"

"You certainly are! Back in line!" She floated away, shaking her head in disgust. "You four, you're next!"

Evie slumped down the hill. A brisk wind chilled the mud leeching through her dress. The girls who had yet to take a turn—their uniforms bright and brilliant blue—cheered for the current team. She, meanwhile, wiped herself as clean as she could, trying her best to ignore the glares of the three girls she had failed.

She retreated to the back of the crowd and found some space near the boy, Basil. Maggie and Anisette were still in front, both cheering loudly. It was crushing. Not to see them so excited, but that she couldn't find it in herself to be a part of it, too.

She looked out over the Dortchen Wild and thought about her home. Life was simpler there. And that simple life was still happening, right at this moment, without her. Somewhere out there, beyond the forest sea, her father was probably fishing in the river, her mother tidying up in case friends stopped by. But even daydreaming of home provided little comfort, because her next thought was of her sister, and how much she would love to take part in this training exercise. She had always been stronger and more confident than Evie.

On the hill, Demetra's team had made good progress. The carriage bobbed toward the summit, steadily, and had already reached the spot where Evie's team failed. Malora had a similar grip to Evie's—using her shoulder for power and the footplate for balance. Even splotched with mud, she carried herself with grace and elegance. Evie could quite easily imagine her helping a family of commoners whose wagon had slipped into a ravine. She certainly looked the part of the princess. Perhaps Evie had misjudged her. Perhaps her hostility only served to mask something deeper. *I may not be around to see it, but maybe, with time, she'll actually become friends with Maggie and the others—*

"Over there, you lummox!" shouted Malora, an insult directed at Demetra. The Fairy Drillsergeant made no move to intervene. She either hadn't heard or had decided to let it pass. Then, to Evie's astonishment, Demetra shifted her hold on the rear axletree. She was actually listening to Malora's barked order. A surge of anger lanced through Evie's stomach. Why didn't Demetra stand up for herself? How could no one have questioned Malora's insult?

"I must know," said Basil, "is that a real dragon scale?" Evie glanced over at him with annoyance. "The blood's real, too, isn't it?"

"Yes," she said, agitated. She had never really looked at him before. His chin faded away to nothing, and his nest of brown hair seemed entirely too big for his head. Still, there was something sweet in his eyes.

"I knew it," he said with an awkward smile. "My brother says there's magic in it, dragon's blood. Says it can show you visions. Visions of what's possible."

She tried to ignore him and focus on the exercise. Demetra and her team had nearly reached the top, and Ironbone Company's cheers had grown louder. *No more about bloody visions,* she thought.

"He says that anything you see in dragon's blood is possible, but only if you make the right choices. D'you suppose I might have a go? Not now, obviously, but . . ."

She walked away, dropping the scale through the neck of her dress.

"Right. Some other time, then," he called.

Could that be true? Could the things she had seen that night by the fire actually be possible? What decisions would she need to make to stop that horrifying witch from sending her minions into the night? And what of the princess forced to her knees?

An exultant cheer went up as the carriage crested the hill and the girls pushing it collapsed. Demetra sat up, mud sluicing from her dress, and beamed down at her friends. *She looks like a princess as well.* Evie was happy for her, of course, but Basil had shifted her thoughts away from the hill. She looked beyond Demetra, beyond the trees that fringed the top of the hill. Her eyes focused instead on the low ceiling of clouds covering the sky from horizon to horizon. Fingers of black swirled through the dull gray, dark and darker rivulets stretching across the entire sky.

One eye remained on those clouds as she and her friends crossed through campus for their first classroom lecture, something called Witch Tactics with Lieutenant Volf. To Evie's frustration, Maggie, Demetra, and Anisette had welcomed Basil into their group. So it was the five of them, sapphire uniforms marred by mud and, in Anisette's case, blood, hurrying across a bailey of packed dirt and gravel toward the Wolfseye Keep, a massive structure with glassy, obsidian walls. While the others bantered about their first successful drill at the Academy, Evie just couldn't wrest her focus from the skies.

"One round of field training and I can't feel my arms," said Demetra.

"Come to me da's shop, hey? We'll show you what real work feels like," said Anisette.

"Or," said Basil with a sheepish grin, "she could send a servant round to do it for her."

Anisette laughed with surprise. "That's quite good, Bas," she said, punching him in the arm.

Evie caught a glimpse of something across the courtyard. She stopped walking while the others continued on. There, partially obscured behind a copse of bloodapple trees, stood Remington. He laughed easily with his companions, and wore the black Thrushbeard doublet like he had been born to it. His smile contained such surety, as though he always knew a secret no one else did. A memory flickered through her mind. His eyes closing . . . his lips lowering to hers . . .

And then a hand fell lightly on his arm. It was sleeved in white, dotted with mud. Malora bent forward, eyes closed in laughter, leaning against him for support. He said something else, and they both laughed even harder.

"Come on, Eves!" called Demetra.

With a frown, she followed her friends into Wolfseye Keep. Through cold passageways and claustrophobic tubes of spiral stairs, Remington remained on her mind. And she was still thinking about him later as she sat behind a carved wooden desk in Lieutenant Volf's classroom. The air was hot and dry, thanks to a small, glowing hearth next to her desk. Out the window, the Queen's Tower shimmered, its spire enveloped by clouds.

"Happiness and joy are as intolerable to the witch as anguish and misery are to the princess," said the old man, his white hair fanning off in all directions. This was Lieutenant Volf, the foremost authority on princess lore and history in all the land. He was slight of frame, with a sharp chin that seemed to pull his mouth into a permanent frown. His voice was mostly breath, and labored breath at that. "Calivigne and her Council of Sisters have only one goal in mind: the extinction of happiness. This is not a choice she has made. This is simply *who she is*.

"It is most important that you understand this concept," he said, brittle joints crackling like firewood as he shuffled around a desk so ancient it looked like it had been cut from the world's first tree. "The witch hates you because she must."

He strode slowly across the front of the room, arms folded behind him. Evie noticed Maggie scrawling notes on her parchment. Nearly everyone else was doing the same. She looked down at her own and frowned. The words *witch tactics* were written across the top and nothing more.

"Many years ago, I had a cadet called Rose-Red who could never appreciate that fact." A silent charge shot through the room. Even Basil, whose head had been moving steadily toward his desk, now looked up with wide eyes. *Another name I'm meant to know.*

"Now, to defeat a witch, one must first understand her." Far more than the mention of Rose-Red, this statement captured Evie's attention. Through all her agonizing about the Academy—whether to stay or go, whether she would ever prove worthy to serve with these girls, whether she could somehow stand before a witch without crumbling into a quivering mess—somehow it had never occurred to her that she might learn the techniques to fight back. She hadn't even considered that a witch might actually be defeated.

"This institution was founded, in part, to help girls like you understand the monsters that roam our world. It is my hope that I shall dispel many falsehoods that have no doubt been forced upon you since birth. To the detriment of humanity, fairies have somehow become the keepers of stories. They are notorious dullards, with memories like houseflies." The class tittered nervously. Unlike Beatrice, Volf made no attempt to keep his personal feelings hidden. "This is why you hear such nonsense as singing axes and dancing mules and other mindless rubbish in our princess stories."

He stopped, leaning on Malora's desk with a desiccated hand. She scowled at it as he patted his forehead with a handkerchief, composed himself, and resumed his slog around the classroom.

"In the pre-princess era, witches roamed the land with impunity. Children disappearing into the night, never to be heard from again, was simply a fact of life. The people were powerless against this dark magic, and life was quite . . . *horrendous* for those who survived. Princess Pennyroyal, the first of the great princesses, discovered the power that courage and compassion can have over the black heart of a witch—incidentally, you must read her story, which you'll find in the third of my thirty-seven-volume series on princess history . . ." He stopped, lost in his thoughts, then shook his head, a memory gone. "But I digress. As I said, Princess Pennyroyal then founded this Academy, where she began training others in the art of courage and compassion. This led to a period known as the Long Sunrise, when witches were banished deep into the forest, no longer free to terrorize the people. And this is how princesses first became the Great Shield to the world.

"It also provided the first recorded instance of witches using organized tactics against princesses. As they were driven from towns and villages, they quite brilliantly began bewitching the forests behind them, filling them with living magic to make it more difficult for a princess to follow. This, of course, is where we get our modern-day enchanted forests."

Quills worked feverishly around the classroom, but Evie just sat and listened and let this incredible history bloom inside her head. In only a few minutes' time, this man had vividly painted an entirely new universe that she had never known existed. Her world up until now had been limited to a small patch of forest, with occasional trips across the mountains. But to think that epic battles had been fought, new techniques had been discovered, heroes and villains had been forged and vanquished . . . It was thrilling.

"From there, we enter the Years of the Missing Sun, when Pennyroyal Academy expanded its scope and began training knights to battle the other great menace of the day: the dragon." Evie wrote the word *menace* on her parchment, then scowled at it. "And then the Classical Princess Era, where a sort of stasis emerged. Princesses and witches developed strategies and counterstrategies to battle one another. Princesses honed courage and compassion, witches fear and confusion.

"And these," he stopped at the front of the class, slowly turning to face them, "are the building blocks of all witch tactics. Fear and confusion. You," he said, looking down his nose at Anisette. "Name for me a witch tactic, if you please."

"Urm," she said with a shrug, "stepmother, maybe? Wicked stepmother?"

"Indeed, indeed. The wicked witch thrives on deception, and a grief-stricken patriarch is her perfect quarry. Marriage allows her entry into a family, a castle . . . perhaps even an entire kingdom.

"I should note that this technique is still widely used. And that is because we have never been able to crack it. The witch, you see, has no heart. So her intrusion into the affairs of the heart often creates a sort of blind spot. Tell me, do any of you know, in the absence of a heart, where a witch's dark power resides?" Only Maggie's hand went up, and Volf ignored it. "In her eyes. Has any of you ever looked into the eyes of a witch?"

Evie's fingernails began to dig into the palms of her hands. She would certainly not volunteer her experience, a moment of utter cowardice that she had survived thanks to a boy in a cage and a mountain of luck.

"Quite right, because had you looked into a witch's eyes you would most likely be made of stone now, wouldn't you?" He chuckled as he started up Evie's aisle, though his laugh sounded like a dying man's cough. "The witch has a whole host of evil magic inside her, of all different stripes. One allows her to disguise the horrific depravity in her eyes. She makes good use of this in the wicked stepmother technique."

His feet shuffled to a stop in front of Evie's desk. He removed a pair of spectacles from his pocket, unfolded an ivory handle, and held them to his eyes.

"You there, name a fairy tale that features a wicked stepmother."

Evie's face went hot and red as the moments clicked by. She heard Kelbra snickering behind her.

"Any will do, Cadet, any at all."

She glanced at Maggie, who gave her a look of encouragement, but she might as well have tried to encourage water from a desert.

"Are you bloody serious?" said Malora.

WHAM! Cadets jumped as Anisette's fist slammed against her oaken desk. She glared at Malora, who looked back with a challenging smile.

"Ladies, please. In this classroom, you will remain silent unless otherwise instructed." Volf turned back to Evie, peering through his spectacles as though she were some sort of rare bird. "Cadet, am I to understand you're unfamiliar with the story of the young girl whose wicked stepmother wouldn't allow her to attend the ball?"

Evie's eyes bored into a swirl of wood grain on her desktop. She wished she could disappear inside of it.

"My dear, if you are unfamiliar with Cinderella, perhaps it's time to reconsider your future here at the Academy."

He didn't send her away, and the class continued on for what seemed an eternity, but Evie didn't add one more word to her parchment.

Later that night, after pushing food around her plate all through supper, then trudging back to the barracks across dew-soaked Hansel's Green, she sat on the edge of her bunk and stared at the floor, at a single red stone mortared amidst all the gray. Around her, cadets prepared themselves for sleep, cracking their necks and stretching their sore muscles before collapsing into their bunks with exhaustion. Her friends had orbited her all night, but at a distance, as though they wanted to comfort her but didn't know what to say. And now, as torches began to go dark, Maggie crept over.

"All right, Eves?"

She nodded, but didn't look up. Maggie gave her shoulder a light squeeze, then went back to her bunk. When every torch except her own had been extinguished, she raised her pewter snuffer and held it over the flame. It flickered and dimmed as she starved it of air, then went black. She sat back down on the edge of her bunk and stared into the darkness.

SHELVES OF DUSTY old books lined the walls. Even more sat in precarious stacks atop a strained oak desk, littered with parchments and quills and wax sticks and other paraphernalia belonging to the most powerful woman at Pennyroyal Academy. Or the second most powerful, if the Queen really was hidden up there in the clouds that swallowed her tower.

"Cinderella," said Princess Beatrice, staring out a panoramic window at the south end of campus. Down the hill and across the plain sprouted the black-green edge of the Dortchen Wild, with endless forest beyond that. All of it beneath a cloak of sagging silver clouds. She turned to scrutinize Evie, who sat in a chair on the other side of the desk, then looked back out the window.

Evie had awoken that morning perched on the side of her bunk, which she supposed was an improvement over the footboard. Anisette shook her awake moments before the Fairy Drillsergeant burst in with blustery shouts to get up and get moving. At least she had been spared another round of that abuse. But before she could leave the barracks with the rest of her company, Princess Hazelbranch stopped her. And when she saw Lieutenant Volf waiting outside, his spine hunched and crooked, she knew her time at the Academy was most likely finished.

He had escorted her here, to the office of the Headmistress, then retreated near the door, where still he stood. Princess Liverwort was there as well, lurking in the dim shadows near the end of one of the bookcases. Everyone kept silent, waiting for the one voice that mattered, that of the imposing woman in gold standing at the window.

"Have you ever been to the sea, Cadet?"

"I . . . I don't know . . ."

"Of course you don't." A triumphant shout sounded from somewhere deep in campus. "There is a stunning piece of technology you'll find there, at the more modern harbors, called a mast crane. By its own particular magic, it can lift things ordinary men cannot. Spokes, cranks, flywheels . . . Somehow this collection of parts works in concert to create the most majestic sailing ships the world has ever seen." She turned to face Evie, her eyes somehow cold and fiery at once. "Each piece of the machine must operate as intended or the whole thing grinds to a halt. I look out over my Academy and everything is, indeed, operating as intended. Yet here in my office sits a piece that just doesn't fit."

Evie flinched to hear someone of such authority confirm her fear. *I know I don't fit, but you didn't need to say it.*

"I understood from the beginning that the Queen's new enlistment policy might lead to some bumps in the road. But how . . . ?" She came around the desk and loomed over Evie. "How is it possible to have drawn so many years of breath and never heard of Cinderella? It's like not being able to name the rain or sky!"

"Let us not forget that memory curse, Headmistress," wheezed Volf.

"Oh, spare me, Lieutenant. Girls with cursed memories forget their ages or families, not the name of our most beloved princess." She took a deep breath, then sat on the edge of her desk, knocking over a small pot of ink. "Blast!" Liverwort moved to clean it up, but Beatrice held up a hand and froze her. "Reports have come in from the Infirmary regarding another curious incident involving you, Cadet Eleven."

"It's Evie, ma'am. Cadet Evie."

"Good, well, at least you'll take something with you from your time here. Tell me, what happened in the Infirmary?"

"I . . . I don't really know. I was looking at all the statues and animals and things, and—"

"Show some respect. Them's people with curses," snarled Liverwort.

"Yes, of course, I'm sorry. But I wasn't really doing anything at all, when this pig started following me. It wouldn't leave me alone. It started screaming and thrashing about and . . . I don't know what happened, but suddenly it was a boy."

"And it is your contention that you'd never seen Prince Forbes before that instance."

"Never."

"Mmm . . ." She moved some sealing wax sticks out of the path of the slow-moving ink. "Although your role in curing a cadet of such respected pedigree was indeed helpful, your astonishing ignorance is not. Perhaps we might consider that curing Prince Forbes was the reason the Fates brought you to us."

"But . . . that can't be right . . ."

Beatrice stood and swept around her desk, where she picked up a quill and fished through the clutter for a specific parchment. Liverwort took the opportunity to begin sopping up the ink. She found the parchment Beatrice was searching for and handed it to her. *How can someone as poised and impressive as Princess Beatrice have such a mess for an office?* thought Evie.

"Cadet, my task this year has been made infinitely more complex by the fact that I must now sift the Warrior Princess from the rest of the silt. You, if you'll forgive my frankness, are silt. Therefore, I see little reason for you to continue on here at the Academy."

"That would've been my advice, too, Mum," said Liverwort.

Beatrice scrawled her signature across the bottom of the parchment, then looked up as though surprised to see Evie still sitting there. "You have been discharged. You may go."

"No!" shouted Evie, surprising even herself as she sprang to her feet. Any thought of caution was viciously drowned in adrenaline. "You can't send me away!"

"You little whelp!" snarled Liverwort, creeping forward. Beatrice again raised a hand to stop her. Liverwort glared at Evie, but retreated to her position near the bookcase.

"I understand how difficult this must be," said Beatrice. "You've traveled a great distance to come here and are no doubt intoxicated by what you have so far seen. But once you're home again, you'll find that—"

"I don't care if I'm a bloody Warrior Princess or not, but I can say for certain that I'm not here just to help some poxy prince!" Her green eyes flashed with righteous anger. "I didn't know what a princess was until I came here, that's true. I didn't know until you said it the other night. And had I understood it meant fighting witches, I never would have come in the first place. But if you're telling me the only reason the Fates brought me here was to turn that pig into a prince, then you'll stop me from ever knowing the real reason." She hadn't expected any of this to come out, but she couldn't bear the thought of her own future being tied to someone she had only just met, someone who had been walking on four legs only hours earlier.

Beatrice dropped her quill into an ink-stained cup with a clink. Her lips were pursed, her eyes sharp. Evie couldn't tell if she was deep in thought or fighting the urge to leap across the desk with strangling fingers.

"Please, Headmistress," she continued, softening her tone. "I know I don't know much, but I do know compassion. And I've—" She choked on her words, but forced herself to spit them out. "I've seen a witch. I looked into her eyes and I know that fear, and I don't ever want anyone to feel it again." The three little girls from Marburg flashed through her mind, dancing with such innocence and joy. If protecting them from the horrors she had felt in that cottage meant staying here to face her greatest fear, then the price was fair.

Beatrice turned in her chair and looked out the window at the slithering clouds. "To have never even heard of Cinderella . . ." She trailed off with a cluck of her tongue, the thought too absurd to finish. She looked to Lieutenant Volf, who kept his eyes fixed on the crossed wooden beams of the ceiling, unwilling to take a stand.

"I take my stewardship of this institution very seriously. I understand well the burden of greatness I must require from each and every cadet who passes through my doors. When the Queen decided to accept commoners, I agreed without question. But I also made a promise to the great princesses who had come before that I would not make special allowances for anyone, despite our desperate situation with the witches. And yet here I am, in the very first week of term, doing just that."

Liverwort gasped.

"You may stay, Cadet."

"Thank you, Headmis—"

"Perhaps you're right. Perhaps there is a bigger reason the

Fates brought you to us. But if I'm right, and your purpose has already been served, then we shan't be seeing much more of each other, I'm afraid." She held the parchment over a candle until it began to blacken, and a small stripe of flame climbed across her signature. "Having little experience with the lowly of birth, I am quite curious to see what lies inside of you, buried beneath untold layers of curses."

Evie nearly ran down a second-year instructor, a young woman with dark features called Princess Moonshadow, as she raced through campus toward the Infirmary. After apologies and angry looks, she continued on, and so did her smile. Yes, she would be allowed to stay, and she was thrilled about that. But the thing that had so energized her on leaving Beatrice's office was that she had found a way to stand up for herself. *I may yet be sent away, but at least it will be because I'm not good enough, and not because I was too scared to try.*

She sprinted around the great bowed wall of Skymeadow Mews, which echoed with the cries of the Academy's hawks. At the far end, a gust of wind hit her with the must of centuries of bird droppings, but even this didn't dampen her spirits. Nothing could bring her back to the earth ... until she reached the Infirmary and saw another of Princess Wertzheim's bitter red potions waiting for her.

"Must I drink another? Nothing happened last time."

"Three times in four this treatment works for restoring missing memories. But it can sometimes take many, many doses, I'm afraid."

Evie fingered the vial, then shut her eyes and downed it in one gulp. "It tastes like blood," she said, wiping her mouth.

"Oh, come now," said Wertzheim, "there's very little blood in there—"

The mournful wail of a horn echoed through campus. Everyone fell silent, save for the ducks and one barking dog. Wertzheim shot up, clapping her hands in sharp staccato.

"Everyone on your feet! I want absolute silence when they arrive. You, move those geese away."

Evie rose in confusion. Nurses scrambled about, clearing a path through the cadets and animals near the stone archway framing the doors. The horn bellowed again. She glanced around, but everyone else seemed as confused and shaken as she was. Then, across the room, her eyes met Prince Forbes's. He had been staring at her from his place with the cursed knight cadets. Uniformed in black and with two days to readjust to life as a human, he appeared rugged and hard, a youthful composite of all the portraits of knights hanging in the castle's rotunda. Patches of dirt marred his humorless features. A long scratch of dried blood ran down his arm. She quickly looked away. Why was he staring at her like that? After the embarrassment he had caused her the other day, she would have been perfectly happy to never see him again.

The doors groaned open, and a blast of wind scattered some parchments. The nurses stood still and tall, and the cadets followed their example. A handful of princesses entered, girls only a few years older than Evie. They were battered and bloodied, their tunic dresses torn and stained. Two of them carried another on a handmade canvas stretcher. Her eyes were closed, a hand draped over the side flopping with each step. Each of these princesses had a haunted look on her face, and Evie knew it could only have been put there by a witch.

"This way, princesses," said Wertzheim, her voice just above a whisper. "Come through."

The princesses trudged across the room toward an archway in the back, the private chambers Forbes had been ushered into after his transformation. Evie studied their faces as they passed. The weariness and loss sent a shiver through her, yet there was something else there, too. Something behind the horrors they had seen.

Goodness. It was the first and only word that came to mind. These were quite simply not ordinary girls; they were *princesses*, and they possessed a grace and nobility that shone through any physical wounds.

They disappeared beneath the archway with several members of staff. Slowly, the remaining nurses coaxed the cadets back to their treatments, and normality returned to the Infirmary. Evie dropped to her chair, despite having already drunk her potion. The eyes of those princesses lingered in her mind, as did the fire that so clearly burned behind them. For those few brief moments, she thought she could actually see the courage, the compassion, the kindness, and the discipline that the Academy taught.

She was so consumed by her thoughts that she hadn't

noticed the corners of her vision beginning to darken. She stared at the lattice of cobblestones at her feet and thought of those burning eyes. And then she saw less and less, and then blackness . . .

"Cadet?" The word wobbled through her mind, and she realized she couldn't breathe. "Princess Wertzheim, over here!"

The whole world fell silent, save for the insistent whistle of wind. From the blackness, a dim light appeared—sunlight— and then a figure. It was a little girl. She had deep green eyes and wore a simple gray dress beneath a woolen mantle embroidered with butterflies. The girl stood on a small mountain meadow of wispy grass and bright blue wildflowers. At the cusp of the meadow, where the earth spilled over a cliff like a waterfall of green, the world fell away into a stomach-clenching valley of tree and rock. In the near distance the mountains roared back up again. Huge, thick cones of trees covered the wall of stone like the fur of some great, green elemental beast. But the girl took little notice of the vastness of her surroundings. She was focused on a small pie with several bites already missing. A trickle of brown gravy ran down her tiny fingers as she happily crunched into the crust for another mouthful . . .

"Cadet! Cadet, you must open your eyes!"

Evie blinked back to consciousness. She was lying on her back on the cold stone floor, and all she could see was princesses looking down at her with sympathy.

"She's back," said Princess Wertzheim. "Easy, girls, help her up."

Evie felt her limp body lift from the floor as they set her in the chair. Someone handed her a glass of water and helped her drink. "I saw something," she said. "I think it was me . . ."

"Ah, good," said Wertzheim with relief. "We weren't certain if it was a memory or some sort of head trauma from when you hit the floor. It's quite rare for a treatment to work this quickly."

Now a throbbing pain started to announce itself on the side of her head. She touched it and winced, her fingers bloodied. One of the nurses pulled back her hair and began to dress the wound.

"You're all right, dear, you just collapsed. Now, tell me what you saw."

"A girl . . . It was me, I suppose. I was eating some sort of savory pie."

"Good, good. What else?" She reached past Evie for a clean parchment and quill, and started scribbling notes.

"That's it, really. Then I heard a voice and . . ." She set the water on the table. Her muscles felt weak, her skin clammy.

"Yes, well, I might have let you remember a bit longer, but as I said, we couldn't take a chance that it might be a head injury."

"So . . . that was a memory?"

"Oh, indeed. And we'll sort through as many as we can until we find out who you really are."

Rather than racing off to join her company in the Dining Hall, Evie lingered for a bit in a quiet part of the Infirmary, her mind swimming with questions. The memory had been so short, so inconsequential, yet it forced her to rethink her entire life. She tried to go back to her earliest memory, no matter how small or hazy the fragment, and all she could recall was a waterfall, and standing knee-deep in a frigid lake. Her father and sister—or was it her mother and sister?—sent waves of spray through the air as they wrestled in the deeper parts. And even this she could only remember by how she felt at the time: shivering and happy and small. This new memory, so clear and complete, had been dredged up from hidden depths of her mind, a sunken ship jarred loose from the bottom of the sea.

Eventually, after one of the nurses hurried her along, she drifted out into the gloom of the day. She walked slowly in the direction of the Dining Hall, still trying to puzzle through what had just happened.

"Hoy, Princess!" called Prince Forbes as he trotted toward her. "Why don't I join you? We are both headed to dinner, are we not?" His voice was as definitive as a wolf's growl, and there was an intensity to him that made her nervous.

"Oh, uh, of course," she said.

"I wanted to thank you for freeing me of my pigskin bonds the other day. It's good to finally be walking on my hind legs again."

She smiled politely, but kept her eyes on the stone path.

"I tried to grip my sword last night and my fingers were so weak I nearly hacked off my foot. I suppose it'll take some time to be completely back on form—"

"I'm sorry, but I don't know you. And you don't know me."

Boots clomped on stone as a knight cadet hurried past,

wearing the pine-green doublet of Winterspire Company. "Move your hooves, Forbes, it's kidney pie today."

Forbes didn't walk any faster. "They all like to have a go," he said. "Apparently I'm one of the few ex-pigs at the Academy, if you can believe it."

They crossed a small bridge, more ornamental than functional, over a tiny drip of water known amongst the cadets as Thumbling Brook. The orange glow of the Dining Hall's torches appeared in the distance. They ordinarily wouldn't have been burning in the daylight hours, but the overcast skies made it necessary.

"We do know each other, actually. We met many years ago, in a manner of speaking, and I was made a pig for the pleasure."

"That's not possible—"

"There's a portrait in my father's castle. A portrait of you."

She looked away with a grimace. "You're wrong. I don't know how else to say it."

He raised his eyebrows and looked at her with distaste. "Look, I understand you've got problems of your own. Healthy people don't tend to spend much time in the Infirmary. But do you honestly believe it's coincidence that my curse was broken when I saw you?"

She opened her mouth to respond, but didn't know what to say. All she wanted was for him to leave her alone. He looked agitated, just as her father used to when she was too frightened to jump from the rocky outcropping into the lake near their home.

"Right. Well, this has certainly been an *enthralling* chat. Thank you for breaking my curse." He gave her the slightest of bows. "And good luck with your own."

He strode away. Despite the grumbles of her stomach, Evie didn't follow. Instead, she sat on a large stone next to the stables and tried to clear her head. How could she reconcile the recovered memory and Forbes's claims about the portrait, about which he was so certain, with the story of her life as she had lived it?

The wispy tendrils of white leeching down from the cloud bank began to release a fine mist. She sat there, breathing in the clean, cold air, and something quite unexpected happened inside her. From her first experience with Remington in the witch's cottage to this very moment, she had felt entirely out of place. But her show of defiance in Princess Beatrice's office that morning had taught her something. Instead of sinking back into despair and self-pity, she forced herself to her feet and marched into the Dining Hall. She found her friends in their usual place at the Ironbone table. They were thrilled to see her, of course, and Maggie even shed a tear when she learned that her new friend hadn't been discharged after all.

As they finished dinner, Evie filled them in on her morning, from her close call with the Headmistress to the recovered memory and the incident with Forbes. This she would not have done only one day earlier, but the elation she felt leaving Beatrice's office had convinced her she needed a new way forward. She had only known these girls—and, of course, Basil—for a short while, but she needed to trust someone to make it to the next day. And the day after that.

Each day got a bit easier to bear, then, and Evie slowly found herself less of an outcast and more of a real third-class princess cadet. And three days after Princess Beatrice granted her a reprieve, Evie did something she would never have imagined doing before.

It happened in a wooded section of campus known as the Pit during a joint obstacle course exercise with the knights of Thrushbeard Company. She had no trouble ignoring Forbes, who seemed determined to do the same to her, but she didn't have quite the same success with Remington. Each time their eyes met and he gave her that half-formed smile, the story Maggie had told about his killing a dragon before the age of twelve faded further into memory. And when he approached her as the cadets waited their turn to attempt the course, all conversation around them stopped.

"It's bloody hard work to talk to someone at this place," he said, eyes fixed on Captain Ramsbottom, a bear of a man in plated mail and a knotted brown beard, and Thrushbeard Company's commanding officer.

Evie's heart began to thump. She was acutely aware that everyone nearby was listening. "Indeed."

"And have you settled in all right? I must say, you've certainly enhanced your wardrobe."

"Yes, thanks," she replied, knotting her fingers together. All she wanted was for him to leave, yet all she wanted was for him to stay. "And you?"

"They're a loutish bunch of brutes over there," he said, casting his eyes on his company-mates, "which happens to be my favorite kind of brute."

She smiled politely . . . until she saw Malora looking at her with cold eyes.

"Well, I'd better get back before Captain Ramsbottom catches me over here and flays me nose to toes. Good luck on the course." He smiled with mischief, then trotted back to his company. Evie glanced at Malora again and found that she was still staring. It unsettled her.

"Next up, OFF!" bellowed Captain Ramsbottom. A knight cadet and a princess cadet sprinted onto the course, and the queue inched forward. Evie was next. With Remington somewhere behind her and Anisette making loud, jesting comments to the others about Evie and him, she felt an extra thump in her pulse.

Suddenly, someone knocked into her from behind. It was Malora, shoving past her to the front of the queue.

"Kingsblood girls first," she said with quiet menace, one eyebrow slightly raised.

Evie clenched her jaw and balled her fists. Kelbra and Sage flanked Malora to form an intimidating wall. The girls waiting behind Evie took a few cautious steps back. Malora stared down at her, icy eyes sharpening to an intensity Evie hadn't seen before.

"Unless you'd like to show your mongrel blood to everyone here, I suggest you unclench those fists."

Evie's heart fluttered beneath her dragon scale. Her nostrils flared. She heard Anisette's braying laughter behind her, and Basil telling an animated joke. Her friends weren't watching, and she was alone. She glared at Malora, with no idea what she was about to do.

"Right, next up!"

The knight cadet in the next queue ran. Malora's mouth curled into a smile of victory, then quickly fell in shock as Evie tore away onto the course.

"Hey!" she snapped, but it was too late.

As Evie scaled a rough-hewn wall, she couldn't keep from smiling. She imagined the smoldering anger on Malora's face, the helpless protestations of Kelbra and Sage. And the same fire of pride she had felt in Beatrice's office flared to life once more.

"My dear, you have all the grace of a giant on ice," said Rumpledshirtsleeves, taking the smooth wooden handle of the flax break out of Evie's hand. She wiped sweat from her brow and watched as he laid the brittle golden stalks across the break's bed. "Observe." With three deft cracks of the blade, the stalks yielded. He gently worked the silky blond fibers free. "Now you."

She picked up another bunch and laid it in the machine. Though clouds still clotted the sky, and the wind that blew brought cold hints of autumn, her linen dress was already soaked through. Invisible grains of dust clung to her skin. Her raw palms had started to callus. All across the orange-brown flax field that marked the northernmost border of the Academy, the cracks of the breaks sounded. She raised her handle, then swung the blade down. The stalks split open, and she slid the fibers free.

"Better, but try not to be such an elephant in heels, will you?"

The old troll tottered away to compliment Basil, whose pile of flax fibers was bigger and more pure than any other cadet's.

"My mother had me spinning flax before I could walk," he told Rumpledshirtsleeves. It was the first time Evie had heard pride in his voice when talking of his mother raising him as a princess.

After an hour of cracking fibers free from shives, Rumpledshirtsleeves gathered the cadets around a massive stack of what looked like blond hair. Two of his tiny assistants stood nearby, flanking a ratty canvas tarpaulin draped over a dress form. Evie knelt next to Maggie and took a long drink from her leather waterskin. Other cadets sat sprawled around their instructor, savoring the opportunity to rest.

"Because you are in your teenaged years, you no doubt wonder why we are out in the fields breaking flax. What does this," he said, pointing a stubby finger at the pile, "have to do with this?" The miniature trolls whipped the canvas aside in a billow of flax dust. The waterskin fell from Evie's lips. She and the others were too entranced to make a sound.

"Remember what I've told you," Rumpledshirtsleeves continued, limping toward the dress form. "Despite Cadet Anisette's protestations, fashion is eminently important to a princess. I created this gown for Princess Blackstone's wedding to the Prince of Rustbark Vale."

He stopped and regarded the piece on the dress form. The gown was simple in its design, and yet unlike anything the girls had seen before. The material itself seemed to have been spun from moonbeams. The silver threads shimmered from within so brightly they were nearly white, yet somehow muted like a cool summer night. He picked at a growth on his chin, rattling his wiry beard.

"The silk is from worms, of course. I bathed it in a proprietary blend of herbs and minerals to help the strands soak up the light." He lifted the skirt, studying the glistening material with a nostalgic smile. "I set it out each month during the full moon until it achieved that rich glimmer. My assistants here had to wait with it through the night to keep the slugs away. It took twelve months of full moons to achieve just the right glow." He let the watery fabric slide through his fingers, then turned to face his cadets.

"So you see, even the most exquisite of garments begins with a tiny, wriggling worm. Linen comes from flax, which sprouts through fertilized dirt. Tulle derives from cotton, which can be beset by fungus and insects. And so on and so forth. Life, splendid and ugly, transformed into transcendence."

Evie blinked, unable to do much else. This simple garment contained all the longing she used to feel as a child staring up into the night sky with her sister. All the conversations, frivolous and meaningful alike, that they used to share as the moon inched across the sky. The heartache of the sudden end of those days was there, too, buried deep inside those delicately woven fibers.

"The proper design is not concerned with itself. It is concerned with the girl beneath. And I don't mean the tailoring or the technique or any of that faff. I mean who she *is*. Her character. *That's* what a properly designed gown will show. As I said yesterday, when a girl feels like a princess on the outside, it becomes much easier to then feel like a princess on the inside. The pod and the pea working in harmony."

He hobbled back to the pile of flax fibers while his assistants snapped the tarpaulin back over the dress, snuffing its luminescence like a candle.

"Why, after all this time talking of fiber and material, have I shown you a gown? Because that is your assignment. Each of you will design and produce your own ball gown, and some of you will have the chance to use them. Has Princess Hazelbranch discussed with you the Grand Ball?"

Several girls said "no," but Maggie clutched Evie's arm with wide eyes and an even wider smile.

"She knows how much I adore being the one to tell you, bless her. The Grand Ball is a competition in the terpsichorean arts. Aside from fighting witches, a princess must engage in a whole host of courtly pursuits. Royal weddings, formal balls, and the like. Ten girls from each company will be selected by Princess Hazelbranch and myself to compete in the Grand Ball. And the winner"—he raised his eyebrows for emphasis—"is exempt from the Helpless Maiden."

Excited murmurs buzzed through the company.

"That's right. The winner of the Grand Ball receives an automatic placement as a second-class princess cadet. There are very few guarantees here at Pennyroyal Academy, but this is one of them. So I suggest you work very thoughtfully—"

"Hang on, you expect us to make gowns from that?" said Malora, scowling at the pile of flax. "I've never heard of a linen ball gown before."

"Damask, lace . . . Use your imagination, my dear. Come, all of you, gather a bundle and I'll teach you the flax comb . . ."

A guaranteed return, thought Evie. None of the staff had hinted at what the Helpless Maiden actually was, but the little bits of gossip she had overheard from some of the second-year cadets made her think this Grand Ball might be her best chance to make it back next year.

That night, while the others compared cuts and bruises and lamented their sore muscles, Evie finished reading the first volume in Volf's epic treatise on Princess History. The stories of children taken from their beds, of mothers and fathers searching the forest by torchlight, chilled her to her bones even beneath her quilt and coverlet.

"I've never had a blister before," said Demetra, sitting at the end of Evie's bunk. "I need that Grand Ball, because my hands won't last to the Helpless Maiden."

"Glamorous life of a princess, hey?" said Anisette. She had borrowed one of Demetra's shoes and was working the heel into the tender muscles of her neck.

Evie climbed out of bed and cracked her back. A dull red

ache spread down her spine when she moved, but otherwise she seemed to be in better shape than the others.

"My brother Barend would never forgive me being this close to dragon's blood without trying it," said Basil, eyeing Evie's necklace. He sat reclined on Anisette's footlocker, picking his teeth with a splinter.

"Enough, Basil. Leave it," said Evie. She set her book on the window ledge next to several other volumes with pages that had been bloated by the elements.

"Don't get cross with me," said Basil. "I was only asking. As far as I'm concerned, you can keep your manky scale."

Maggie looked up from a letter she was writing to her father back home. Anisette, meanwhile, plopped onto her canvas mattress stuffed thick with feathers and began kneading her foot.

"I'm sorry," said Evie. "I just . . . My nerves are a bit worn, that's all." Her eyes flicked across the room to Malora, who was laughing with Kelbra. She had been much more aggressive toward Evie and her friends since the incident on the obstacle course, and had shown an uncanny ability to know when the Fairy Drillsergeant wasn't watching. Maggie had even started taking a longer route around the Bramblestick Company table in the Dining Hall just to avoid walking past her.

"Ah," said Basil, following Evie's eyes across the room. "Princess Manky herself."

"I can't understand why she's here. All I read about in these books is a princess's natural kindness. There's not a drop in her."

"Reckon she's here for the same reason we all are," said Anisette. "She don't want to live in a world of witches."

Evie frowned. *I think she's only here to make herself look good, and to meet a knight of proper breeding. Like Remington.*

"Look, back in the Blackmarsh we've been hearing about witches coming down the Slope for months now, yeah?" said Anisette. "And naught for us to do about it but sit round and wait for her sister to save us." She flicked her head at Demetra, who just stared impassively at the floor. "When I heard us without the kingsblood could enlist, I was the first queued up. I only wanted to *do something,* like Princess Camilla. Your sister's a real hero to all the girls of the Blackmarsh."

"Indeed," said Demetra without looking up. The word hung there, begging for more to follow, but none did.

"Well, I'm not here because of witches. Unless you count my crazy mother," said Basil.

Anisette and Evie chuckled, but Demetra and Maggie did not. A heavy silence followed, the only sound the tapping of Basil's boot on the floor. Then, from the next bunk, Maggie spoke.

"I suppose I'm here for my mother as well." Her expression was hard to read in the dim torchlight, but her voice sounded a bit more strained than usual. "She . . . passed on a few months ago."

Basil's foot stopped. Demetra turned to look at Maggie with great sympathy in her eyes.

"Blimey," said Anisette.

"I'm sorry, Maggie," said Evie. "Really."

"It's all right. I still have Dad around to be my tailor's dummy." She smiled, wiping a tear from her eye. "Oh, who am I kidding, I made him do that when Mum was alive, too. So did Mum." She laughed away her tears, and a warm atmosphere settled over the group like an invisible campfire.

"I'm really sorry about your mum, Maggie," said Demetra.

"Enough," said Maggie with a sniffle. "She's gone and there's nothing to be done. What about you, Evie? What brought you here?"

Evie froze. Her stomach coiled like a pile of snakes. *Don't do it, Evie, do not do it . . .* She formulated lies, searching her brain for a story tame enough that they might hear it and move on. But when she looked at Maggie, she saw such vulnerability beneath the torchlight reflected in her teary eyes. She saw a person who had lived a life unique from all others, and had come to the Academy for reasons that were hers alone. All of them—Anisette, Demetra, Basil . . . even Malora and her friends—every girl at the Academy, and every boy, as well, had specific, personal reasons for being there. Why should her own story be so special?

"I suppose I'm here because I've got nowhere else to go." A torch went dark at the end of the barracks. Girls had started to settle in for the night. Maggie came around to join Anisette on her bunk, and Evie sat down next to Demetra. She took a deep breath and continued in a soft voice only their group could hear. "I love my father, mother, and sister more than anything in this world. But . . . they're not my family anymore."

Demetra's hand hooked through Evie's elbow.

"I suppose I always knew I was different. I've known it my whole life. But it only got worse as I got older. And I finally found out why . . ." She looked up and met Basil's eyes. Then Maggie's, and Anisette's. "I found out why when my sister learned to fly . . ."

Wind screamed through fissures in the rock below. It lashed the girl's face as it bellowed across the mountaintop. She opened her eyes, eyes as green and mysterious as the forest shivering behind her.

There is nothing to fear, she told herself, even as she peered down the sheer rock face. Hundreds and hundreds of feet of cold, bald stone fell away beneath her toes. She filled her lungs with bracing mountain air and looked up to the ocean of sky. The clouds and their happy blue background seemed closer and altogether more peaceful than the hard earthen floor so far below. Still, she had climbed this mountain for a reason. *The only way I'll fly is if I have to,* she told herself, and she leaned forward and fell off the world.

Before her feet even left the ledge, she knew she had made a terrible mistake. In a moment of panic she tried to will herself back onto solid ground, but it was too late. She plummeted with dizzying speed, angry winds blasting her face. All she could do was hold out her arms and wish for it to end quickly. The slope of trees that had seemed so far away only moments ago now rushed toward her, only seconds away from impact. *Father will be so angry* was the last thought she had before—

Something broadsided her with such force that it froze her lungs. She couldn't breathe, and neither could she see in the sudden blackness. She tumbled end over end inside some hard, rough container until she heard a concussive explosion so loud it drowned out her own screams. She slammed into the side of whatever now held her, then tumbled in sickening swoops. Outside, the crashing booms continued, but these at least were sounds she recognized. Stone against stone. Large chunks of falling mountain. She slammed down once more, and then everything came to a stop. All around her, she heard rocks thud and crunch to the ground. *I've survived the fall, but I'll be crushed to death anyway.*

She found a sliver of light and crawled toward it, coughing from the white dust swirling in the air. She wedged her head through the opening. The mountainside looked as though it had collided with the moon. Chunks of what had been a long, flat wall were broken away. Whole trees had been uprooted and tossed aside like dandelions. She forced the rest of her body through the opening, and her heart broke.

She had been inside the taloned claw of a dragon. He was an eighty-foot drake, one horn sheared off at the tip in a long-ago battle. His scales were a tarnished, faded white that had at one point been green. His body contorted hideously beneath giant chunks of mountain. She could see one wing, mangled and shredded, and a stream of shimmering black blood running from his neck down the sun-bleached stone.

"FATHER!" she screamed, the call echoing across the countryside, and each time ignored. "FATHER, NO!"

She grabbed a motionless claw, curved like a scimitar, and lowered herself to his muscular leg.

"FATHER!"

She slid down the beast's bulging shoulder and slammed to the ground in a puff of dust. She found his head, long and reptilian and motionless, and her eyes moistened with grief.

"Oh, Father, what have I done?"

She tried to pull away the crumbled stone, but a piece that looked like a pebble next to him was a boulder to her. She fell to her knees, overcome by helplessness, and that was when the damaged wing began to flutter. She thought perhaps it was just the wind, but then it shot up into the sky, the membrane stretching taut like a ship's sail. The damaged sections of the wing snapped loudly in the wind, but the dragon was clearly alive.

With the fluttering of small stones falling, then the heavy thud of bigger ones, the dragon unfurled himself from where he had crashed. Black blood stained the rock face and streamed down his neck. He pulled himself free of the debris and rose to his full, terrifying height. Aside from the horrendous gash in his neck, the damaged wing, and other assorted injuries, he seemed to be in fair condition.

More stones showered down as the great drake's weathered,

saurian head snaked toward her, black smoke wafting from his nostrils. His snout, bigger than the girl's entire body, nudged her, knocking her backward.

"I'm sorry, Father," she said. "I'm so sorry." And from the remorse on her face, there could be little doubt that she meant it.

That night, squatting on a water-smoothed shelf of limestone blanketed with moss and tiny orange mushrooms, the girl slept. Next to her, another dragon perched in the same position. This was a hornless female, her scales the bright green of youth. Her neck folded in half, causing a rumbling snore with each breath. She was smaller than the other dragon by half, but still dwarfed the girl next to her.

A long, rough tail snaked free from the stone shelf. It belonged to the girl's father, lying on the ground nearby, his body wrapped loosely around the sleepers. He lifted himself as quietly as he could, then lowered his head to nudge the younger dragon. She stirred a bit and straightened up, and her snoring stopped. Then he swiveled to look at the girl. His face contained the primitive coldness of any lower species, a blank expression concerned only with survival, but after considering her for a moment, his eyes softened with affection. An almost human tenderness transformed his face. He rubbed his cheek against her side as gently as a cat's paw, careful to keep the smoke from her face. She didn't stir, but her sleepy hand rose up and rested on his lip. He held there, savoring the moment just as any human father would have done, then gently slipped away and left the two to sleep. But when he stalked away to the next chamber, the crash of his footfalls resounded through the cave.

The girl's eyes fluttered open. She heard the thundering movement of another dragon with her father in the next chamber. Her mother. Then, she heard the harsh, rasped rumble of voices. After a lifetime of passing flame through their throats, the dragons' voices sounded scorched and charred.

"It was a foolish act and nothing more," said her father.

The girl crept down from her perch and hopped across the boulders scattered across the cave floor until she reached the entrance to the next chamber, a jagged hole worn through the stone by centuries of dripping water. She peered over the bottom of the hole and saw her father sitting near a massive fire. Her mother, nearly as big and the yellow-green of dying leaves, cleaned his wounds with small blasts of liquid flame. This chamber, the central feature of the family's cave, was enormous, big enough to stand the two biggest pines in the forest atop each other with room to spare.

"We can't go on like this. She'll kill herself, or one of us," said her mother.

The girl's heart thumped. She knew beyond any doubt they were talking about her.

"It had to have been an accident," said her father, recoiling as a blast of fire torched his neck. "Why in the world would she jump?"

"Because her sister can fly so well. Do you think she doesn't see how far behind she is?"

"But she hasn't even got wings."

"Yes," said her mother. The sudden gravity in her voice sent a chill up the girl's spine. "And we know why that is, don't we?"

Her father growled and turned his head.

"It doesn't mean we love her any less. It only means we must face facts and start treating her like what she really is: a human."

"What do I know about raising a human?" snapped her father. "How are we supposed to prepare a human for the world?"

The girl's lip began to tremble. As the firelight danced across her face, she fell silently to pieces. She hid in the shadows, knees pulled tight to her chest, until her parents had finished their conversation and retired to their own chamber. Then she raced through the cavern and splashed up the slope that led to the surface. A blast of cold air hit her as she approached the cave mouth. Everything was covered in moss, and trickles of water sifted through the rock teeth. She stepped out into the night, the waxing moon bathing everything blue. Wearing only her spiderweb covering, she tracked along the base of the mountain until the stone gave way to forest bracken.

What is a human? What am I?

She gasped, and her breath caught in her throat. There, just ahead, was the broken part of the mountain where her father had saved her life. The explosion of boulders and trees. The splashes of black blood sparkling in the moonlight.

It was my fault. He could have died, and it was all my fault.

As she approached the crash site, the degree of devastation pierced her heart. This might have been her father's gravesite, and all because she chose to jump. *How could I have been so selfish?*

There, wedged into the stone, beneath a slash of blood, she saw something. She clutched the sharp edge and pulled loose a scale. It was one of her father's, broken off in the violence of that morning. Blood had dried across one side, shimmering in the light like stars.

She had crept out of the cave that night not knowing what to do. Now, as she worked dead bileberry weeds through a hole in the scale and lashed it around her neck, she knew she could never go home again.

They're better off without me. All of them. I won't hold my sister back any longer, and I won't trouble my parents.

She slipped into the black of the forest, the most difficult place for them to track her, and ran straight on for hours. The rain started to fall shortly after she entered the trees, building in intensity as the night wore on. She was determined to get far enough away that her parents would never find her, but the storm soon built to a raging frenzy. Lightning strobed the forest, and rain made climbing near impossible. Everything became a shiny wet blackness, lit up time and again by bolts from the sky. Thunder pounded from the heavens. And still she ran.

She scrambled down the bank of a dry riverbed that was quickly filling with runoff. She sploshed across, but a wall of floodwater suddenly cascaded through, knocking her down and sweeping her away. She fought the river, but was powerless against the rampaging waters. Finally, hundreds of feet off her original course, she managed to grab hold of a dead branch and pull herself from the rapids.

She slopped up the far bank and tried to run again, but the intensity of the tempest frightened her. Wind howled through the trees, throwing sprays of rain in all directions. She would scarcely open her eyes before another gust spattered them with water. Lightning and thunder assaulted the forest. And all she had to protect herself was a thin layer of wadded-up spiderwebs.

She staggered toward a sprawling beech for shelter. Instead, the crackle of splintering wood tore through the air, and a massive branch crashed to the ground behind her. She tumbled into the undergrowth. When she turned back, the branch was lifting off the ground in a rustle of leaves and a groan of wood. It rose high into the black sky above. Lightning flashed, and she finally saw the tree for what it truly was.

This tree is trying to kill me.

The lightning blast struck the tree in an explosion of flame, sawing off the branch. It sailed back to the earth, serenaded by a furious roar of thunder. She dove out of the way just before it would have crushed her to death. The way the huge branch landed left a small gap underneath. She wormed through the muck and into this new shelter.

Oh please oh please oh please, get me out of here!

A colossal gust of wind blasted the forest. Leaves and detritus swirled through the air, and the girl thought she might be swept away into the night sky. As she clenched her eyes and held on to the broken branch, she heard a slap against the wood just above her head. She looked up and saw something that didn't belong. Something man-made. A parchment.

Something on the parchment caused her such astonishment that it drowned out the tempest that had nearly killed her. It was so unusual, so unthinkable, that she couldn't make sense of it. *Perhaps I am already dead.*

It was the Pennyroyal Academy notice, with its picture of the princess in front of the castle, pinned to the branch by the wind.

She reached up with shaking hand and peeled the notice from the tree. As rain sluiced down her face, she stared at the princess with such confusion that she forgot to breathe.

She looks like me. She looks exactly like me.

10

"A GOBLIN HELPED point me toward Marburg, but I never would have made it without Remington," said Evie, her voice just above a whisper.

She paused and waited for a reaction, but found only the soft snoring of the girl in the bunk next to Anisette's.

"All the stories my mother and father told while I was growing up were about knights killing dragons. I couldn't believe it when I found one who actually wanted to help me."

Still no one spoke. Her heart began to pound. *Why couldn't I have just kept my mouth shut?*

"You lot are the first humans I'd ever seen," she said with a nervous quiver. "When Remington brought me to enlist . . . it was as though I'd been dropped into an entirely new world—"

"I'm sorry, Evie, I'm having a hard time understanding," said Basil. "When you jumped from the cliff, you were trying to . . . end it all?"

"What? No! No, I did it to make my father proud," she said, stumbling slightly over her words. "I suppose a part of me knew

I wouldn't be able to fly, but I couldn't bear their looks any longer. Sympathetic and worried and . . . My whole life I knew I was the part of the family that didn't belong, and if I could only fly, then perhaps . . . I guess I wasn't thinking clearly."

Basil crossed one leg over the other, still picking his teeth. "Well . . . beats my story."

Evie looked to Maggie, to Anisette, to Demetra. All were deep in thought. It was Anisette who spoke first.

"Right, Eves, are you saying you was raised by dragons?"

Evie cringed and checked the nearby bunks, but no one was listening. *Why did I open my mouth? I knew they wouldn't believe me.*

"Dragons eat people, yeah? So how come they didn't eat you?"

"Curious, isn't it?" said Basil. "They must have warped her mind somehow—"

"No, you don't understand. They're good to me—*were* good to me. Better than I deserved."

"I've heard of wolves raising cats and things before, but dragons? Dragons as a species are mindless, murderous monsters—"

"Stop it!" said Maggie a bit too loudly. "That's her family!"

"Yes, but they're dragons—"

"And what does it matter?" She climbed off Anisette's bunk and sat next to Evie, pulling her into a protective embrace. "They raised her and cared for her, and she loves them." Evie had started to feel as helpless as she had tumbling through the raging river waters. And Maggie had just become the branch that saved her.

"Fair point, that," said Anisette.

"Your family may be dragons, but they still sound better than mine," said Demetra.

Basil chuckled. "Now *that* I can agree with. Sorry, Evie, I didn't mean anything by it."

"Everyone's got strangeness in their family," added Anisette with a shrug. "Yours just had scales as well."

"So you don't think I'm mad?" said Evie.

"The first thing you need to know about humans?" said Maggie. "We're all mad."

Evie spent that night cocooned tightly in her blanket. If she could only get through one night lying down like the others, perhaps she could break the impulse to perch. But long after the final torch had been snuffed, sleep still didn't come. She lay awake in the darkness listening to Anisette's snores and the distant singing of frogs. Memories swam through her mind hour upon hour, and none needed to be prompted by a bitter potion—her father teaching her and her sister to scale a tree . . . her mother guiding her up the rock to the top of the cliff . . . her sister darting a claw into a lake and pulling out a flopping silver fish, bigger than Evie. Her life had been a happy one. Even as she dissected it into its smallest parts, she could find only one complaint from her days in the cave, and that was her own body. No wings. No scales. And a fraction of the size of her sister. Had she only looked like a dragon, all would have been bliss. Instead, she had chosen to leave her father, her mother, her sister, and the only home she had ever known and come to this strange place to learn to fight witches. What were the Fates playing at?

At some point in those quiet hours, her memories became dreams. And as the first gray light of dawn streamed through the window, a voice from the next bunk pulled her back into consciousness.

"Eves! You did it! You're off the perch!"

She opened her eyes to Anisette's smiling face, sideways in her vision, as though she were sitting on the wall. As her mind emerged from the swamp of grogginess, she realized she was still lying down. Her right arm was numb, and as she sat up, sharp stings of pain started to attack it.

"I did it," she said. "I did it! My head feels odd. Like I was in a deeper sleep than usual or something."

"That's because you had blood in your brain, like you're meant to. Come on, let's get ready before the Fairy Drill-sergeant turns up."

As the weeks began to roll from one to another, the canopy of clouds remained. Some days the cover would be cottony white-gray; others, great roiling mountains of black in the sky. The air became colder, the rains sharper, and the clouds never broke.

But beneath them, in the packed dirt and mortared cobble alleys that snaked through Pennyroyal Academy, Evie gradually began to feel more at home. Revealing her secret to her friends had lightened her burden. She found herself better able to focus, and her mind became a dry sponge soaking up knowledge.

Lieutenant Volf may have been a brittle old man with rotten breath and a short temper, but he had managed to produce a sea of fascinating work about princesses and witches. She read the next two volumes in his collection in less than a week each, then skipped ahead to one of the later tomes. During an exercise in the dungeons of Thorn Keep, a small fortress behind Pennyroyal Castle, Maggie had told Evie of a modern-day princess called Princess Middlemiss, the only cadet ever to successfully escape these bare stone cells. Evie had become so intrigued by the idea of a princess who was still alive and out there beyond the Dortchen Wild fighting witches that she needed to know more. She read Volf's book through, then went back to page one and started again, though this time she skipped past the stories of missing children, taken into the forest by moonlight and never heard from again. These kidnappings provoked such heartache and anger inside her that she would read on and then realize she hadn't absorbed a word of it.

She enjoyed learning of the exploits of the great princesses of the past, and about the tidal shifts in the world that resulted from the witch-princess wars, but studying a real person who had roamed these buildings only a few short years before somehow made Princess History more real and immediate. According to Volf's text, Middlemiss had only been an average cadet at the Academy, one of the worst in her class to be commissioned as a Princess of the Shield, yet she had proved to be one of the best in the real world, single-handedly ridding the coastal kingdoms of the One-Shore Sea of witches. If Middlemiss could find a way through the Academy and carve out a place for herself in the world, then perhaps Evie could, too.

She hadn't seen much of Remington, aside from brief exchanges in the Dining Hall, and that suited her just fine. Between memory treatments, worrying over her Grand Ball gown, and keeping up with the physical demands of her training, she had begun to think he would be nothing more than a distraction, anyway.

But now that she stood only a few yards away from him, she realized how much she had missed that glint of mischief in his eyes. She stole a glance at him and he was already looking at her. She quickly looked away.

"Pay close attention, all of you," said the Fairy Drillsergeant, floating near the hulking, bearded Captain Ramsbottom. "This is not a game."

Ironbone Company and Thrushbeard Company had gathered beneath a thin, octagonal tower called Joringel's Stem. There were other, bigger towers nearby—the tallest being Dapplegrim Tower, so disjointed and crumbling it looked like giants had been bashing at it—but standing at its base, Joringel's Stem seemed high enough. Particularly when a small figure in silver stepped onto the ledge of the highest window, framed by the swirling black clouds above. Then, to gasps and screams, she fell.

A horse tore across the courtyard ridden by a knight cadet in matching silver and chain mail, leaning forward to slice the air. Just as the princess was about to smash on the stone, the horse galloped past and she landed on its back. The Thrushbeard knights cheered as the horse curled back around and trotted to a stop before them.

"And that's how you escape a tower," said the Fairy Drillsergeant. "Thank you, cadets."

The knight and princess bowed their heads, then rode off and disappeared around the tower.

"It takes timing and trust to execute this type of escape. But if you don't master it, you could be spending the bulk of your career trapped in a tower." A ripple of nervous whispers broke out on the princess side. "Relax, you sorry wumpers, I've got a wand, haven't I? Those were first-class cadets. They're the only ones to do this without safety precautions."

Evie noticed Demetra standing near Maggie, eyes fixed on a lone dandelion. She looked ashen. *There's something the matter with her lately,* she thought. *I must remember to try to talk to her during free hours.*

"Today, you'll be working with partners." Evie looked to Remington. He gave her a smile and raised his eyebrows. As she grinned back, Malora took a half step forward and blocked their view. Evie couldn't say for certain if it was intentional or not, but she suspected it probably was.

To her consternation, she hadn't been paired with Remington, but with Forbes. Judging by the flat acceptance in his reaction, he was none too thrilled with the pairing, either. She and the other Ironbone girls followed Demetra and Maggie up the twisting turnpike staircase that seemed to stretch on to the heavens.

"Come on, Demetra, there's nothing to worry about," came Maggie's voice from above, bouncing off the tubular stone walls. They passed a small diamond-shaped window, and Evie caught a glimpse of the knight cadets below. They already looked small and distant, and there were many more stairs left to climb.

Finally, they crested the staircase and emerged into an empty lookout room, where most of the walls had been cut away into pointed arches to create panoramic windows. Maggie dragged Demetra across the hollow wooden floor to the window overlooking the courtyard. Evie followed. Behind her, scattered members of Ironbone Company emerged, huffing for breath.

"Look, there's my knight!" said Maggie, pointing to the ground below.

"*Whenever you're ready, Cadet!*" came the ghost of the Fairy Drillsergeant's voice.

Maggie turned to Evie with wide eyes and an excited smile, and a moment later she was gone.

"Maggie!" screamed Demetra.

Evie leaned over the rain-smoothed ledge and saw a flash of motion in the courtyard below. A moment later, the horse traced a wide arc into the field beyond, carrying both Maggie and her knight.

"Brilliant, Cadet!" shouted the Fairy Drillsergeant. "Who's next up there?"

A small contingent of Ironbone girls huddled near the top of the staircase, with others sporadically joining them. Most were hunched over or leaning against the wall, struggling for breath. Others looked in no hurry to take their turns.

Evie turned to Demetra. "Reckon it's us."

"Shouldn't kingsbloods go first?" said Kelbra to Malora. Evie looked over, ready for a fight. Instead, Malora gave her a sly smile.

"Let them," she said. "We won't get any of their splatter on us up here." Evie scowled, but Malora didn't seem to mind.

"You go ahead," said Demetra.

Evie gave Malora one last glare, then put a foot on the window ledge. But before she could jump, something stopped her. Something she had glimpsed in Demetra's eyes.

"Demetra . . . are you all right?" She stepped down into the lookout room.

"I can't." Demetra slowly shook her head. Her lip trembled and her eyes welled with tears.

"What do you mean?"

"I can't do it. I'd rather go home."

"Demetra, listen, all you have to do is close your eyes, take one step, and it'll be over in a moment." She put a hand on her friend's arm. "Trust me, I've done it from a higher place than this."

"It's not the fall, Evie, it's . . . They're on horseback down there."

"Go on, will you? It's getting crowded up here," said Malora as more Ironbone girls reached the top.

"Demetra." Evie gripped her shoulders and looked straight into her eyes. "What's wrong?"

"*What's going on up there?*" shouted the Fairy Drillsergeant. "*Do I have to come up and throw you out?*"

"I should just go home and save everyone the bother," said Demetra with a sniffle.

"I don't understand. You're one of the best in the company—"

"But I'm not my sister, am I? I'll never be my sister. I can't even ride a bloody horse." She took a deep breath and looked out the window, and the daylight lit up the pain in her eyes. "I used to go riding all the time until my horse threw me. I don't even remember why it happened, but I'll never forget it. I couldn't breathe. I tried to scream to my father that I was dying, but I couldn't speak."

"Are you seriously crying?" said Malora, incredulous. Kelbra laughed, and so did a few others.

Evie glowered at her. "Quiet, Malora, can't you see she's scared?"

Malora's jaw tightened in anger, but she didn't say anything.

"My father picked me up and put me back in the saddle. I still couldn't breathe, but he said I had to toughen up and keep riding. The horse threw me again, and I . . ." She swallowed back the horrible memory, but couldn't stop tears from falling. "The look on my sister's face . . . like it was somehow *my* fault . . ."

"Forget your sister. This is for you. None of us is going to make it through this place without confronting our fears."

"Bloody hell, girls, all you have to do in this exercise is FALL!"

"You just have to step through and do it, that's all there is. Besides, you can't go home. What if you're the Warrior Princess?" said Evie with a smile.

Demetra laughed and wiped her eyes. "And afraid of a horse? I think Basil might have better odds."

"Hey!" he said. "I'm sitting right here!"

A blast of wind shot through the window. "All right," she said with a shiver. "All right." She put her hands on either side of the arch and stepped into the window.

"Look, there's your horse there," said Evie, pointing to Demetra's knight at the courtyard's edge. "That horse is going to keep you alive, do you understand?"

Demetra nodded. She looked out at the distant horizon, where the charcoal clouds sawed the Glass Mountains in half, and she was gone.

Her screams pierced the campus, and behind Evie the girls who were already nervous about the fall shifted uncomfortably. Down the side of the tower, Evie saw a glimpse of whipping golden hair and a galloping horse, and then she was on its back riding into the green expanse beyond.

"That's what I like to see, Cadet! Perhaps I've underestimated Ironbone Company, have I? Who's next?"

Evie didn't wait for discussion. She stepped onto the rain-smoothed stone and crouched in the window. The winds swished in and out of the lookout room, playing havoc with her balance. From these heights, the undulating peaks and valleys of the Dortchen Wild looked like a tempestuous green sea. She could even see the slight curve of the earth as she looked from one end of the world to the other. She closed her eyes, ignoring the pig snorts and laughter behind her, and let the wind rush across her face. She pulled the dragon scale from her dress and put it to her lips.

"For you, Father," she whispered. And then she leaned out into empty air and fell.

As she plummeted toward the ground, she had none of the terror of her fall from the cliff. This was different. She let the wind push her arms away from her body and felt the adrenaline course through her blood. With her eyes closed, she could almost imagine that she was flying. It was a blissful weightlessness she had never experienced before, and it felt so entirely *right*—

Her body slammed to a sudden stop, and her neck snapped forward. *I've missed my horse*, she thought. *I'm dead.* She tried to inhale, but could only manage a tiny wheeze of air. She opened her eyes and saw . . . grass?

"WHAT IN BLAZES DO YOU THINK YOU'RE DOING?" screamed the Fairy Drillsergeant, so incensed that her voice rasped away to nothing.

Gradually, Evie's lungs began to draw air again. She looked around and realized she was floating only inches off the ground, spared from a horrible death by the magic in the Fairy Drillsergeant's wand.

But why am I above grass and not cobblestones?

"ARE YOU TRYING TO GET YOURSELF KILLED? AN-SWER ME, CADET!"

"I . . . I'm sorry, Fairy Drillsergeant, I don't know what happened." She coughed, and her breathing returned to normal.

The Fairy Drillsergeant flicked her wand and Evie fell the last few inches to the ground. She pushed herself to her knees, and that's when it dawned on her.

I've just flown.

Forbes sat on his mount near the tower, a look of utter bafflement on his face. Somehow, she had overshot him, overshot the entire courtyard, and had ended up in the middle of the field.

Fates be praised, I've just flown.

She caught the eyes of Maggie and Demetra, both looking back at her with astonishment.

"GET IN THERE AND RUN THAT STAIRCASE UNTIL I TELL YOU TO STOP! I WILL NOT HAVE . . . *WHATEVER THAT WAS* IN MY COMPANY!"

Evie staggered to her feet. Her muscles felt weak and shaky. She started to run back to Joringel's Stem, and a smile bloomed across her face. With each quivering step, it grew bigger and the Fairy Drillsergeant's screams faded farther away.

I did it, Father. I flew.

As she passed through the tower door and started up the turnpike stairs once again, the exercise slowly returned to normal operation. Evie ran the stairs, up and down, for more than an hour. And she felt so light and free that she could have easily done twenty more.

I flew, Father, and I am your little girl after all.

EVIE SAT on a low wall bordering one of the Academy's many baileys, this one accented with spindly, leafless fruit trees. The unhewn stone of the wall was dry, though heavy black clouds above bulged with rain. Her breath puffed in the crisp air as she turned another page of her book. She had spent so much time reading about Princess Middlemiss and other contemporary princesses that she had fallen behind on her actual class work. She didn't mind having to catch up, though. The story she was reading now had her riveted. It told of Princess Pennyroyal's very first discovery of courage, a seminal event in Princess History. She had only been two years older than Evie was now when it happened. A wicked witch had enslaved her village and killed her beloved grandparents, who had raised her from birth. This act triggered something inside her that had snuffed her fears and allowed her to stand face-to-face with the witch. Armed with nothing but her own courage and the memory of her grandparents, Pennyroyal had become the first princess ever to drive a witch from a kingdom. It was the purest display of courage Evie had ever heard told, made all the more miraculous because of where she was reading it. She ran a hand over the flagstone wall, pocked with divots caused by years and weather. It had new meaning to her now. Every stone, every building, every concept in this Academy could be sourced to the story she now read.

"*Volume Three: A Narrative History on the Origins of Courage* by . . . Volf. Sounds absolutely horrendous."

Evie looked up to find Remington, dressed in a black tunic beneath his black leather Thrushbeard doublet. A tarnished bronze scabbard at his hip housed a sword.

"Hello," she said.

"Aren't you a bit cold out here?" He cupped his hands and blew into them.

She closed her book and said nothing. Perhaps it was that she had been so deeply engrossed in the book, or perhaps it was something else, but she found herself at a bit of a loss for words.

"Oh, that's right," he said, eyeing a flapping banner in the distance, "you don't particularly feel the cold, do you? I remember that from our first frigid swim together."

Something near a barren apple tree across the way caught her attention. Three girls in emerald tunic dresses, shivering and pretending not to, seemed to be having a chat. But Evie noticed that they kept glancing over. Remington followed her eyes and saw them, too.

"Bloody hell . . ." He shook his head. "All right, ladies?" he called, and they scattered, mortified to have been spotted. "Honestly, what is it about your kind? They seem to think I'll be their Grand Ball escort if they only lurk about and make me uncomfortable enough."

"Perhaps they're waiting to see if you'll need rescuing from a witch," said Evie. Immediately after the words were out, her face fell. She had meant it to sound flirtatious, but then realized she had no idea how to do that. Still, her worry vanished when he laughed.

"Is that so? Well, when the final songs are sung, we'll see who saved whom."

Their eyes held for a moment, and neither spoke. It was only a second or two, but something remarkable passed between them. His swagger fell away and she glimpsed a completely different person underneath.

"Besides, I've retired from the witch game," he said in a clumsy attempt to cover the moment. "I'm on to dragons now."

She cringed, and her spine straightened just a bit.

"Speaking of which," she said, "I believe you owe me an apology."

"Do I?"

"You lied to me when we first met. You said you weren't a knight."

He glanced around the bailey in confusion, as if only now realizing where he was. "This is the training academy, is it not? Or else I've been horribly misled."

"I heard about your . . . that you've . . ." She choked on the words. *"Killed a dragon."*

"Where did you hear that?" he said, his face darkening. "Honestly, the gossip is endless. No, my lady, I haven't killed any dragons. Or giants or tigers or sea serpents, either."

She studied his face, trying to read his truthfulness. His anger over the rumor seemed genuine. Was it possible it really wasn't true? They stood there a moment, neither sure what to say, until finally the bong of a bell echoed deep in campus.

"Ah, the chimes of the late cadet, forever ringing, forever ringing," he said as his eyes lightened and his smile returned. "Try not to freeze out here. I didn't rescue you from a witch only to see the elements get you."

He flicked his dark eyebrows, and then he was gone. A smile crept across her face as she watched him go. If Maggie really was mistaken, if he hadn't actually killed a dragon . . . well . . .

Her smile blossomed until her lips parted and she was beaming. As she was replaying the conversation in her head, three figures in green dresses scurried past, and she burst out in laughter.

That night in the Dining Hall, she caught herself staring over at him all through supper. Unless she consciously forced herself to listen to her friends—and tonight's topic of conversation was Maggie defending to all others that the white-furred snowbear really did exist in the lands of the south—her eyes always found their way back across the room to his table.

Over the next few days, her thoughts kept returning to the bailey. *He hasn't killed a dragon after all.* And with that fact dispensed, he came to mind at meals, during drills, in classrooms, and in the Infirmary. But unlike the distractions she had battled during her first few weeks at the Academy, this one was quite welcome.

Anisette turned many nighttime conversations to the knights. She and Maggie seemed to take particular pleasure in teasing Evie about Remington, which usually drove Basil out of the barracks to his storehouse. But Evie kept her feelings to herself, and responded with nothing more than a smile.

She was smiling still as she and her company followed the Fairy Drillsergeant up a rain-slicked road to the Armory, a brown dome that lay on the ground like a fallen shield, glinting in the wet.

"Inside, all of you," said the Fairy Drillsergeant, who seemed in an even fouler mood than usual.

The cadets poured through the iron-studded doors and into a vast circular chamber with a low, curved ceiling. The walls were ringed with every type of armor and close-combat weapon imaginable. Spears and spikes and swords and maces and shields. Pennyroyal banners streamed down the walls, separating the various families of weaponry. The center of the Armory was dominated by a worn sparring pit of scarred cobblestones, crisscrossed with the chinks and slashes of weapons slapping rock.

"We get to fight!" said Anisette. As cadets wandered the room inspecting the weaponry, she and Basil started arguing about the merits of a broadsword versus a great sword.

Evie, however, stopped just inside the doorway. Something across the room unsettled her. Two large statues, one around ten feet and the other half that, rested beneath a thin slit window. The smaller of the two was a little girl playing with a frog, her face permanently frozen in the wonder and innocence of childhood. The larger was a witch, feeble and cloaked. The way the statues were positioned, the little girl faced away from the witch, blissfully unaware of what was forever creeping up behind her.

"Gather round, ladies, gather round," said the Fairy Drill-sergeant. Her sparkling dust fell atop a wooden rail that ringed the sparring pit, broken sporadically to allow fighters to enter. "Right. Hessekel. Gisela. Step forward, please."

No one moved. The girls looked around in confusion.

"That's right. They're gone. I discharged them last night."

The shock was palpable. Evie had been partnered with Hessekel in a drill about navigating enchanted forests a month ago, but hadn't spoken to her since. Gisela she didn't know at all. Yet they were Ironbone girls, and now they were gone.

"The Grand Ball has only one winner," said the Fairy Drill-sergeant. "The rest of you will have to fight your way through the Helpless Maiden." She folded her arms behind her and began floating slowly back and forth. "It's time to get serious, ladies. The world is falling apart out there. Remember Marburg? Where we first met? The witches are there."

Several girls gasped, and Demetra called out, "No!" Evie's mind immediately went to the three little girls dancing on the high street. And what must their faces look like now?

"Marburg will be exceedingly difficult for the witches to take—Princess Gabriela is one of the best there is—but the simple fact that they're there is troubling. And that's why we're here today. I want to give you a taste of a second-year drill to remind you what your training is all about."

Those three laughing faces spun through Evie's mind, whirling faster and faster to the fiddler's tune.

"What is a princess's first option when confronted by a witch?"

"Evasion," said a smattering of cadets. Even as a chorus, their voices were grim.

"And if she's seen you?"

The little girls vanished, replaced by yellow eyes veined with red. *If she's seen you, it's too late.*

"Perhaps you'd opt for a sword, yes?" The Fairy Drillsergeant flicked her wand and a massive broadsword sailed across the room, the steel throwing off sparks as it clanged into the far wall and spun to rest. "A pike perhaps? A mace?" A swirl of the wand launched a wooden spear and spiked ball through the air. Evie glanced at Maggie, and even she looked frightened. "Any witch worth her salt has far more powerful magic than I do. Those weapons," she said, thrusting a finger across the room, "are useless. Your battle isn't fought in a tower or village. It's fought in here." She thumped her chest with a closed fist. "And your weapons have been with you since the day you were born.

"The witch's weapon is fear. She aims to put as much into your heart as she can before she takes it. Either that or she'll simply turn you to stone. If that sounds preferable to death, it is not. The skin hardens to rock. The blood stops flowing. The living flesh is petrified, but the mind is not." The dull patter of rain was the only sound in the cavernous Armory. None of the girls moved. Most stared at the discarded weapons strewn across the floor.

"The witch uses fear, but so do we. And there's nothing she fears more than love." She continued her slow patrol, locking eyes with whichever cadet was in front of her. "She has no answer for it. *That* is the magic of a Princess of the Shield. *That* is how you defeat a witch. Whoever scares the other in the core of her heart first, wins. That's the game."

She aimed her wand and gave it a flick. The statues began to grind across the floor into the sparring pit. Several girls screamed and covered their ears from the horrible grate of stone on stone. Finally, the statues reached the center of the pit, and the horrific sound stopped with a lingering echo.

"These statues were created to simulate real-world conditions. Our dissident witch helped us design and enchant them to feel authentic. When you step into this ring, you need only remember two things: compassion is your shield, and courage is your weapon. If you can't draw it, you'll feel hers. Know yourself and trust yourself, ladies. Let's find out who you really are."

Evie studied the malicious grin on the witch's face. Her eyes were wide, hungrily looking down on the innocent girl.

"Cadet Magdalena, step forward, please."

Maggie entered the pit through a gap in the rail. The floor had the slightest of grades, like a shallow bowl, sloping away to the center where the statues now rested.

"Are you frightened, Cadet?"

"Yes, Fairy Drillsergeant."

"Wait 'til you've got to find your courage with a twelve-foot mountain witch standing above you." She flicked her wand again and the statues came to life, a small billow of dust wafting off each. The horrible grinding of stone resumed. *Do your best, Cadet!* she shouted over the din. The figures moved slowly, as though submerged in quicksand. From Evie's vantage point, she could see most of the right side of Maggie's face, and there she saw fear.

"*Courage cannot coexist with self-doubt!*" shouted the Fairy Drillsergeant.

Maggie stood alone before the moving statues. She didn't move, just stared at the unfolding scene. The witch eased her shoulders back, and her cloak slipped slowly to her feet. The little girl reached out a delicate hand to stroke the frog's back.

"*What's she feeling, that little girl? Does your heart ache for her?*"

The little girl's head turned, agonizingly slowly, and the lightness in her eyes faded, replaced by an expression of pure terror, an anguished scream. The witch, meanwhile, raised her bony arms, her eyes and mouth pulling even wider until her face was a distorted mask of horror. Spider legs of fear crawled up and down Evie's body. *And I'm not even the one in the pit.*

"*Now . . . draw your weapon, Cadet,*" said the Fairy Drillsergeant.

Maggie closed her eyes and disappeared inside herself. Her hands trembled at her sides. Her eyes squinted tight. The other cadets looked at one another with frightened anticipation, no one quite sure what was happening. But, as certain as the sun, *something* was happening . . .

A strange glow flickered in the air near Maggie's chest. It was faint, yet undeniably there.

"*That's it, Cadet! That's it!*"

The pale light intensified, as though each beat of Maggie's heart made it stronger. The cadets watched in awe, eyes wide, as it pulsed into an illuminated bloom of wafting strands, like a jellyfish of stars.

"*There it is, girls. Courage!*" called the Fairy Drillsergeant.

Maggie's jaw quivered and her eyelids went white, so tightly were they closed. As a princess's magic undulated in the air, the witch's bloodthirsty smile and hate-filled eyes began to shift away from the little girl to focus on her. With the full force of the witch's dark magic trained on her, every part of Maggie's face quivered. Untold stores of darkest terror were hurtling, invisible, straight into her heart.

"*That's her weapon. Suffering . . . despair . . . Only compassion can block it! Look at that little girl!*"

Maggie's body shuddered from the extraordinary effort.

Still, the bloom in front of her chest began to spatter and dissolve, like rain on snow. She opened her eyes to focus on the little girl, tears streaming down her cheeks, but it was too late. Her frail blossom of courage faded to deep gray. And then it was gone.

She yelped in pain and fell backward. Then she scrambled up the pit until she backed into one of the rail posts, pulling her knees in tight. The Fairy Drillsergeant flicked her wand and the awful grinding sound echoed to a stop.

"Compassion and courage are the only weapons you'll have against a witch," said the Fairy Drillsergeant. "I take that rather seriously. Hessekel and Gisela didn't. What about you? The spell on that statue over there is a quarter of what a real witch can do. It's time to stop mucking about and commit yourselves, ladies."

Demetra helped Maggie to her feet. Evie was so shaken that she didn't even join the chorus of, "Yes, Fairy Drillsergeant." If good, kindhearted Maggie suffered that much in a simulation, what chance would Evie have when confronted with a real witch? The progress she had made since arriving at the Academy now seemed so fragile. Would it hold up under those piercing yellow eyes? Or would it crumble like so many kingdoms already had?

12

"PRINCESS CADET MAGDALENA!" called Beatrice.

A flurry of voices became a wild cheer, snapping Evie from her reverie. She was in the Royal Hall and Maggie had a grip on her arm, her eyes as wide as the sun.

"She called my name . . . but those are all princesses of the blood up there . . ."

Cadets congratulated her and guided her away from Evie, down the row of benches toward the center aisle. Only once she was gone did it dawn on Evie that her friend had just been selected to the Grand Ball. She'd been a million miles away, thinking about that day in the Armory. Thinking about courage, or lack thereof.

The entire third class had gathered to hear the announcement of the Grand Ball competitors. Forty knight cadets, ten from each company, stood on the dais in their mud-spattered uniforms. One by one, they had heard called the names of the princesses they would be accompanying. And one by one, elated girls had popped up from the crowd and made their way forward. They had been selected by a small committee of instructors and House Princesses for their effort and dedication to their training thus far. And now each of them had earned the chance to win a coveted place in the second class.

As Maggie's auburn curls bounced toward the dais, trembling hands hovering near her mouth, Evie felt a twinge of regret that she had been too distracted to congratulate her friend. The applause and the hooting—mainly from Ironbone Company—began to die away as Maggie took her place with her partner, Cadet Stanischild, a rugged boy with thick arms that strained his black tunic. He looked utterly petrified.

Evie glanced across the dais as though she had just woken from a dream, which, in a sense, she had. Nearly all of the knight cadets had already been partnered. Only one remained at the far end. He wore the black of Thrushbeard Company and a half smile. His eyes were on the ceiling, and he looked as though he was struggling to keep from laughing. Girls from all companies leaned forward ever so slightly, desperate to hear the words that would launch a thousand letters home, as though marching down this aisle to become his Grand Ball partner was only the first step toward the inevitable march down the matrimonial aisle.

Evie scanned the blue dresses and found Malora sitting a few rows back. She looked serene, like the cat who knew where the fish swam, the whisper of a smile on her face.

Let it be anyone but her.

Princess Beatrice returned to the lectern. "The final competitor in this year's Grand Ball . . ." She took a gilded card from one of Rumpledshirtsleeves's miniature assistants, bedecked in a stylish suit of carmine and pink. "From Ironbone Company, to be escorted by Knight Cadet Remington of Thrushbeard Company . . . Princess Cadet Basil."

A confused murmur spread through the hall. Evie glanced at Basil, who sat with his arms crossed, a look of supreme annoyance on his face.

Beatrice, taken aback by the crowd's reaction, only now realized what she had said. She checked the card again, then began lambasting the hapless troll. He held out his upturned hands to show that it wasn't his fault.

Evie glanced back at Malora, perched at the edge of her bench, frantically scouring the hall for someone to set this horrible injustice to rights. Princess Hazelbranch hurried to the dais and whispered something in Beatrice's ear. With a glare of furious reproach, the Headmistress raised her hands for quiet. Evie's eyes met Remington's, and he gave her the slightest of winks. She didn't know what it meant, but her cheeks flushed red.

"It seems a mistake has been made," said Beatrice. Evie didn't turn back, but she could imagine the smug look on Malora's face. "The final competitor is not, indeed, Cadet Basil. It is Cadet Eleven."

Scattered applause broke out. A sea of faces turned toward

Evie. She had forgotten that Cadet Eleven was her. Anisette pulled her to her feet and ushered her down the row. "Go on, Eves! You made it!"

The Ironbone girls clapped her back and shouted her name as they helped her to the center aisle. It was only when she stood there, with nothing between herself and Remington except Princess Beatrice, who had resumed her scolding of the poor troll, that she finally understood. She, not Malora, would attend the Grand Ball with Remington.

She began to walk toward the dais, and heads turned to watch. As she mounted the stairs, Hazelbranch gave her a proud nod. For the first time since she had arrived at the Academy, all eyes were on her and she didn't mind. She stepped past Maggie, who gave her an ecstatic smile, and filed in next to Remington.

"I do sympathize with that bloke, but it had to be done," he said softly.

"What had to be done?"

"*That*. All this formality gives me a rash."

She turned to him and saw a mischievous spark in his eye. "*You* changed the names? But how?"

"Secret methods," he whispered.

Beatrice spoke, calming the murmurs of the crowd. "The winner of the Grand Ball brings great honor to her company—and his, of course—as well as the Grand Ball trophy, now housed in Stonewitch Company barracks."

A cheer went up from the girls of Stonewitch.

"Cadets," she continued, still scowling at the miniature troll, "these are your champions."

The Royal Hall filled with applause. Girls called out the names of friends lucky enough to have been chosen. The first few rows of cadets stood, then the rest of third class joined the ovation. Goose bumps rose on Evie's arms as the sound of mass approval enveloped her. Summoning courage was forgotten. The spiderweb dress was forgotten. Her memory curse was forgotten.

This is what it feels like to belong—

"*IT'S NOT FAIR!*" screamed a voice of venomous passion. The shriek was so loud that it pierced through the applause. "*SHE'S JUST A BLOODY PEASANT!*"

The clapping died away and heads swiveled to see who was responsible. A small ring started to open in the Ironbone blue.

"*SHE DOESN'T BELONG UP THERE WITH HIM!*" wailed Malora, her hands clutched tightly at her chest. Her face was twisted in rage, tears streaming from red eyes. "*SHE DOESN'T BELONG UP THERE AT ALL! SHE'S NOTHING BUT A CURRISH, LOWBORN FREAK!*"

"THAT IS QUITE ENOUGH!" boomed Princess Beatrice.

"It's me ... it's me ..." cried Malora, but her wave of fury had already crested.

"I SAID THAT'S ENOUGH!"

The Royal Hall was thick with tension. Though everyone was looking at Malora and trying to make sense of her shocking outburst, Evie had never felt such humiliation in her life.

Like a castle in the sand washed over by the tide, her fledgling confidence had vanished. Gradually, the curious eyes shifted her way, as though the cadets needed to see for themselves if the horrible things Malora had said were true. The girl who had been a dragon, then a human, was now something else entirely. She had been made subhuman. An object of ridicule. A freak.

Malora's sobs echoed through the hall. Red heat climbed Evie's chest and neck and into her face like flames in a building soon to crumble. She couldn't move.

"Now," said Beatrice, and from the sound of her voice, even she was a bit shaken by the outburst. "Where were we . . ."

As Beatrice read out an explanation of the Grand Ball's scoring system, Evie scanned the hall. Every set of eyes she saw was looking straight back at her. Some with sympathy. Some with amusement. Some with vicious whispers to the friends seated next to them.

"Forget it, Evie," said Remington, leaning in so closely she could feel his breath on her neck. "No one will remember—"

Suddenly, she leapt from the dais in two great bounds, sprinting down the aisle and out of the hall.

"Evie!" shouted Remington. But she was gone.

Her footfalls echoed through the rotunda as she burst out of Pennyroyal Castle, then ran past the fountain and its towering princess statue and down the hill through the swaying grass. She had already leapt the crumbling stone wall before anyone else even started down the hill. By the time they reached the edge of the clearing, she had disappeared into the thick green shadows of the Dortchen Wild, exposing herself to whatever creeping things waited beyond the magical protections of the wall.

She ran and ran and ran, her feet crunching through rust-colored oak leaves. She ran through low red spikes of deadnettles into a valley walled with green. She ran, but her heart was still in the Royal Hall, still trapped in that awful moment of humiliation. Phantom insects crawled over her body and she ran to shake them loose. She ran over hills and splashing streams, through white-flowered viburnum and thick tangles of chokeberry. The hairy arms of the beeches waved above as chill winds blew, and the sky faded from the bright gray of seaside sand to the ominous dark of fresh smoke. She ran until hemlocks slashed her arms and maidenhair ferns grew so thick she couldn't see the ground beneath.

If this is how humans treat one another, then I'd rather be a dragon.

She ran until her lungs burned and her uniform was soaked through with gossamer mist. After hours of pure flight, she trudged to a stop. Great, heaving sobs wracked her body. Running hadn't gotten her one step further from the thing she meant to escape.

A loud crackle tore through the air. She dove to the side as a swinging branch caught her leg, spinning her through the undergrowth. The bark tore her dress and opened bloody scrapes along her calf. She scrambled to her feet and raced to the tree's trunk, where its branches couldn't reach.

What have I done?

She wiped the bleariness from her eyes and surveyed the gloom of the forest. All around her, in every direction, was a perfect sameness. Spidery tree limbs and treacherous bracken and walls of forest and gullies and stones. She looked to the sky for guidance, but even the bits that showed through the canopy had faded to dusk. She was well and truly lost in a forest the Fairy Drillsergeant had described as the single most dangerous in all the land.

"Oh no . . . no no no no no no no . . ." Her breath came in white plumes where it hadn't only moments before.

A twig snapped in the distance. She searched the empty spaces between trees, but found only gathering darkness. She slid to a knee and hunched against the trunk, trying to make herself as small as possible. Her heart hammered inside her chest.

If she finds you don't look in her eyes don't let her see your fear or you're dead you're dead you're dead . . .

She knew it was a witch, and that everything she had been training for had deserted her. She was still the same frightened girl she had been in that cottage, shivering beneath the candy crank machine.

A cold, desolate cackle crept out from the dark, and Evie's last flicker of hope was snuffed. There, hobbling down a gentle slope, a shrouded figure lurched in the murky green. Evie was frozen, unable even to blink.

Something moved in her peripheral vision, and her eyes darted left. There, another figure, as formless and hunched as the other, trudged from the trees. This one, too, cackled with menace.

"Lost your way, young one?" said the first creature. It was the voice of a kindly old lady. A kindly old lady with blood under her fingernails.

"My word," said the second. "It's a Pennyroyal girl."

The witches were close enough now that even in the gloom she could make out the pale yellow orbs of their eyes.

"Fates be praised," came a third voice. Evie wheeled, eyes darting from one hag to the next. "Calivigne shall reward us proper for this."

The three witches staggered ever closer, and each step gave Evie the acute panic of drowning. Everything—the forest, the witches, even her own hands—now seemed to be stretching away, as though she was falling down a well. She could smell the pungent mustiness of wet earth, could see the scabbed cracks in the witches' lips.

And then she saw nothing.

From the darkness, a face appeared, no more than a dim halo of light. She couldn't discern the features, but the figure seemed to be young. A woman.

Mother, she thought. *Mother, is it you?*

"Awake now . . ." came a soft voice, and the face disappeared into the blackness.

"Awake . . ." It sounded small and distant, as though it were coming from inside a cave. Evie fought through the void to find it, to understand what it was saying.

"Awake, little one . . ." The voice became clearer. She had almost found her way out.

"That's it . . ."

She could smell fire, then, and taste something on her lips. She swallowed, and found a grainy substance on her tongue, bitter like an olive but with a hint of meaty iron.

"Awake . . ."

Slivers of light blinded her. She squinted to allow her eyes time to adjust. Tears tickled the skin near her temples, and she knew she was lying down. A wooden spoon split her lips, filling her mouth with another scoop of the putrid, curdled substance. She spit it out and forced her eyes open. One of the hags loomed over her, holding the spoon. The other two tended a steaming cauldron near a crackling fire.

Evie tried to sit, but she was bound to a bed with a rope as harsh as corroded metal. She writhed against her restraints, but to no avail.

"Yes, yes! Feel the fear in your veins!" croaked one near the fire. "It will only add to the value of that lovely heart."

Evie stopped struggling, but her muscles remained as tight as the ropes. All three witches leered at her with hungry smiles. They looked like corpses, interred and buried, that had risen again. Their skin, waxy and drooping in parts, was so attenuated across their skull bones that it looked like the slightest touch might tear it apart. White hair wisped from their heads and chins, and their wide mustard eyes were shot through with blood vessels.

"Our Sister should arrive momentarily," said the witch with the spoon. "It would be quite nice if you were properly terrified—"

A soft rapping at the door interrupted her. The witches threw up their hands and danced around with excitement.

"She's here! She's here!" they sang.

One crossed to the door, but didn't open it just yet. "Now remember what we discussed, girls. We have a price in mind . . ."

". . . and we intend to get it," finished the other two.

Dozens of thoughts flickered through Evie's mind. She tried to focus on one thing—escape—but it was only a word, quickly shunted away by visions of what waited behind that door. She spit again, trying to clear the vile taste from her mouth.

The door creaked open and the cottage fell silent, save for the pop and hiss of the fire as the witches' stew bubbled onto the coals.

"Good evening, Sister," said the witch at the door. She staggered back, clearing a path. The other two huddled together. Evie thought they looked frightened, and if they were frightened, what did that mean for her?

Cold night air poured into the cottage, followed by the most frightening thing Evie had ever seen.

A witch floated inside, her feet dragging limply across the floor beams. Her skin had the lumpy, slimy texture of sludge on a stagnant pond. Her jaw hung free in a wide smile, and her bright yellow eyes were trapped in a permanent stare because she had no eyelids to close. The instant she crossed the threshold, those eyes fixed onto Evie, who recoiled as though she had been bitten. The witch had only just entered the cottage, but already she had gone inside Evie's eyes, probing toward her heart, searching for courage.

"Welcome to our humble home, Sister. We trust your journey wasn't too difficult?" said the witch near the door.

The Sister ignored her and floated to the bed, her decaying tree-bark slippers scraping slowly across the floor. The stench of mold and rot filled Evie's nose, and the whole world started to blacken at the fringes of her vision. The witch noticed and hurried over with her spoon, forcing more of the bitter potion into her mouth. It shocked Evie back to consciousness. Tears streamed down her temples and into her hair. She had the same panicked feeling as when she had jumped from the cliff . . . a cold certainty that she was about to die.

"Our dear Sister," said the hag with the spoon. "You can see she's a Pennyroyal girl. Quite valuable, indeed."

The Sister's eyes bored into Evie, her mouth hanging wide.

"She's obviously yours to keep, m'lady, as we three are loyal to none but Calivigne."

The longer Evie's eyes remained locked on the Sister's, the more complexity she could see. Beyond the cold hate there was an unexpected depth of anguish, as though this witch was bound to roam the land seeing everything, every act of evil, without ever being able to close her eyes. And all that wickedness, despair, and madness now beamed straight from the Sister's eyes into Evie's heart. She had never felt so utterly meaningless in her life.

"If it please you, we should like to discuss a price, m'lady," said the witch, causing the other two to clench each other even more tightly. "Of course, we mean no insult to a witch as eminent as yourself. We are but three humble sisters struggling to make our lives in the dark forest."

Evie's strength began to drain. The ropes slackened, and her head sank back to the straw-stuffed pillow.

"Do you know," spoke the Sister in a low whisper, "how a witch is made?"

Don't listen! screamed Evie inside her head. *Look away!* Somewhere inside of her, a small spark of fight still remained.

"She is born from a cauldron," she continued in a strange, unplaceable accent, "the product of her ingredients. First, the heart of a dragon. Older dragons make the best witches, for they have seen the worst of life. The fury in a dragon's heart is unmatched."

"We have a fine selection of dragons' hearts as well, if you'd—"

"The second ingredient we require is a righteous heart," said the Sister. Evie realized that her jaw was barely moving, as though the words were being formed somewhere else, somewhere deep inside of her. "Innocent children, good men and women. All are acceptable, but most desired is the heart of a princess. It beats strongly with virtue, goodness, and innocence."

Tears streamed from Evie's eyes. She managed one last struggle with the ropes, but it was so feeble the witches didn't even notice.

"To create a truly cruel witch, one must find a virtuous heart bathed in fear. As yours is now. One dragon's heart of fury, one virtuous heart awash in terror. This is the recipe for the most wicked witches in all the land."

"And all we ask for this girl's heart is placement in a kingdom," said the witch with the spoon. The other two cowered as though the Sister might strike them dead at any moment. "Forgive me, m'lady, but our bones are too weary for this forest life."

The Sister's eyes remained on Evie's, which had started to flutter closed, like a butterfly slowly dying.

"Your price is fair—"

"We should also like an audience with Calivigne," continued the witch. Her eyes went wide and her shoulders crumpled. She realized she might have overstepped. "Simply to show her our potions . . . to see if we might be of use . . ."

"You shall not receive an audience with Calivigne," said the Sister. Her arm rose, skeletal fingers clacking as the joints snapped open. She slid a bony finger under the dragon scale necklace. "But I shall reward your loyalty with this."

With an abrupt flick of her wrist, she tore the necklace free.

"No . . ." muttered Evie, barely mustering the energy to speak.

"Oh, thank you, m'lady, thank you!" said the overjoyed witch. "Look, girls, dragon's blood and all!"

With a casual toss, and to the delight of her sisters, she lobbed the scale toward the cauldron.

"No!" said Evie. Her eyes shot open. A dying spark erupted into a flame. "No! No! No! No!"

The scale arced through the air, sinking into the boiling stew with a puff of rancid brown smoke. Evie held her breath and let the flame inside her build into a fire. Her mind was clear. Her eyes were open. Her fear was gone.

"NO NO NO NO NO!"

She pulled on the bindings with all her strength, then let herself go slack. She clenched again, feeling a kind of power she had never known course through her muscles. As the last ridge of the scale disappeared into the cauldron, something exploded inside of her.

"NO!"

A brilliant flash of electric light detonated in front of her chest. The bonds that had held so tightly ripped away like spiderwebs, and she was free. And then, like lightning, the white flash was gone.

She leapt off the bed and threw her shoulder into the witch nearest the cauldron, knocking her into the flames. The old crone shrieked as the fire sizzled her gauzy skin into a fine green mist. Evie plunged her hand into the boiling sludge of the cauldron. The pain was so intense it registered only as a bolt of shock in her brain. She couldn't feel her hand, but knew she had a grip on the scale. She ripped it from the stew and fled out the open door.

She tore through the black forest. True, shocking pain began to settle around her hand like a thousand tiny insects eating her flesh. She clutched the dragon scale in her other hand, the one that could still feel. Her foot found a goblin's hole and she went sprawling face-first through the rotting black leaves beneath the undergrowth.

She spit out a mouthful of muck and looked for a route of escape. But instead she found something else. Something that brought back the old familiar fear, that hopeless, helpless terror of witches that she just could not escape.

It was the sickly, pale glow of two yellow eyes. She flipped onto her back and found two more sets of witches' eyes.

"Leave me be!" she cried. Something grabbed hold of her leg, though nothing was there. The Sister began to pull her back through the bracken with some ancient, unknown spell.

"No! Please, stop!" She tried to kick free of the witch's magic, to roll and scrape and scream and struggle, but it was no use. The Sister dragged her closer and closer, using a black magic that only compassion and courage could defeat. And Evie was in no state to summon either.

Suddenly, she had the strangest sensation that she wasn't

moving anymore. A moment later there was an explosion, a concussive crash that rumbled the entire forest, as something elemental slammed to the ground only yards away.

Evie screamed and covered her head with her good arm. She was free, the witch's spell having somehow been broken. She scrambled away in a blind panic until she slammed into something big and solid and rough with scales.

"Sister?"

Evie's dragon sister contorted her face in serpentine rage and unleashed an unholy roar into the trees.

"Begone, wretched beast!" shouted one of the witches as the roar's echo faded into the night.

"We'll kill you and take your heart just for the fun!" called the other.

The dragon spewed a blast of flame into the trees, the smell so acrid it singed Evie's eyes. She heard the witches' shrieks of pain and terror, and couldn't imagine the fireball exploding around them. The thought of that—of those hideous witches that had been so close to killing her, fearing for their own lives—emboldened her. And then, through a mystery of the human mind, the faces of the three little girls of Marburg came to her again.

"Away with you, witches! Do you hear me? Away with you!" She took a step forward into the black, and something moved with her. There, yards ahead, an invisible shield seemed to mirror her every step. She couldn't be certain if it was real or just a product of her exhausted mind.

"I am not afraid of you!" she shouted, and with this, she knew the thing was real. A weapon born inside her that she had never known existed.

"Dragons and princesses have no alliance!" shrieked a voice so awful Evie knew it could only be the Sister's. "Calivigne shall hear of this!"

There was a flurry of movement, like bat wings flapping, and then silence. Evie stood in the dark for several moments, waiting for some sound to tell her the witches had truly gone. Finally, her dragon sister stomped forward and lowered her great head.

"Come, before the trees awake."

13

Beyond the green ripple of ferns, beyond the stand of bristlecone pines that marked the forest mouth, the towering shoulders of a mountain range loomed in the near distance. The peaks wore hoods of snow, and the trees were outlined in white nearly halfway down the valley.

Evie studied this swooping landscape of blacks and greens and whites as though she had never seen it before. But, of course, this was the same view she had woken to every morning of her life. She was home again, in the old familiar cave. Something about it seemed strange, though. *It's the sky,* she thought. *I haven't seen a sky of blue in months.*

She turned her head, wincing at a sharp ache that ringed her neck. Ignoring the pain, she saw that she was sitting on a mossy ledge. This had always been one of her favorite places to fall asleep as a girl. Here she would listen to her father tell stories of the great dragons of the past while the stars rolled slowly by. Her mind began to emerge from sleep, and the details of how she got back to the cave returned. Her sister had come out of the night to save her. She must have wrenched her neck running headlong into the dragon's leg during her scramble from . . .

Oh yes . . . the witches. It was the second time she had narrowly evaded death at their hands. But this time she had escaped by entirely different means.

She glanced down at her hand, the one that had rescued the dragon scale from the cauldron, and found it wrapped in a huge, gray verbascum leaf. She peeled the wet layers away until the chill of mountain air bit her sensitive skin. With great care, she stretched her fingers, then balled them into a fist. The skin felt tight, the muscles stiff, but only the dull echo of her horrific burns remained. This was her sister's work, she knew. Dragons were born with fire inside them, and as pups they learned to treat all manner of burns.

She uncurled her fingers once more. The sensation was dulled, as though her hand belonged to someone else. The skin was unnaturally smooth scar tissue, mottled with streaks of brown and red. *It was worth it,* she thought, *to rescue . . .*

Her other hand shot to her neck, and a moment of panic died away as quickly as it had come. The scale hung there, right where it belonged. She ran a thumb across its rough ridges and felt an immense sense of gratitude. If all she had to show for her encounter with the witches were some scars on her hand, then she would count herself lucky.

"You've been asleep two days," came the dry rumble of her sister's voice.

She wheeled and saw the great lizard curled in a trough of cool stone. "Sister!"

"It was all I could do to keep you on your perch," she said, pulling her huge green body from the rock. She lowered her head. Evie ran her good hand down the dirt-crusted scales of her sister's cheek.

"How did you ever find me out there? They were going to kill me."

"Something drew me. I never venture that far from home, but . . . I don't know, really. It was as though I could *feel* Father." She hooked Evie's scale with one of her talons. "I think it was this."

A shadow crossed the cave mouth as the sun traveled behind a cloud. Evie shivered, but more from something ominous in her sister's words than the cold.

"What do you mean you could 'feel Father'? Where is he?" She glanced deeper into the cave and saw nothing but stone and moss and rippling water. "Where's Mother?"

Her sister's obsidian eyes, ringed by heavy folds of tan flesh and scales, wilted. *Something's happened,* thought Evie. Even if her sister couldn't find the words, her eyes spoke volumes.

"Where are they?" She stood up on her perch.

"I'm sorry, Sister," said the dragon. "I'm sorry."

Evie's knees began to flutter.

"Father's . . . dead."

"What?" said Evie, her voice breaking at the end.

"He was killed by the Sisters. Months ago. Mother refuses

to believe it. She still goes away for weeks on end searching for him, but ... he's gone."

Evie leapt from her perch and bounded across the stones to the cave mouth. The sun reemerged and lit up the mountainside with colors so vibrant they hurt her eyes. Her sister stepped out next to her.

"I don't understand," said Evie. "How could witches ... do that? He's the strongest dragon I've ever known. He must be out there ... somewhere ..."

"It was that storm. Mother said it was the worst she'd ever seen. Flooded out most of the cave. We couldn't find you anywhere."

Evie collapsed in a small patch of weeds. Her sister's words cut straight to her core. Despair crashed over her like ocean waves. *He was looking for me.*

"We kept watch, Mother and I, hoping he'd bring you back, but ... he never did." Her tail swept across the gravel and rested along Evie's thigh. "Our friends beyond the mountain heard from others who had heard from others that it was a lightning strike got him. And as he lay injured, Calivigne's witches closed in."

Evie's scarred fingers wrapped around her dragon scale. *This is all I have of him now.* A shimmer of light pulsed through the fading black stain of her father's blood. She wiped the tears away, but more kept coming. Her heart had been broken clean in half. She didn't know what she was supposed to do. She stared deep into the forest, silently listening to its sounds as the minutes clicked by. Intermittent whistles of birdsong. The distant hum of a waterfall. Leaves rustled by the breeze. Everything was just the same as it had always been, yet entirely and irrevocably different.

"I hate witches," she spat. Her tears had already started to transform from pure grief into contempt. "I've never hated anything in my life, but I hate them."

"They say our kind are leaving the lands of the north because of witches. Imagine it, the Dragonlands without dragons. It's only a matter of time until they're here, in our woods."

"I'll die before I see that happen," said Evie.

"I'm afraid there isn't much to be done. They have the numbers and the will."

"The place I've been, they train us to fight them."

"What, fight witches? That's brilliant! I thought there was something different about you. You look bigger, somehow. Stronger."

"I'm not," said Evie, hanging her head. "You need courage to fight a witch. The only time I ever had any was back in that cottage, and even then it was only because of this." She lifted the scale.

"Bah, you've got plenty of courage. Remember when you fought off that hawk to get her egg?"

"That hawk nearly killed me!"

"Yes, but she didn't, did she? Come, we've got to take you back."

"I can't go back. I don't belong there, either."

"Our father was the most courageous dragon the sun has ever seen, you said it yourself. If it's courage you need, then take him with you. In here." She rested a claw against Evie's chest. "He'll help you find your courage."

Evie filled her lungs with the air of newborn winter, then slowly let it out again. "Sometimes I feel like there's too much dragon in me to ever be a princess. But then there's too much princess in me to really be a dragon. I don't know what I am."

"The witches must pay for what they've done," said her sister.

The faint ember of those words glowed inside Evie. Images of her father—her dear, sweet father who taught her to see the world in all its horror and beauty, to strive for the good and fight back against the bad—flashed through her mind.

The witches must pay.

Now thoughts of the witch with no eyelids crept in, one of Calivigne's Council of Sisters. The ember inside her ignited, burning with cold rage.

The witches must pay.

Her anger piled on top of itself like sticks on a fire until it consumed her from the inside with pure dragon fury.

"I am the daughter of dragons, and no witch will ever frighten me again."

They set off that very afternoon. Evie's sister, by virtue of the dragon's innate sense of navigation and orientation, found her way back to the Dortchen Wild, to the spot where she had charred the forest to scare off the witches. After that, it was only a matter of covering huge, swooping arcs of the forest until the lights of Pennyroyal's towers appeared above the canopy. By the time they set down at the edge of the great clearing, night had fallen.

Evie peered out from the trees, her sister next to her. Crickets sounded from the grassland beyond the wall, but not from the enchanted forest behind them. The Academy shimmered atop its hill, torchlight glowing from windows. To Evie, it really was beautiful, a light of goodness in a world of dark. She saw it and knew that her sister had been right to bring her back.

"Do you really think this will work?" she said. "We were warned about leaving the grounds."

"What other choice do we have? Besides, after what that girl said to you, no one could fault you for running off. And it's just your bad luck there was a vicious man-eating dragon waiting to snatch you up. If we can get you inside, they'll keep you."

Evie studied the dim flicker of the towers. Her heart was thumping. She longed to be back inside, but something about this plan frightened her. She put a hand on her sister's foot. "The instant they lift the barrier, you've got to go. All right? Promise me."

The dragon's face softened. She touched a talon to Evie's cheek. "A witch fighter. He would have been so proud."

Her wings sprayed out into the pines, and with a mighty flap she lifted into the air. Evie's breath caught in her throat. She wanted to call her sister back, to stop this whole foolish plan,

174

but it was too late. A tree crackled, then crashed to the ground as the dragon lifted free of the forest canopy.

Then, in a violent spray of noise and fire, she swooped down from the clouds. A shower of glowing liquid streamed from her throat, leaving trails of burning pines and grass. She roared with the primeval ferocity of the fires at the heart of the world. Up on the hill, two horn blasts bellowed and torches began to move about. Her sister's plan was already working.

Evie nearly fell to the ground as the dragon rammed her body into the invisible wall of fairies' magic. Dots of orange light poured down the hill like a meteor shower. It wasn't just staff, it was the cadets, as well. Apparently, no one wanted to miss the rare sight of a rampaging dragon. *This changes nothing,* Evie told herself. *Get through the wall, that's all that matters.*

"*Get those girls back!*" came a voice. Evie recognized it as the harsh snarl of Corporal Liverwort. "*Boys as well! Get away from that wall!*"

And now Evie could see faces in the bright flash of her sister's fiery jets. There stood Remington with the other knight cadets, shielding his eyes. Members of staff shouted indistinguishable things as they tried to formulate a plan. Her heart thumped like a war drum. It was her turn now.

Then she saw something that made the blood rush from her head. Staff pushed cadets aside to allow an intimidating fleet of horsemen through. Their bodies were covered head to toe in glassy black armor, as were their horses. In the glint of firelight, they looked like something from another world, like riders made of ice. Each of them carried a steel-tipped lance, with other weaponry strapped to their mounts' tack.

"Dragonslayers . . ." she said. These were men who had long ago graduated from the Academy. They had gone out into the world as the elite dragon-killing force for the kingdoms in which they served, then returned to teach the next generation their secrets. Only the steel at their hips knew how many dragons this squadron had put to ground. Evie looked up at her sister, diving in for another assault on the wall, and realized she had no idea what waited beyond it.

Evie broke from the trees and raced for the wall. "*Help!*" she shouted. "*Help me!*"

Her screams were drowned out by another roar from her sister. The dragonslayers hadn't yet moved, perhaps waiting for word from Princess Beatrice, or in a case as extreme as this, the Queen herself. Evie's feet couldn't match her panic and she stumbled forward, her face plowing through the hard dirt.

"*There's someone out there!*" Even through the screaming pain in her chin, Evie recognized the voice of the Fairy Drillsergeant. "*Get up, Cadet! MOVE!*"

Evie staggered to her feet. She scrambled ahead, wiping a smear of blood from her face. The fall had cluttered her head and she was having trouble focusing, but she knew one thing for certain. *The barrier has been lifted and I must get through.*

The dragon soared low across the clearing. Cadets screamed, convinced she was about to be taken in the creature's jaws. Staff shouted urgent orders. And her eyes caught Forbes's just as his mouth broke open with the word "ATTACK!" In the confusion, he took the lance off a distracted knight and mounted his horse, then broke from the crowd.

"Forbes, no!" shouted Remington. He knocked a young knight instructor aside and swung atop his black charger, following Forbes over the wall.

Run, Evie. Run faster and you can stop this.

"DRAGONSLAYERS, AHEAD! STOP THOSE BOYS!" came the panicked voice of the Headmistress.

The dragon swept into the air and unleashed another terrible roar. She hadn't seen either of the boys come over the wall, and was oblivious to the fleet of dragonslayers now doing the same. Suddenly, the field was full of very dangerous moving parts.

Evie ran as fast as she could toward the wall, but rough clumps of ground kept tripping her up. She fell onto her shoulder, then rolled to the side to see the horror unfolding before her.

Forbes charged at the huge, falling shadow of the dragon as she plunged in for another run of flame and thunder. Behind him, and closing fast, galloped the dragonslayers, their armor shimmering in the burning trees of the Dortchen Wild.

"SISTER!" screamed Evie. "SIS—"

Something ripped her from the ground. Pain fired through her ribs and she heard the sounds of tearing fabric and clomping hooves. Remington had grabbed her by the dress and hauled her onto his charger in one frantic pass.

"Hold on!" he shouted.

But Evie had lost all strength. She bounced limply on the horse, caged by Remington's arms, as they raced back to the wall. Another violent roar flattened the grass as the dragon swooped wide of the men waiting below. Her tail slapped into Forbes, launching him and his horse to the trees.

The metal tip of a dragonslayer's lance flashed upward, and a monstrous screech blasted across the clearing. Evie saw her sister's body recoil and knew she had been pierced.

"NO!"

And then she could hear nothing. Not the screams of the cadets as Remington's horse raced under the magical barrier. Not the roar of flame at the charred forest edge. Not the shrieks of her sister as she lurched off the ground and wobbled in the air, just beyond the reach of the dragonslayers.

Maggie, Demetra, Anisette, and Basil led the group that raced to help Evie from Remington's horse, but they were quickly pushed aside by staff. Hazelbranch and Wertzheim broke through next, lowering her limp body to the grass. They checked her for injury and covered her torn dress with burlap blankets. She didn't hear their questions. Her eyes were focused on her dear sister as she tried to flap her wings to escape, dropping in sickening jags back to the ground.

"Are you hurt?"

"What happened?"

"Clear some space! Give her air!"

"Your hand! What's happened to your hand? The dragon's scalded her!"

The wounded dragon desperately flapped her wings, finally building enough lift to clear the treetops. With erratic dips and bobs through the air, she disappeared into the low silver clouds.

"I'm sorry . . ." said Evie. "I'm so sorry . . ." The words were meant for her sister, but the staff heard them differently.

"You've nothing to apologize for, Cadet," said Hazelbranch. "You haven't done a thing wrong—"

"What's happened here?" demanded Beatrice, shoving through the crowd with annoyance.

"She's in shock," said Hazelbranch, dragging Evie to her feet. "We've got to get her to the Infirmary."

"Everyone, back to your barracks!" shouted Beatrice. "Get the water butts down here and put out those fires! You, clear this hillside!"

As Hazelbranch and Wertzheim helped Evie stagger up the carriage ruts toward campus, she caught a glimpse of her friends up ahead. They were trying to break free from the herd to come to her, but the staff wouldn't let them through.

"You're all right, Eves!" shouted Maggie, and then they were shoved ahead with the rest of the cadets.

Evie's mind had gone flat and empty. It was all she could do to bring breath into her lungs.

Amidst the chaos on that hill, she glanced over and saw

something entirely unexpected. Something so surprising she couldn't even comprehend its meaning. There, walking up the hill in the great migration of cadets, was Malora. Her eyes met Evie's, and in them was compassion. True, real, human compassion. It only lasted a moment, but in that compassion Evie saw that Malora understood. She understood the trauma of Evie's plight, and that she had been the one who had caused it. After that momentary connection, where Malora had allowed her vulnerability to shine through, Evie looked up to the black dome of clouds just as they began to drop white flakes of snow.

14

EVIE STAGGERED through swirling snow, her dress a punch of blue against the gray. Winds howled, throwing icy waves of powder through the air. She saw something in the snow ahead, a splash of black on the ground. It shimmered like the silvery snowflakes drifting all around her.

Dragon's blood.

She looked to her left, then her right, but the flurries washed past so swiftly it was impossible to judge direction. Something had crept up behind her—she could feel it there—and she turned to find her sister. The swampy green of her scales looked almost black in the whiteout. A horrendous gash in her side was washed with blood.

"Find Saudade . . . find yourself . . ." she growled.

"Is that where Father is?"

"That's where you are."

A gust of wind howled, blasting the dragon to snow. Evie turned back and the blood was gone as well. She stood alone in the frozen heart of winter.

Then, so faint they could have been the shadows of snow-drifts, figures began to appear. Dozens of them, lurching forth from the white. They came from all directions, swaying like ghost ships in frozen seas. Witches.

There, beyond their slow, ragged advance, one towered above all others, her face obscured in the shadows of a thick black cloak—

Evie startled awake. She was asleep in her chair in the Infirmary waiting for another round of treatment. She wiped a bit of spittle from her chin and sat up. Though it had only been a nightmare, the image of Calivigne's grim silhouette lingered.

"Good, you're awake," said Princess Wertzheim. "Just in time for this." She set a small vial of red liquid on the table and made some notes on her parchment. Evie picked up the potion, rolling the smooth glass between her fingers, then set it down with a clink.

"I'd rather just get back to my company, if that's all right."

"And you shall. Once you've had your treatment." Wertzheim sat behind the table and busied herself with her notes.

Evie scowled at the tiny stoppered vial. In the weeks since she had awoken here after the assault on the wall, she had returned to the Infirmary each day for treatment. And each day when she stepped through the doors, the awful memory of her sister's screams washed into her mind like seawater into a tidal pool.

"It's not brewed for its flavor. Go on."

Still, Evie didn't move. She stared into the depths of that

liquid and could think of nothing but her sister and her father and her red hatred of the enemy.

Wertzheim lowered her parchment. "Drink the potion, Cadet."

"No. I don't care about some make-believe past. I don't care about potions or memories or any of it. All I want is to fight witches."

"Cadet Eleven—"

"I've been drinking these bloody things for months and I've had one memory." She jabbed a finger in the air. "*One*. About a bloody pie—"

"Watch your words, Cadet," said Wertzheim, her demeanor hardening. "You will treat every member of staff with respect, and that includes me, or I shall be forced to send you home—"

"Then do it!" spat Evie, shooting to her feet. *Why am I acting this way?* she thought. She had nothing but affection for the Academy's nurses, but a reckless part of her had been unleashed and she didn't know how to control it. "I'm not drinking that bloody potion—"

An arm snaked Evie's waist, pulling her back from the table.

"Forgive her, Princess, she's under duress," said Forbes. "Loads and loads of duress."

The sight of him enraged Evie. She tried to worm free of his grip, so he pinned her arms to her sides and lifted her off the floor.

"What are you doing? Let go of me!"

"Cadet Forbes, release that girl!"

"I'm only trying to save her from herself."

"Put me down!" She thrashed and wriggled, but his grip was too tight.

"All right!" he said. He gently lowered her to the floor, but kept his arms clamped around her. "All right, but just, please, calm yourself. Before you say something you'll regret."

He eased his arms open. She shoved him back, fixing him with a dark scowl.

"That's enough!" shouted Wertzheim.

"Perhaps we might forgo this round of treatment, Princess?" he asked.

"You don't speak for me, Forbes!"

"Our companies have joint exercises this afternoon. Let me take her now, and I assure you she'll return for her next treatment in an entirely different frame of mind."

Wertzheim glared at Evie, then gave Forbes the slightest of nods.

"She does apologize, if not with her mouth, with her heart." He took Evie's hand, but she shook him off. "Come with me now or you'll do something you cannot undo," he said. The intensity in his eyes cut right through her anger. She knew what he was saying was right.

He thanked Wertzheim again, then ushered Evie away. She opened her mouth to shout at him, but he had already shouldered through the door. He didn't hold it for her.

"Ah, lovely. Clouds."

"Who do you think you are, handling me like that? You have no right—"

He stopped, and she nearly crashed into him. "Right, shall we just go back in, then, and you can complete your self-destruction?"

She had no words at the ready. She hated the way he made her feel like a child.

"Those ladies have cared for me these five years gone, and I don't like to see them mistreated. Especially by some stroppy cow who shouldn't even be here in the first place." His boots ground the frosted dirt as he turned to march on.

"Oh, so you'll judge me by my blood as well!"

"I'm not judging you by your bloody blood, I'm judging you because you ran away. You quit. A Princess of the Shield never quits, highborn or otherwise."

She trudged to a stop. Once again, he left her with no response. It would have been easier, and perhaps hurt a bit less, had he just been one of the aristocracy who looked down on commoners.

"Come on, it's cold," he said, annoyed. "Or do you want to lie down in the road and have a sulk?"

He disappeared around a corner, and she quickly realized she didn't know where she was going, so she chased after him. He had already started walking along the top of a stone wall, deteriorating and covered in leafy gray lichens, with gnarled roots pushing through the rocks. The wall had been built to brace a stand of trees that had long since outgrown it, and rather than take it down, the groundskeepers had decided to let it crumble away on its own.

"Where are we going?"

He didn't respond. She stumbled along the wall behind him until they were even with the peak of Stendal's Forge. The Forge wasn't a particularly high structure, but it was high enough to break a bone. Eventually the wall leveled off and Forbes hopped into the grove of trees behind it. She followed, tracking his black doublet through the green.

"The staff attempted to enchant these trees years ago for training, but they never got the magic quite right. They decommissioned them, and they've just been growing here untouched ever since."

Evie's attempts to stay angry began to falter. She had been in so many forests that wanted her dead that the sensation of being in one safe behind the Academy's protections was bizarrely soothing. These were oaks and spruce, red firs and giant's-toe pines. Calm, peaceful trees that reminded her of home.

"Believe it or not, I do have some sympathy for you," said Forbes, ducking the lower fork of an oak branch. "I understand your aversion to the potions. The *uncursed* watch us go off for treatment like we're some sort of curiosity." He couldn't disguise the contempt in his voice.

"I don't care about them," she said. "I'm here to fight witches, not piddle about with curses and potions and other distractions."

"You have quite a high opinion of yourself, don't you?" he said with a laugh that dripped arrogance. "I suppose you'd classify me as a distraction as well?"

"As a matter of fact, I would." *And I'd also like to punch you right in the mouth.* She might have enjoyed this walk if he weren't so skilled at making her angry. Everything about him, from his condescending sneer to his ease in weaving through the trees, was just so . . . *certain.*

"My father is one of the great military strategists of our time. He's led armies in countless battles, some of the most famous ever fought. My mother died when I was quite young, and he took it upon himself to teach me the ways of men, but most of these lessons came from his absence. He'd be away weeks on end, sometimes months, collecting lands and treasure. Prestige, as well. It was difficult to understand as a boy, but it was always made right when I'd see his sails on the horizon. I was in awe of him, really. I understood quite early on that most boys didn't have fathers like mine."

Suddenly the trees ended. Evie and Forbes emerged into the shadow of a behemoth structure of cut yellow sandstone.

"See there? The Bronze Keep. Just round this way."

They followed the wall, then emerged into a cobblestone hub with roads that spiderwebbed in every direction. Without hesitation, he selected a path and led her into a serpentine alleyway flanked by white plaster buildings crisscrossed with dark brown timbers.

"After my father returned from his last campaign, something

had changed," he continued. "He didn't greet me at the port or take me riding, as he normally did. There was no treasure in his hulls, and there were no tales of faraway lands to send me to sleep at night. There was only a portrait."

Evie grimaced. *That bloody portrait again.* He hadn't had a chance to bring it up since their walk to the Dining Hall that day, and she was hoping she had already heard the last of it.

"My father is a hard man. He's a noble man, but not exactly a good man. The portrait, which he'd won through some unscrupulous deal or another, had been cursed by a witch. She told him if he ever laid eyes on it, he'd be punished for his greed. So he locked it away deep in the castle and forbade anyone from entering, on penalty of death. I saw even less of him then, though I always knew exactly where he was. Just sitting there outside that door. The portrait consumed him, though he was destined never to see it. It was all he thought about."

Evie said nothing. She despised Forbes, but there was something quite genuine in his voice.

"I had to know what had taken my place in his heart, so I went down there one day when I knew he was away on some diplomatic mission or another. I snuck past his guards and got inside. It was a dusty old room, no windows, no furnishings. Just a lone portrait sitting on an easel. I lifted the cover, and that's when you and I first met. And that's when I earned my hooves." He paused and turned to face her. The smile on his face was the thinnest of covers for a poorly buried anger. "You'll forgive me if I've been a *distraction*."

Her eyes fell to the cobblestones. He glared at her for another moment, then charged ahead. She followed, winding past unknown structures until quite suddenly the Queen's Tower loomed overhead. It looked like it had been spun of the most delicate glass, a perfect, crystalline structure buried in the clouds. Unfortunately, Forbes marched right past its astonishing beauty.

"I didn't mean to insult you," she said, leaving the tower behind to keep pace. She felt chastened, as though she was partially to blame for what had happened to him. "I just . . . I have had other memories, but I lied to Princess Wertzheim about them because they don't matter."

"Oh?" he said without breaking stride.

"They're just flashes of things, and none of it makes any sense. A table, a mountain, a man with a beard . . . a screaming dragon."

"Did you hear that monster scream the other night?" She couldn't see his face, but she could hear the smile in his voice. "He nearly got me, but the dragonslayers made up for it. I only wish it had been me who put the lance in him."

"In *her*," said Evie, and whatever thaw had started between them iced right back over again. "And I suppose there's some honor in murdering dragons?"

"Murder, is it?" he said with a laugh. "And why are you suddenly so concerned about dead dragons?"

Evie faltered. She didn't trust Forbes, and she certainly didn't want to reveal that she was the daughter of dragons to someone with so much hate in his heart. "Some knights care more about chivalry and honor than killing, that's all."

"And I shall do my best to avoid their bones as I kill the dragons that killed them."

She wanted to throttle him, to say she wished her sister had killed him that night, but she didn't dare. "You may be a human, but you're still a pig!"

"Is that so?" he said, turning to face her with a scowl. "Well, mark this: I wouldn't be able to slay a single dragon had you not given me these back." He flexed his gloved fists in front of her face. "Thanks for that."

He set off down the hill and left her reeling beneath the statue of a man in smooth, impenetrable armor, the granite draped in a fine layer of snow. He was a knight, lance in hand, grave frown forged in the blood of a thousand dragons. She lingered there a moment, staggered by the implication of what Forbes had said, and when she finally stumbled through campus and rejoined her company for the joint training exercise with Thrushbeard Company, she received the crushing news that he was the only knight cadet still without a partner. But for her sister, she made up her mind that she would do whatever it took to succeed, even if it meant working with a pig.

And so, as she struggled to slither under a downed tree, she refused to take his hand. She could feel her strength being sapped away into the black mud beneath her, but would rather have been stuck there forever than accept his help.

"Hurry up, will you?"

The knight cadet next to her squirmed under easily, then reached back to drag Basil through.

"In a life made up of humiliating moments, this beats all," he said as his partner hauled him out of the slop.

Evie twisted her body until she was on her back and kicked into the mud. Finally, she began to slide through. She grabbed the rough bark of the log and pulled with all her remaining strength until she came free, then scrambled to her feet, great walls of black slopping off of her. They ran; she was tied to Forbes by a long rope, most of which was coiled around his shoulder. Up ahead, there loomed a thirty-foot wall topped by a crenellated parapet. It was scorched and battle-damaged, and a fetid moat intersected it to the right. But the cadets they were chasing had gone left, to an outbuilding that housed a staircase up to the wall walk.

"*Move, Cadets!*" shouted the Fairy Drillsergeant behind them. "*All of you run the Woundwort Tower spirals today except the first team up! LET'S GO!*"

Evie and Forbes paused at the base of the wall. He began cutting himself loose with a blade from his belt.

"Hurry, you bloody idiot!" It felt good to insult him, even though he wasn't doing anything wrong. She glanced at the staircase and frowned when she saw Remington helping his partner, Malora, mount the first step.

Forbes slapped the coil of rope into her chest. "Would you rather kiss him or beat him? Go!"

She hauled the heavy rope to the stairs and sprinted up,

taking them two at a stride. She and Malora reached the wall walk at the same time. Only a handful of others were there. *I'm going to win this challenge,* she thought as she raced past the first crenellation. Demetra was there, her rope taut across the battlement, already struggling under the weight of her knight.

Evie leaned into an open crenel and saw Forbes waiting below. She threw the coil over the side, wrapping the other end from palm to elbow. Moments later, he began his climb, jerking her into the stone.

"Bloody hell!" she heard him yell.

She regathered the rope and braced herself. *This will be harder than I thought.* He began again. She gritted her teeth, leaning into his weight. The rope dug into her shoulder. From her neck through her back and down both legs, her muscles screamed.

"What are you doing?" It was Demetra, and there was distress in her voice.

Evie glanced over and saw Malora standing in Demetra's crenel with her rope over the side. Other blue dresses scurried past down the wall walk, but there was plenty of open space along the battlement. Malora had intentionally chosen that one to harass Demetra, and had already started edging her to the side.

Evie's arms shook from exertion, yet she eased back until she could see down the wall. There, not quite halfway up, Demetra's knight was nearly on top of Remington.

"Keep 'er steady!" he called in a thick brogue.

"Malora, give me some space!" shouted Remington.

Evie looked back to the crenel and saw Demetra struggling mightily to maintain her grip. Malora, also having a difficult time with the rope, still managed to land a kick to Demetra's shin.

"Malora!" shouted Evie. "What's the matter with you?" She was so disturbed by the assault that she lost focus. The rope fibers began to eat at her fingers.

"Shut it!" yelled Malora as she forced Demetra to the crenel's edge, where her arms would soon meet stone and she'd have to drop her knight. The girls grunted, each trying to protect her space, but Malora was taller, her will stronger.

"Can't you even hold a bloody rope?" called Forbes from down the wall.

"COME ON, LADS, CLIMB!" yelled the Fairy Drillsergeant, and Evie's heart sank. If she was still down at the bottom of the wall, there would be no help coming for Demetra.

"Malora, please!" said Demetra. "I'm going to drop him!"

But it was Malora who lost her grip and tumbled to the wall walk, her rope whizzing across the stone and disappearing over the side.

"Remington!" shouted Evie. She leaned against the coarse limestone, the rope biting her shoulder. He was sprawled on the ground, rubbing the back of his head, dazed but alive.

She pushed back from the wall and peered to the next crenel. Demetra was struggling mightily under the weight of her knight. Her eyes were clenched, her teeth were gritted, and her arms shuddered like dragonfly wings.

"He's almost to the top, Demetra!" called Evie. "Just hold on!"

Malora scrambled to her feet and charged at Demetra, knocking her into the stone battlement. Demetra's rope zipped over the side, and the thud of her knight hitting the ground followed.

"WHAT'S GOING ON UP THERE?"

Demetra put a hand to the back of her head. It came back slick with blood. Her face hardened and she shoved Malora, leaving a dark smear across her dress. "Don't ever touch me again, you cow!"

Malora lunged. She clutched Demetra by the shoulders and hurled her into the crenel. Demetra tried to grab the stone, but her momentum was too great. She toppled over the side.

"DEMETRA!" shouted Evie. She dropped Forbes and leaned over the battlement.

"*Aahhh!*" he shouted from the ground, clutching his leg.

The Fairy Drillsergeant, meanwhile, caught Demetra with her wand only a moment before her neck would have snapped on the ground. "HOW IN BLAZES DO YOU FALL OFF A WALL, CADET?"

Something flared up inside Evie. She charged at Malora and they both crashed to the wall walk.

"Oi, Evie! Stop!" called Anisette.

The girls grappled. Evie reached for any sort of leverage—linen, flesh, or hair—as Malora clawed a line of blood into her face.

"Get your hands off me!" she snarled.

194

"You could have killed her!" shouted Evie, enraged.

Anisette dove on top and tried to force her body between them. Others stood and watched, holding their ropes as best they could.

"That's enough, girls!" said Anisette, jerking Malora's arm back and freeing Evie's hair from her grip. Malora shrieked and tried to claw Anisette's face. Evie reached up to grab her wrist, and as Anisette tried to push them apart, her elbow inadvertently smashed into Malora's eye.

"*THE THREE OF YOU, GET OFF MY WALL!*" bellowed the Fairy Drillsergeant, who had arrived on the wall walk just in time to see Anisette strike Malora.

Evie scrambled to her feet, then helped Anisette up. Malora, feeling around her tender eye for blood, pushed herself to a sitting position.

"We're sorry, Fairy—"

"*GET OFF MY WALL!*"

"You can't send me home," said Malora. Even through labored breath, her voice remained calm and defiant. "My mother will never—"

"I don't care if your mother is Cinderella herself! I want you off my wall! NOW!"

Evie, breath pluming from her mouth in the bracing winter air, suddenly realized what she'd done. *I'm being discharged. I've got myself thrown out of the Academy, and now I'll never learn to defeat a witch.*

Behind the Fairy Drillsergeant's trail of sparkles, Maggie

finally arrived at the top of the staircase. She looked horrified by the scene she found waiting on the wall walk.

"It's not Evie's fault, is it?" said Anisette. "I started the fight."

The Fairy Drillsergeant turned her ire full on Anisette. "Good, then we're agreed! *GET OUT!*"

"With respect, it ain't fair to send her home for what I done. It's my responsibility—"

"Anisette, what are you doing?" said Evie, but Anisette cut her short with a glare.

"GET OFF MY WALL, CADET! I WON'T SAY IT AGAIN!" Then the Fairy Drillsergeant turned to Evie and Malora, jabbing her tiny finger at them. "You. And you. We'll let the Headmistress sort you out."

"But it's not Anisette's fault!" said Evie.

"Eves. Enough."

Anisette limped across the wall walk past the Fairy Drillsergeant. Down below, Captain Ramsbottom shouted at the knights in an attempt to restore order, but up on the wall, the only sound was the steady huffing of Evie and Malora.

Evie found Maggie's eyes, but there was only helplessness there. Anisette paused next to her, at the head of the stairs, and turned back. She was crying. A small circle of red had already started to rise from a knock on her forehead. She laid her hand across her heart, smiled through her tears, and vanished down the staircase.

WITH HER HANDS interlocked behind her, Princess Beatrice glowered at the two girls standing in front of her desk.

Evie's eyes hadn't left the floor since she and Malora had been summoned, but she could *feel* Beatrice's glare, and knew she deserved it. Her dress was torn, and so soon after Rumpledshirtsleeves had given her thread to repair the damage from the night she had returned to the Academy. She tried to conceal her left hand with her right, but the stains of dried blood seemed to be everywhere. A tangle of hair fell across her eye, but she left it; at least it prevented her from seeing the girl standing next to her. The girl who had just gotten one of her only friends discharged from the Academy.

The door snapped open and Evie jumped. "Discharge papers, Mum," said Liverwort. She strode to the desk, knocking into Evie as she did, and set two parchments atop the heap of clutter.

The Headmistress walked deliberately around her desk, lips pursed. She stepped in front of Evie and Malora and let her hard blue eyes linger on each of them. Then, like a viper, she snatched up Evie's scarred and bloodied hand. "Is this the hand of a princess?"

Evie grimaced. "No, Headmistress."

Beatrice threw her hand down and turned to Malora. "And you. Would the Queen be proud of your actions today?"

Malora's eyes fell to the worn beams of the floor. She didn't respond.

"Cadet Anisette is gone, and quite rightly so," said the Head-mistress, and Evie finally placed the particular tone she heard in Beatrice's voice. It wasn't anger or disappointment; it was disgust. "I see little reason to keep either of you—"

The door flew open and a woman entered, her face drawn in urgent concern. "Malora?"

"Mother!" She ran to the woman's arms. Beatrice opened her mouth to protest, but stopped herself. Evie studied Malora's mother. She had clearly been a staggering beauty in another life, and had aged into the cold elegance of a porcelain vase. She had eyes as dark as her hair, which spilled over a shawl that was wrapped around her shoulders like a web around a fly.

"I assure you, Headmistress, this is not how I raised her."

"Yes, well," said Beatrice, "you have long been a friend to this institution, Countess Hardcastle, for which we are forever in your debt . . ."

Evie stood transfixed by this woman, this Countess Hardcas-tle. The others kept talking, but she was so deeply mesmerized that she heard none of it. There was something about Malora's mother . . . a strange familiarity . . . a nagging sensation that perhaps they had met somewhere before. And the longer she studied that face, the more certain she became.

She reached behind her for a chair, for something to lean on, but before she could steady herself, she was rocked by a memory so clear and total that it eclipsed everything else . . .

It was her, the younger Evie, from her very first recovered memory in the Infirmary. She stood in a cozy room with a wood-burning stove, an oaken table, and two grimy windows flanking a heavy door. The walls were covered in cabinets and hooks and all manner of cookery gear. It was dark and warm, and she was about to take a bite from a golden-crusted pie . . .

The memory faded, and she was back in Beatrice's office, disoriented and dizzy—

But another came right after the first. A bear of a man with a hearty smile in light mail armor. She had seen him before as well, only as a wisp of a vision after one of her treatments, and never so clearly as this. He sat atop a huge white palfrey with black mane and hooves. And she sat behind him, the young version of herself, clutching him around his thick middle, grinning ear to ear . . .

Words began to mix with memories and reality, and all she could do was stand there and stare at Countess Hardcastle and wait for it to stop. ". . . but fighting another cadet," came the muted voice of Princess Beatrice, "*that* is something a Princess of the Shield would never do . . ."

Another memory now. A stately manor of white plastered

walls crisscrossed with deep brown timbers nestled high above a valley. The walls were punctuated with large, iron-framed windows. Two redbrick chimneys spired from opposite ends of the roof like horns—

And another: two little girls running through a meadow near a wood. One was Evie. The other had long, black hair—

". . . and here is the other player in our great drama. May I introduce Cadet Eleven . . ."

Hardcastle's eyes, the dark umber of rust, met Evie's. There was a flicker of recognition, but she couldn't place Evie, either—

The memories came faster now. Countess Hardcastle, ten years younger, slipping a pie from the wood-burning stove. Evie was there watching as she set it on a stone to cool—

Little Evie throwing a ball of snow at the great bearded man. He roared with laughter, then dropped a scoop of white flakes over younger Hardcastle's head—

Evie and the black-haired girl sitting on either side of Hardcastle as she taught them to play a harp . . .

Evie's eyes bored into Hardcastle's as the memories started to pool together like liquid mercury.

"What are you doing?" said Malora. She had finally noticed the peculiar looks Evie and Hardcastle were giving each other. Evie turned to her now, and another memory came—

The black-haired girl climbing into a small larchwood bed next to Evie's. She turned with a smile, and there was simply no question. This was Malora, ten years ago . . .

Evie's face went white. Her eyes swung back to Countess Hardcastle...

"Mother?"

No one spoke. Then, in a faint whisper, Hardcastle said, "Nicolina?"

"What's she talking about?" said Malora. Despite the hint of panic in her voice, everyone ignored her.

Evie was staggered. That word—*Nicolina*—was so foreign, yet so entirely loaded with meaning. Beatrice caught Liverwort's eye and flicked her head, sending her assistant scurrying for the door.

"Countess," she said. "Do you mean to say you know this girl?"

"I should say so, Headmistress," she replied, her voice soft with wonder. "This girl is called Nicolina, and she is . . ." She nearly choked on the word. "She is my daughter."

The next few minutes blurred past. Beatrice ushered Evie into a private room adjoining her office. She collapsed into a plush chair and listened to Malora's frantic voice muffled through the door. Beatrice poured her a cup of passionflower tea, and her mind seemed to go blank after that . . .

"My darling Nicolina, I thought I'd lost you forever."

Evie looked down at her hands. They were enveloped inside Countess Hardcastle's. *I must have fallen asleep,* she thought, *but, then, why isn't this a dream?* She glanced around and found Beatrice and Liverwort huddled over a massive tome with ancient, brittle pages. Sure enough, everything that had just happened was as real as the scars on her hand.

"Would you mind calling me Evie?" she croaked. Her voice was dry, like the pages of the book.

"Of course, my darling, whatever you prefer."

Thank goodness. I couldn't bear changing my name again. She felt as though she should say something, to explain somehow this incredible thing that had just happened, but her mind was blank. She glanced up at Hardcastle, cringing when she saw her muted smile. How could this woman—spindly, hard-edged, and pale as fog—possibly be her mother?

"Registry of Peerage proves it. That there's Countess Hardcastle's little one," proclaimed Liverwort.

"Peerage?" said Evie. "But isn't that for the highborn?"

"If you please, Countess," said Beatrice, motioning to the ancient book. Liverwort stepped aside, and Hardcastle scrawled her mark with a quill, which she then handed to Beatrice to witness. Once the Registry had been updated, Liverwort closed the cover, tucked the book under her arm, and exited.

"Young lady, it is quite right you should be confused," said the Headmistress. "You were cursed at some point in your young life, and it stripped away your every memory." Hardcastle returned to the chair across from her, but Beatrice remained standing. "This woman is your mother, and you are terribly fortunate for that. She's a fine woman, a true friend of the Academy."

"Thank you, Headmistress, you are most kind." Now that

some of the initial shock had worn away, Evie could hear the same silky ribbon running through Hardcastle's voice that was present in Malora's. "Your sister is quite . . . *unsettled* by all of this, as you can imagine. The physicians said she had blocked all memory of you when you went missing, and I had always believed that to be for the best." She shook her head, her eyes haunted. "I couldn't bear the thought of her feeling such grief as I had. She had found her own way round the pain, and for that I was eternally grateful. My only wish was for her to be able to live as a normal girl." Beatrice put a hand on Hardcastle's shoulder. Her smile was tinged with sadness. "Tell me, Nicolina—er, Evie . . . is there nothing *you* remember?"

Evie seemed to remember many things all of a sudden. More in the last hour than in all the rest of her time at the Academy. But most were only flickers of things—faces and places and images—but nothing of substance.

"Quite often in cases such as these, a sudden event will jar loose other memories," said Beatrice. "Take a moment. Breathe. Think back."

Evie inhaled deeply and closed her eyes, only too happy to escape the scrutiny of that room. After a moment, a scene began to form from the black of her mind. It had the same disconcerting familiarity of all the other memories . . .

She was in that small kitchen, the one with the dingy windows. Only now, she was actually there. The room felt wide and deep and safe and warm. The slate floor was scattered with lavender-scented rushes, and the windows weren't dirty, but layered with frost on the outside. Other scents filled the room, warm smells of baking and stewing. She was really there, a little girl, in that kitchen with her mother.

She had just placed a wedge of white cheese into a lashed straw basket, and was waiting for more. Hardcastle, softer and younger and lighter behind the eyes, wrapped a small pie in linen, then handed it to her daughter. Evie gave her a cheeky, sidelong glance, then took the steaming pie from its sleeve.

"Aha, young lady, it may be your birthday, but you must still wait 'til you get there."

"One bite?"

Hardcastle gave her a stern look that the little girl knew wasn't real. "All right," she said, breaking into a smile. "But only one."

Evie shoved the pie into her mouth and bit off a huge piece. As she struggled to keep it from spilling onto the floor, Hardcastle laughed with delight. "You're a naughty one."

The big bearded man barreled into the room. He had a voice ripe with laughter and authority, cheeks permanently reddened from hours on horseback, and a twinkle in his eye for the little girl with the basket. "Pie, is it?" he bellowed, grabbing it out of Evie's hands. He took a huge bite of his own, and just like that, half of it was gone.

"Daddy!" she said, admonishing him.

"There won't be any left for the picnic," said Hardcastle, putting the rest in the basket.

"All right, all right." He wrapped his thick arms around

Hardcastle and pulled her tight. "You're certain you don't mind, my lovely?"

"No," she said, then pecked him on the lips. "You must go. We've been promising this one her birthday picnic for weeks, haven't we?"

"My stars, is it someone's birthday?" he roared, releasing Hardcastle and scooping Evie off the floor. She giggled with delight as he swung her through the air.

"Your map to the picnic ground," said Hardcastle. She handed him a rolled parchment. "And your expertly packed picnic." She hung the handle over his forearm. "And, please, don't worry about Malora. I'll find a way to break that fever."

He raised the parchment like a sword and aimed it at the door. "Very well, then, let's be off . . . for adventure!" And he charged out into the biting autumn air.

Hardcastle squatted down and embraced Evie, then looked at her with a mother's bittersweet awareness of the passage of time. "My little girl, five years old already. All our plans will one day come and go, won't they?" Little Evie kissed her mother's cheek, then galloped to the door . . .

"Ah, yes," came a distant voice. "King Callahan."

Evie opened her eyes, as disoriented as if she had woken from a deep sleep. It took her a moment to realize that she had been recounting the memory aloud. Everything had felt so vivid and so *real* . . .

"What a lovely man was he," said Hardcastle.

"She's on an aggressive treatment plan, Countess, and more

memories should return as the days pass. But I'm afraid for now I must cut this wonderful reunion short."

"What?" said Evie. "But we've only just—"

"I know this is all quite strange for you, Cadet, but you must understand that we deal in recovered memories as a matter of course. It's best you continue your training as before and let the memories sort themselves out. There will be plenty of time for reunions after term."

"It's all right, my darling," said Hardcastle, rising from her chair. "I'm content in the knowledge that for the first time since your fifth birthday, I know where you are."

"One last thing, if you please, Countess."

"Of course."

Beatrice looked down at Evie. "As I said to Cadet Malora, you have now used your final chance. Should I see you in my office again, it will be with discharge papers in hand. Am I quite clear?"

"Does that mean Anisette gets to stay as well?" asked Evie.

"Former cadets are no longer your concern."

No longer my concern, thought Evie. *One of my very best friends is no longer my concern.* It was all she could do to keep from crying.

After a protracted series of hugs and farewells, Beatrice enlisted one of the Academy's administrators, a young princess only a few years removed from graduation called Princess Rahden, to escort Evie back to her barracks. But Evie was so shaken by everything that had just happened that she didn't say a word the entire hike across Hansel's Green. And, somehow, when she stepped inside, Hazelbranch already seemed to know about her new family situation. She took Evie's hand and led her through the empty barracks. When they passed Anisette's bunk, Evie's heart broke anew. There was her ball gown, draped over its dress form. It was sloppy and poorly constructed—Anisette had never done well at Rumpledshirtsleeves's lessons—but it was *hers,* and now she would never have the chance to finish it.

Hazelbranch took Evie into the latrine, then sat her down on a stool in front of the mirror. Using scalding water from a bucket, she began to scrub away the dirt, the blood, and the tears that were all that remained from the fight.

"Your ball gown is coming along nicely," she said. "Rumpledshirtsleeves has really developed your talents." She took a boxwood comb off the countertop and began unsnarling Evie's hair. "I suspect, however, that there might be more on your mind than fashion."

"I already have a sister and I don't want another. Especially one as vile as Malora."

Hazelbranch smiled as she began running the comb from root to tip. It felt like music, so smooth was her technique.

"Why? Why is *she* still here and Anisette isn't?"

"Perhaps there's something inside her we haven't seen yet." The delicate comb clinked on the stone, and she started to pull Evie's hair into loose strands. "That's the way it is with people, you know. When I was a girl, my mother died quite unexpectedly. She meant the world to me. To my father as well. But in his grief, he consented to marry another. She was a dreadful woman, and her dreadful daughters became my stepsisters. They lived to torment me. Each morning I'd wake and wonder what I'd done to make them hate me so. Eventually I came to see that I hadn't done anything at all. Something somewhere in their lives had hurt them—I could see that even if they couldn't—and I made up my mind to treat them decently, as others so clearly hadn't." Evie studied her in the mirror. She could live to be a thousand years old and she'd never be as kind as Hazelbranch. It seemed to come naturally, as though it was a part of her, like hair or skin.

"Each of us is blessed with the ability to control our own decisions," she continued, "but cursed with the inability to control the decisions of others. I couldn't do a thing about the way they treated me, but I got to choose the way I treated them. And do you know what happened? As we grew into adulthood, one of those wicked stepsisters became the best friend I've ever had."

Evie scowled and looked to the floor. She had no interest in being the bigger person. She despised Malora, and was comfortable in her anger. "It isn't fair. Of all the people here . . ."

"Life isn't fair, Evie. It never has been and it never will be. You can sit back and moan about its unfairness while the witches roll across the countryside, or you can pick yourself up and get on with it."

She took a step back, and Evie's eyes went to the glass. The girl staring back at her was a stranger. Where moments ago there had been a rough, filthy girl streaked with blood and grime, now sat the most beautiful version of herself she had ever seen. Hazelbranch had plaited her hair into a delicate braid across the top of her head like a crown. Comets of wispy brown fell behind her ears.

"Mirrors show what our eyes cannot see. Mirrors reveal the truth."

There was something more to this new person in the mirror than her hair. Something unseeable. Something had changed deep inside the girl in the spiderweb dress. She looked, somehow, more herself, like the wolf pup that has learned to hunt its own meal.

"You get to decide who you want to be. No one else."

16

"SHE WOULD'VE BEEN on her third pheasant by now," said Basil. "Nothing made her hungrier than a lecture on the mechanics of the spinning wheel."

He and Demetra and Evie sat in their usual place in the Dining Hall, only now there were noticeable holes in the blue around them. Others companies were thinner as well. Discharges had increased since Hessekel and Gisela became the first to go, but none stung quite like Anisette's.

"I love to spin," he continued, "but bloody hell, how many times can he show us how to hang a distaff?"

"I heard some girls nattering in the privy this afternoon—I think they were from Goosegirl Company. They said every peasant sent away puts them closer to being Warrior Princess," said Demetra. She pushed her plate away with distaste. "I wanted to throttle them."

Evie glanced down the table at Malora. *My sister.* But thinking it didn't make it any less ludicrous. She supposed they had a connection now that hadn't existed before, but even her talk with Princess Hazelbranch hadn't blunted her animosity. It also hadn't answered the one question she now feared the Fates would leave forever unanswered: *why?*

"Evie! Evie, you *must* see this!" It was Maggie, charging toward them with a leather-bound book.

"There you are," said Basil. "We looked all over for you."

Maggie sat next to Evie and shoved cutlery and dishware aside to clear a place for the book. "I didn't want to disrupt you kingsbloods now that I'm the only commoner left."

She was still smiling, but pointedly didn't look any of them in the eye. Evie glanced to Demetra and Basil. Their confused expressions confirmed that they had noticed as well.

"I remembered something I read long ago about curses and their cures, so I decided to go to the Archives to see if I could find any more about it. It's absolutely incredible down there. They must have copies of every book and scroll ever written."

The three of them exchanged another uneasy glance. She seemed to be taking Anisette's dismissal rather . . . strangely.

"And that's when I found this." She placed a hand on the warped cover. "It's about Forbes. Or his portrait, rather."

"Really?" said Evie.

"Listen to this . . ." She skimmed the pages until she found the passage she was looking for. "'The confusion caused by its derangement will lead the mind of the cursed to seek to explain the unexplainable. Often it is not the object itself that provides the cure, but a small, seemingly insignificant aspect of the object. Yet the cursed mind clings to that which is plainly manifest before it.'" She turned to Evie with wide, expectant eyes.

"Urm . . . what?"

"It's like that girl Volf told us about," said Demetra. "Princess Dalfsen—"

"Dallefsen," said Basil.

"Right, Dallefsen. Remember, Eves? She searched the land for the perfect bite of bread, convinced it would restore her sight, but in the end it wasn't the bread at all . . ."

"It was the knife she'd used to cut it," said Evie.

"Exactly!" said Maggie. "Perhaps your hair is the same shade as the girl Forbes saw in the portrait. Or the way you smelled reminded him of the room where it was kept. *You* weren't the cure, something *about you* was."

"So . . . it wasn't really me in the portrait?"

"Of course not! Forbes was so dazzled by his recovery he convinced himself it was you that cured him, when it could have just been a fly sitting on your shoulder, or any number of other things."

Evie weighed the book's assertion against Forbes's theory. One made sense—he only *thought* she was the cure. The other required strange leaps in logic and time. "Oh, Maggie, you've no idea what this means!" she said, pulling her friend into a tight embrace.

"It means Forbes is nothing to you," said Demetra. "We've all seen how you agonize over him, like you're somehow responsible for every crude, boorish thing he does. But, Evie . . . he's meaningless to you now."

"And you're meaningless to him, he just doesn't know it yet," added Basil.

Shivers raced across her skin. She felt lighter than she had before. "With Anisette going," she said, shaking her head in disbelief, "and the Helpless Maiden looming, and finding out I'm sisters with *her* . . . this really is the best news. It gives me one less thing to worry about." She kissed Maggie's cheek. "Thank you."

"You should go over there and shove that book in his stupid face," said Basil with a cheeky grin.

Evie smiled deviously. It was a thrilling prospect, finally cutting herself free from him. But as she was considering it, she noticed Lieutenant Volf shuffling to the exit. "I'll be right back. There's another box I'd like to see if I can tick . . ."

She rose and hurried after him, ignoring the glares from Malora and Sage as she passed. The bracing night air struck her the instant she pushed through the door. Her eyes followed twin trails through the snow on the cobblestones, and there was Volf, trudging into the fog beyond the light of the Dining Hall's torches with an apple in his hand.

"Lieutenant?" Breath streamed from her mouth.

He turned, his face drawn and ancient. In the torchlight, his wrinkles seemed to be etched even deeper. "Well? What is it? I have a date with a warm fire and some even warmer brandy."

"Do you know of a place called Saudade?"

He blinked, then let out a wheezing chuckle. She had never seen him smile before, and it looked so painful, she didn't want to see it again. "Saudade, did you say? There's an old one."

"So you do know it?"

"Saudade is a mythical water kingdom. A fiction. It doesn't exist."

She frowned in confusion. The word that had haunted her for so long was only a myth?

"According to legend, Saudade was looked upon with disfavor by the Fates, who sought to destroy it at every opportunity. When finally they succeeded, the kingdom burst apart into the Great Tide that washed the world clean, ushering in the Age of Kings. It's yet another fairy's flight of fancy," he said with disgust. "Really, child, have I taught you nothing? You mustn't believe a word you read in those stories."

"I didn't read it. I saw it. Here." She pulled the dragon scale from inside her dress.

"Ah," he said with a nod. "Dragon's blood. Only marginally more reliable than fairies."

"There was a vision. It said I would be Princess of Saudade."

He clucked with disapproval. "Tell me, my dear, how many decisions have you made today since reveille? Dozens? Hundreds? Thousands, even? And how many more will you make tomorrow? Dragon's blood will show you the possible, that much is true, but only if every decision you make falls precisely into place. If even a single choice is different, your vision will have no more truth in it than the brandy I am off to drink."

He began to turn toward the dark of campus. "Good night, Cadet—"

"I've dreamt of it as well. More than once."

His eyes, usually so aloof, sparkled in the firelight with something like sympathy. "And did these dreams occur before or after the dragon's blood put the word in your head?"

She said nothing, because his implication was correct. She had first heard the word in the blood, and all the dreams had followed.

"Princess Snow White once ate an apple that had been poisoned by a witch. That does not mean there is poison in this." He held up his apple. "Do you understand what I'm saying? Simply because there is magic in the world does not mean everything is magical." A cough rattled from deep in his lungs as he turned and trudged up the cobblestone path, disappearing into the foggy night.

Evie stood beneath the crystal flakes blowing off the Dining Hall's roof, replaying the conversation in her mind again and again until she had satisfied herself with what he had said. Then, she took a deep, cleansing breath and looked up to the clouds. A smile broke across her face, then spread to her eyes.

"It doesn't exist," she said softly. And a second lingering riddle floated from her shoulders and vanished into the night.

Even the Fairy Drillsergeant noticed the change in Evie after that. Without those twin mysteries troubling her mind, she was free to focus on the one thing she really wanted, the singular reason she had returned to the Academy with her sister: to battle witches. The scale she wore no longer held power over her. It was simply a reminder of the family that she so dearly loved. It contained lies and visions and other troubles she needn't bother with, so she ignored the blood and kept the scale close to her heart. Each time she began a drill, she repeated a silent promise that she would do her best to honor her father, her mother, and her sister . . . those of the dragon variety. She always included a plea to the Fates that her sister might be safe and warm and happily eating roasted bear in the family cave with their mother. And she quickly became one of the most dedicated, disciplined cadets in the entire company.

As for her new human sister, the revelations of Beatrice's office held an unintended consequence that suited Evie well. She and Malora worked hard to stay clear of each other, as if acknowledging the other's existence would make the whole sordid thing real.

Saudade meant nothing, and the portrait in Forbes's childhood castle meant nothing. She was free.

She began to excel in other areas as well. She could now turn raw, brittle stalks of flax into linen in less than five minutes, beating, combing, and spinning the fibers with remarkable efficiency. She stayed awake long after dark, retraining herself to pinch a needle with fingers that had only become more rigid and numb since their plunge into the boiling cauldron. Her ball gown was nearly finished, a strange design, though beautiful in its own way, with reds and oranges swirling around the body like flame.

Together, Evie and her friends survived cut after cut. They soon became inured to those dramatic moments when an instructor would halt an exercise, point to a cadet, and end her dream of becoming a princess. The bunks in the barracks began to empty, and the constant threat of snow didn't help to warm any of their hearts. Still, Evie had managed to become one of Ironbone Company's surprising successes. Maggie, Demetra, and Basil excelled as well. Though they never spoke of their prospects in the Helpless Maiden, perhaps out of some superstitious fear that it might put them on the next coach out, each of them could see in the others a new toughness. A toughness rooted in those four magical virtues every princess needed: courage, compassion, kindness, and discipline.

Though she felt faster, smarter, and more self-assured in virtually every way, one weekly event tested her patience. After exceedingly dry sessions with Princess Doberan in the stables, where cadets learned the art of animal husbandry, Evie and Maggie would leave the others and make their way to the Piper of Hamelin Ballroom, a grand structure of cut stone, white as chalk, flanked by dangling willows. Inside, the ballroom was immense, layered with seven tiers of polished oak flooring arranged like a stream flowing from pool to pool. A minstrels' gallery ringed the entire hall. Here, she and the other Grand Ball competitors were shown the fundamental principles of dance.

Evie spent those hours with one hand inside Remington's and another on his shoulder, but she wasn't allowed to say more than a few words to him. All communication was done through glances, for Sir Osdorf, the Knight of Jasmine Pass, allowed absolutely no conversation during his instruction. *How are we meant to be partners if we can't even talk?* she thought, tripping over the hem of her dress once again. Remington was good about not laughing, though she had caught the mirth in his eyes more than once.

Still, all things considered, the weeks following her introduction—or reintroduction—to Countess Hardcastle were some of the best she had had at the Academy. And it was with contentment and a measure of pride that she lay down in her bunk, like all the other cadets, and drifted off to sleep the night she was awoken by the croaking of a frog.

She hadn't noticed at first. None of them had. The guttural grunt had simply blended into the fabric of dreams. But after a particularly loud croak, Evie's eyes popped open. She waited in the dark, unmoving, to see if the sound would come again, but all she heard was the soft rhythm of Maggie's breathing. She was just about to close her eyes when the frog croaked again. She sat up and quietly drew back her blanket. There it was, sitting on the ledge between her bunk and the one that had belonged to Anisette. The window was partially cracked to allow fresh air. That was where the frog had entered.

And it was looking right at her.

She crept out of her bunk with the soft creak of wood and went to the window, but the frog leapt into the night before she got there. She pushed the window open and saw it sitting on the frosted grass staring back at her.

I must be mad, she thought. *I could swear that frog wants me to follow it.*

She glanced around the barracks, though it was difficult to see anything in the darkness. All sounded quiet. She eased onto the stone ledge and climbed through. As she dropped to the ground, she held her breath and pressed her back against the barracks.

Someone's awake. And they've seen me.

It had been the flutter of a sheet, perhaps, or some other movement across the room. Or maybe it was only the shadows playing tricks. The frog let loose another rumbling croak, then turned and flopped away past the other barracks.

She took a deep breath, then hurried after it. *What am I doing?* Though the moon was only a muted dot in the sky illuminating the blue edges of the clouds, she tried to stay low. If any member of staff saw her, she would almost certainly find herself in the Headmistress's office, and then on the first coach out.

She tracked the frog by streaks in the snow and its chirping song. After several minutes, she realized exactly where it was going: the Grennilieu Bog, a restricted area of campus used only for specific training exercises.

"This is madness," she whispered. *Especially if someone really has seen me leaving.* "Is there something you want?"

219

The frog took a final, lazy hop, then flopped around to face her. The membrane beneath its throat distended with a low chirrup. She studied the creature with rising panic. *What am I doing out here with a bloody frog?*

It called again, more loudly this time. And then the croaks kept coming, each more insistent than the last, the frog's vocal sac swelling bigger and bigger. Evie's eyes went wide with horror as its head bent back at an unusual angle, forced that way by a dangerously inflated throat, which looked like a swamp bubble ready to pop.

"Please!" she said. "Stop doing that!"

The grating rasp went on, and the frog's throat continued to expand. Evie was certain the whole campus could hear. She eased away, ready to scramble back to her barracks, but her foot tangled in the knobby root of a fig tree. She fell to the ground, and that was when the membrane swept up from the frog's stomach and washed over the head of . . .

"Remington!"

He stood, pulling the cloak that had been a frog's throat back from his shoulders. "Not bad, eh? My great-grandfather was the original Frog King. Taught me all the cheeky family secrets."

"You're . . . a frog?"

"At times. But no one knows that other than my great-grandfather and my brother. And now you. So," he said, extending his hand, "come with me before we add to that list."

He pulled her to her feet and led her into the bog. They

passed decayed trees, fallen and eaten away, turbid waters gurgling with mud, and dangling moss so long and thick it looked like the branches were melting. She stopped, suddenly, and looked back.

"What is it?"

She listened for another moment, but thought it must have been her imagination. "We really shouldn't be out here."

"I don't care," he said. "It's so bloody difficult to have a proper chat in this place. I stand face-to-face with you in the ballroom and can't even ask about the weather." A chill ran through her, less from the biting air and more because she'd been on his mind. "I never got to tell you how sorry I was for what happened in the castle."

She frowned, trying to understand what he was referring to, and when she did, her hand slid free. "You mean with Malora."

"I tried to find you afterward, but you didn't even have the decency to leave a trail of crumbs. Then I saw you with that dragon, and—"

"Could we talk about something else?"

"Better yet, let's do something else. Come on."

He swung over a deadfall and disappeared into the darkness. She did the same and found him standing at the edge of a great, glassy pool of water, dotted with dozens of lily pads, each as big as a carriage wheel. He raised his eyebrows, then started to step into the water.

"What are you doing?" she said, putting her hands against

his chest. He took her wrists and pulled her out with him. Her breath caught and she cringed for the splash of icy water, but it didn't come. They were standing on one of the lily pads. It gave a bit beneath her feet, but supported both of them without buckling.

"Stoneflower lily pads. They can hold a horse if need be. It's how Sir Isaac escaped the dragon in the Battle of Innisglen. Learned that at Pennyroyal Academy." He folded his fingers between hers and pulled her to the next one. "Come on, trust me—"

"*Wait!*" she hissed, jerking his arm back. He nearly fell in, but regained his balance in time.

"Are you mad?"

"*Shh!*" She peered into the darkness. A distant shadowy figure bounded away through the undergrowth. "There—did you see it?"

"You're awfully paranoid for a girl who follows strange frogs into the night."

She stared into the dark corners of the bog, but nothing else moved. "Perhaps it was a deer or something."

"Good. Let's not let some rogue woodland creature ruin our evening."

He guided her from lily pad to lily pad, and with each step the calm of night returned. It was one of the strangest sensations she had ever experienced, as though she were walking on water without breaking the surface. Each lily pad absorbed her weight with barely a ripple. But the even stranger sensation was the one in her stomach. It fluttered and twirled like a cage of butterflies, and all because her fingers were enmeshed with his.

"I'm glad for it, you know."

"What?"

"That you're the sort of girl to follow strange frogs."

She laughed, quite possibly for the first time since leaving home. It was a lovely feeling, and sorely missed, like a forgotten childhood toy rediscovered.

"Could I ask you something?" she said. Her heart pounded like it had when she had attempted to flirt with him in the courtyard what felt like a million years ago. "There are dozens of girls back there who would give anything to be standing here. And from what I've heard, thousands more across the land. So . . . why am I?"

"Ah," he said. "Why have I reached down from my golden tower to pluck you from the muck?"

She laughed again, but not because he was wrong.

"I don't know, really," he said. "You're a bit dangerous, I suppose."

"*I'm* dangerous?"

"How can I explain? Everywhere I go, people know more about me than I do. My mother has my life planned out to the hymns they'll sing at my funeral. This, right here, is a choice I get to make for myself. And that is, unfortunately, a rarity."

The soft music of rippling water accompanied them as they stepped from one lily pad to the next.

"Choices aren't always so good," she said. "It's far too easy to make a bad one."

"The first bad choice I ever made was that shortcut through the enchanted forest. But even though I nearly died and got turned to candy, I still got to rescue you."

She swatted his arm playfully. *This,* she thought, *this is a moment I'd like my memory to keep.* Though the night was still black and her bunk far away, she already knew this would be one of her most revisited memories, one she'd want to examine from all angles and one whose afterglow she'd want to enjoy for a long time to come.

They circled back to the shoreline, but Remington stopped her from stepping to dry land. He unwrapped his hand from hers and slid both arms around her waist. Her heart stopped. She looked into his eyes, and something else happened on this night of new things.

"Oh . . ." she said lazily as something passed between them. Without another word spoken, the flirtatious lightness of the moment matured into something more. She saw beyond the self-assured smirks and the family name and the charmed life that would take him anywhere in the world he wanted to go. Her eyes fell closed and her lips fell open. He pulled her body to his own . . .

A low, furious snarl, the sound of flesh about to be torn and blood about to be spilled, rumbled up from the trees behind Evie. She opened her eyes and saw Remington looking past her. There was no panic in him, but there was the unmistakable urgency of adrenaline.

"Evie . . ."

She slowly turned around—

And the fairy tale evening ripped apart in a terrifying flash of white daggers. Two hulking, shaggy wolves leapt from the depths of the bog with soul-chilling roars.

She reacted instinctively, throwing Remington to the shore as one of the wolves knocked her into the bog. She glided through the icy water like a snake, another latent skill she had learned from the dragons. She could swim faster and more fluidly than any human—or wolf—alive. Within moments, she pulled herself to shore.

"Evie!"

The muscular beasts splashed after her, snarling and roaring and snapping their jaws. She grabbed Remington's hand and they ran into the trees. Behind them, teeth crunched with sprays of froth.

No roots no rabbit holes no rocks oh please oh please oh please!

She scanned the bog for any sort of cover. In her mind, she could see the elegant forms of the wolves behind her, graceful creatures of death bounding through the darkness, waiting for the slightest misstep.

As they tore through a sheet of hanging moss, she noticed something and reacted. She swung her body, throwing Remington off his feet. One wolf dove at him, catching the back of his knee with a claw just as he tumbled into a small cave between boulders. A fraction of a second later and he would have been dragged into the night and his bones stripped clean.

Evie broke left, and the other wolf pursued. She glanced back to see if one had stayed behind, but both were there, snarling and chomping, hot spit flying from their razor teeth.

"Evie!" she heard Remington call in the distance. "*Evie!*"

She slammed into a branch, caroming through the sedges until she fell. The first wolf was on her immediately, and the second bore down with furious intent. She rolled onto her back, pinned beneath the wolf's massive paw. Its great jaw opened, teeth flashing forth that promised death before pain could even arrive.

But something had started to gurgle deep in Evie's stomach. It rumbled up through her throat and came flooding from her mouth before she even knew what she was doing. It was her voice, only savage, and inhumanly louder. She was roaring. From the dragon parts of her heart.

The wolves recoiled, pinning their ears back as the roar poured from her throat. Then, with frustrated yelps, they scampered over a stone and vanished into the bog.

Evie lay on her back, choking for breath, astonished by what had just happened. She had survived, somehow. The bestial roar echoed in her head. How could that possibly have come from her? She didn't know, but the power of it still coursed through her veins.

"Remington!" She scrambled to her feet. As she raced back

to where she had left him, a cold panic washed over her. Had he heard the roar? Of course he had, but how could she ever explain it?

"Evie!" he called again, and she ran toward his voice. He sat on the ground, a torn piece of black tunic wrapped around his leg. It was soaked through with blood.

"Are you all right?" She dropped to a knee and tried to examine his wound.

"What was that?"

"I think I scared them off, but we'd better go. Someone had to have heard that." She put his arm around her neck and helped him to his feet.

"Blimey, was that you?"

Don't say it. Don't say it. "My parents were dragons."

"What?"

She gave him a look, at once helpless and exasperated. There was no taking the words back now.

"Well," he said, "looks like we're both reptiles, then."

"No. You're an amphibian. Come on . . ."

And they hobbled into the night, aglow in the crackling rush of life that came from cheating death.

EVIE SCANNED the crowd for Remington, but didn't see him anywhere. The whole of Pennyroyal Academy had gathered in the Royal Hall to hear news of what had happened in the night. Second- and first-class cadets and members of staff lined the walls surrounding benches filled with third-class cadets. Rumors circulated about the wolf attack, but the bits Evie overheard were almost all wrong. One girl, a top cadet in Schlauraffen Company, said with great authority that it had been giants.

As she continued her search, she found Malora staring back at her from across the room. Her eyes were raw and ringed with red.

Princess Beatrice's heels clicked across the stone, and the buzz of the crowd quieted. She was trailed by the most senior staff, including several white-bearded knights Evie had not seen before. These were big men, strong and comfortable with death, and she shuddered to think how many dragons they had bloodied between them.

Beatrice approached the lectern and unfolded a parchment. She seemed somehow smaller than she had before. Perhaps it was the short night's sleep or the frantic conversations that had surely been held at the highest levels of the administration. Evie's musings were quickly answered.

"From the Queen," said Beatrice, and then she began to read. "Approximately three hours before morning reveille, two wolves from the Dortchen Wild were found inside Pennyroyal's walls."

There was a flurry of voices as people realized they were more vulnerable than they had thought.

"Commander Muldenhammer and his team have dispatched them, and the grounds are now secure." She nodded to the man behind her. He must have been closer to seven feet than six, and his hands were the size of melons. She turned back to the crowd, pausing to acknowledge someone approaching the dais. It was Countess Hardcastle. She mounted the stairs and joined the House Princesses, who didn't seem at all surprised to see her.

Evie glanced at Maggie, sitting at the end of the row with Demetra, and gave her a look that said, *What's she doing here?*

"The Queen does not take this breach lightly. She is therefore suspending all Academy business until an investigation is completed and she can ensure the safety of every cadet under her command." More mumbles of concern rippled through the room. "Return to your barracks. We are clearing the campus, and the coaches for Castle Waldeck leave shortly. Marburg is . . . no longer a viable option."

The staff began shouting orders above the confused and frightened mutterings of the cadets. Beatrice and her advisers huddled on the dais as, slowly, the crowd emptied into the rotunda. While Evie waited for her row to clear, she looked at Hardcastle, standing at the fringes of Beatrice's group. Her eyes were filled with a mother's compassion, and when Evie followed them across the hall, she found Malora.

Back in the barracks, she finally had a chance to tell Maggie, Demetra, and Basil what had happened in the bog. But her story was cut short when Hardcastle arrived, escorted by Hazelbranch. She had come to collect both of her daughters. And so, with immense apprehension, Evie said goodbye to her friends and followed Hardcastle and Malora across Hansel's Green. Malora stomped off well ahead of them, then darted into her mother's carriage. It was round and black, with delicate silver ornamentations. Three windows shimmered on each side, flanked by massive wheels, nearly as big as Evie herself. Above the horse team sat a detached dickey box for the coachman, who was introduced as Hardcastle's valet, Wormwood. He stowed Evie's knapsack, then took her hand and helped her inside. Twin benches lined with goose-down cushions faced each other. Malora already sat on the rear-facing side, staring coldly out the window.

"There, Nicolina, sit with your sister."

Evie sat next to Malora, who pulled her dress in tight, as though she didn't want even her clothing to touch her sister.

Hardcastle took the opposite bench. She folded her hands primly in her lap with a look of supreme contentment.

"Lovely," she said. "Our little family, reunited at last."

The coach lurched away, wheeling around the fountain and down the hill toward the Dortchen Wild. No one spoke. Only the dull thud of hooves in the mud spoiled the silence. And before long, Evie was back in the woods once again.

She pretended to fall asleep as they began the long, lurching ride through the climbs and drops of the Dortchen Wild. Beneath the twin blankets of cloud and canopy, and inside the tiny warm shell of the carriage as it traveled through wintry forest, sleep seemed a plausible excuse to avoid conversation. The carriage bounced along on its undergear as hours passed in near silence. Hardcastle occasionally asked a question of Malora, whose grunted responses stopped the talk cold.

Evie tried to relive the previous night in her mind, specifically the part before the wolves attacked. What had happened between her and Remington? She couldn't say, really. He was clearly going to kiss her, which was thrilling in itself, but something more had passed between them. She knew almost nothing about him, yet found herself passing that long ride trying to imagine what his home must be like. Who was he when he was there? Was he different amidst the formalities of court? Would the sparkle in his eye and that half smile fade away under the scrutiny of an adoring people? Or was he always just Remington, confident and charming and sharp as a rose's thorn?

Hours passed in minutes with these thoughts, and before long the carriage began a long ascent into a range shrouded with powder-coated pines. She looked out across the valley, deep green at the bottom where it was not yet cold enough for snow. At the higher elevations, the emerald forests turned smoky white, and she was surprised to see the faint outline of the sun already dropping to the top of the far mountains. She had been drifting between dreams and daydreams for most of a day.

Finally, after climbing so high that the air became thin and sharp, the carriage swung onto a gravel path. There, perched at the end, was the manor house Evie had seen in her memory. But time had clawed away at it. It looked tired, the plaster cracked and some of the fir beams rotted. The once-beautiful gardens, draped in snow, were overgrown with weeds and dead things. The majesty of the estate was buried beneath rust and decay.

The carriage swung around and stopped. Malora shoved past Evie and raced up the walk to the entrance. She looked quite ashen, as though the long, jostling carriage ride had made her queasy.

"Here it is, Nicolina," said Hardcastle. "Callahan Manor."

Evie stepped out of the carriage, Hardcastle following behind, and took in the magnificent sweep of the horizon. The world fell away in nearly every direction, giving the manor impressive views over primeval forest valleys.

"It's Evie . . . please."

"Yes, yes, of course. Evie. I'd forgotten. Come, let me show you your home."

Wormwood busied himself with the baggage and horses. Hardcastle took Evie's hand in the crook of her elbow and walked her up the path. This was her ancestral home. The place she had been born. *This is where I lived with Countess Hardcastle and King Callahan and Malora,* she told herself, but it felt more like a story in a book than reality. Until—

A memory flashed into her consciousness. The manor was pristine, shimmering and polished and chirping with life. The King, bearded and jolly, sat atop his palfrey with Evie behind him. He fastened the picnic basket to one of his weatherworn saddlebags, then looked to Hardcastle, who stood in a vestibule off the side of the house. She blew a kiss and waved as the horse trotted toward a thin trail that disappeared into the woods . . .

The memory jarred Evie. Somehow she felt certain that as she rode away that day, it was the last time she would see Callahan Manor. Until now.

Hardcastle excused herself to light fires and warm the bones of the old house, so Wormwood guided Evie to her bedchamber. The Manor was dark and drab and filled with dusty relics and ornate furniture. He led her upstairs to her room at the end of the hall, bowed, and closed the door behind him with a soft click. At last, she was alone. She took a deep breath, hoping it might clear away some of the melancholy that had settled over her. It did not.

Her bed was massive, at least three times as big across as her bunk at the Academy. The walls were covered in faded brown oils of men in military uniforms and women with serious faces wearing tight, corseted dresses. An elegant armoire and matching dresser lined the walls. A mirror sat atop the dresser, dusty bottles of long-evaporated perfumes scattered beneath. She would have been perfectly happy to climb into that bed and sleep until morning, or perhaps even try to perch on the footboard, but Hardcastle had made it clear she expected to see more of her daughter after she had settled in. And so, she opened the door and went back down the staircase. She walked gently, as though she were sneaking somewhere she wasn't meant to be. No one seemed to be around, so she thought she might get some air. Through a tarnished glass door, she found a terrace of polished marble. She walked to the edge and peered over the balustrade, where a valley of trees fell away so sharply it took her breath away, and even more so when the setting sun peeked through the clouds and painted everything purple.

"It's magic, isn't it?" said Countess Hardcastle. She stepped to the balustrade next to Evie and looked out at the mountains. "This is where we were meant to live, all of us, happily to the end of our days."

Evie said nothing. A hawk cried in the distance, its echo filling the valley with sorrow.

"It's quite cold out here, isn't it?" she continued. Evie smiled, but didn't respond. "Princess Beatrice says I'm to let you ease into life at your own pace, but I . . ." She paused to compose herself. "I want you to know I never stopped looking for you."

Evie could feel Hardcastle studying her, but kept her eyes on the bloodred orb settling onto the horizon. It was the first time she had seen the sun since her return to the cave. Before the lance had pierced her sister's flesh.

"Is there anything you'd like to know? Anything at all? As I said, this must happen at *your* pace—"

"What became of my real father?"

"Ah . . . a rapid pace, then."

"I'm sorry," said Evie. She hadn't meant to blurt it out like that, but it was hard to know how to act.

"I assume you're referring to your father of the blood?"

"Yes. You said the King was my stepfather."

"Indeed, that is so. As for your blood father, well, it was an arranged marriage, you see. I'm afraid I didn't really know him. He was killed by a giant before you ever entered this world."

So she would never know her blood father. Truth be told, it didn't bother her, particularly since the dragon would always be her one true father, and, judging by her memories, she had loved and been loved by King Callahan as well. Her blood father felt so abstract in her heart as to be nothing more than a character in a story. True, the story was hers, but he simply wasn't a major player.

"It was only you and me until I met King Callahan. I'd received an invitation to a ball at his palace. We fell desperately in love. He, too, had lost a spouse, and when we married, he became your stepfather and I Malora's stepmother. He may not have been your blood, but that is how he loved you.

"When he . . . *died*, I went from Queen Hardcastle to Queen Dowager Hardcastle. As if it weren't painful enough to have lost him, I lost my name as well. *Dowager*," she spat, shaking her head ruefully. "My new title became such a painful reminder of that awful day that I decided to go back to Countess."

Evie stole a glance at her mother, who looked off at the sun, eyes glistening. She felt a wellspring of tenderness for this woman, for all the hardships she had endured in only a few years' time. *What would my life be like now had her vision of a happy future come to fruition?*

"And now might I ask a question of you?"

"Of course," said Evie.

Hardcastle smiled, as though ashamed of what was to come. "I don't quite know how to say it." She turned to face Evie. "Might you consider . . . staying? Here with me, I mean. Princess Beatrice has agreed to let you reenlist next year—"

"*What?*"

"It's just that . . . I've only just got you back. The Academy might reopen tomorrow, the next day, the day after that . . . and I'll lose you all over again."

Evie turned away, lines of worry etched across her forehead. Clouds had begun to encroach on the sun, like spider's silk around prey. "You won't lose me," was all she could think to say.

Hardcastle paused, then joined her daughter in watching the sun's last light. "It's yours, you know. All of this." She swept her arm across the wintry paradise below. "I'm just an old Queen Dowager, and I might not be around much longer."

"You're not old."

"I don't mean to make you uncomfortable, my darling. I'd just like to taste the life that *dragon* took from me. The life that was mine by rights—"

"Dragon?"

Hardcastle bit back tears. Whatever memory had come to her stung as sharply and deeply as the day it was born. "Wormwood?" she called. "Wormwood!"

The valet stepped onto the terrace. "Yes, madam."

"Fetch the King's portrait."

He bowed and disappeared into the glowing warmth of the house.

"Your memory, the one that came to you in Princess Beatrice's office. I've had that same memory every day since you rode off for that picnic. It's become an eternal nightmare." She took a deep breath and held the balustrade to steady herself. "It was your fifth birthday. The day the King died."

Memories swirled through Evie's head. A flash of that moment in the kitchen, only a short flight of stairs beneath where she now stood. Her joyous giggles as the King swept her into the air.

"We were all meant to celebrate together, but Malora fell desperately ill. We decided it would be cruel to keep you from your picnic after we'd talked about it for so long . . ."

237

Another flash of memory. Evie and her stepfather on a mountain meadow looking out across the basin. An immense waterfall plunged hundreds of feet into an ice-blue lake below. The picnic basket sat open at her feet.

"When the King's men went in search of you, they found . . . true horror on that mountaintop . . ."

And now the memory became real, just as her memory in Beatrice's office had. She was there, standing in the grass. The wind tousled her hair, carrying the scent of honeysuckle and deathribbon flowers. The waterfall rumbled distantly, a stripe of white down the black mountain face. And the King . . . the King . . .

She looked up at him, and what she saw in his face chilled her to her bones. Beneath the furs of nobility, beneath the beard and the scars and the rough red skin, the King's sapphire eyes stared at that waterfall with complete emptiness. He looked lost, vacant—

And then the trees behind them began to crackle down like dead sticks. A wall of pale green scales burst into the meadow with a piercing roar.

"*GET AWAY!*" bellowed the King. His broadsword flashed as he loosed it from its sheath. She ran, diving into a tangle of greenbrier. She covered her ears and clenched her teeth against the horrific sounds of violence. Streams of flame spewed through the grass, leaving thick trails of liquid fire and smoke. The King's shouts and the crash of steel told her he was still alive. The dragon shrieked in pain as the King landed a blow.

Then his body flopped through the undergrowth only yards away from where she hid. He scrambled to his feet, diving away before another fiery burst lit up the meadow.

Evie was too terrified to move. She could only see flashes of the battle, but had trouble imagining how the King would be able to withstand an assault from a creature that stood as high as the treetops. And yet, his brave shouts kept coming.

Finally, the dragon screamed so loudly that she clutched her head. When it stopped, she opened her eyes and saw the great beast lurch into the air, the wind of its wings pressing down on her. To her horror, the King dangled from the hilt of his broadsword, the only part that wasn't buried in the dragon's shoulder. She couldn't move, couldn't breathe, couldn't even blink as the dragon flew across the valley, carrying her stepfather to what would certainly be his death . . .

"I thought that dragon had erased half my family that day, and yet . . . here you are . . ."

Evie stood on the terrace, staring at the final, fading corona of sun as it slipped behind the mountain. Her eyes were wide with shock, and her skin had gone ashen.

"Where have you been, my dear?"

One piece of the memory flashed through Evie's head again and again. It was the only glance she had gotten of the great drake as it crashed out from the trees. His eyes, red with fury . . . his horns, so crooked and battle-scarred . . . the familiar bend in his neck and the divot in his snout . . .

It was her father.

Evie's eyes began to tear. The shock on her face twisted and contorted into betrayal as the ramifications of it all kept pouring in. It was her own father who had orphaned her that day.

The door clicked open and Wormwood returned. He carried a piece of tattered canvas no bigger than the dragon scale around Evie's neck.

"Ah, here he is. Your true father."

Evie, devastated, took the ragged portrait. It was the man from her memories, King Callahan. He stood atop a mountain, eyes skyward, jolly and laughing. Her father. Her true father.

"I'm sorry ... I don't feel well ..." She raced past Wormwood and disappeared inside, leaving Hardcastle alone once again.

Back in the confines of her bedchamber, she sat at the edge of her bed, gripping the dragon scale as if to choke the life out of it. Tears of anger and betrayal streamed down her face.

"I am daughter to the King. I am a princess. I never was a bloody dragon."

She threw the scale at the wall, and it clacked to the floor. She wrenched loose a rusted iron bar and opened the shutters to let in the frigid air. The moon, shaded by clouds as wispy as an old woman's hair, soaked the valley blue under the black sawtooth outline of a distant mountain range.

An animal shriek shot through her mind. Then came that horrible vision of the dragon carrying the King high across the valley, her two fathers bound together in a mortal struggle that only one would survive. Silence settled across the meadow after that, with only a whisper of wind across the grass and the soft crackle of fire. She crept out from the greenbrier, her arms and face slashed by thorns. The meadow, the bucolic patch of green where she was to celebrate her fifth birthday, was destroyed. Streaks of char and fire. Giant waves of earth plowed up through the grass. Blood, both black and red, marring the green.

Now, looking back, she could remember standing there staring at the devastation. But even then it felt distant, like a story told around a fire rather than a horrific scene of violence and death. A movement in the trees caught her eye. She was not alone. There was a second dragon, a smaller one, bright green and no bigger than a carriage. The dragon, a female, stepped out from the trees and regarded her. She pawed the earth with a great olive-green talon and gave a purring roar. Evie wasn't frightened or angry or any of the things she was now. She felt nothing as she stepped toward the beast. The dragon retreated a few steps, then stopped. Finally, sensing the little girl wasn't a threat, she turned and crashed into the forest. Evie, as though sleepwalking, followed.

"Sister," she said, for that was who the juvenile dragon would one day become. As the memory faded into the night, she lifted the small portrait of King Callahan to the moonlight. She studied his rugged features, the proud curve of his back, the mirth in his eyes. "What do I do?" she said in a cracked voice. "Is *this* where my life is meant to be?" Princess Beatrice had supposed once that the Fates had brought Evie to Pennyroyal Academy to help Forbes, but perhaps it was to lead her back to her true mother. Her true life. Perhaps she *was* meant to stay at Callahan Manor and help heal the scars that encased her mother like a shell.

From the corner of her eye, she saw a faint light ripple through the dragon's blood on the scale. She picked it up in her scarred fingers, and a wave of anguish crashed over her.

"You stole me . . . You stole me from my life . . . You made everything a lie . . ."

The great fractures in her life, the strange things that had never quite made sense, began to snap back into place. She had loved her dragon family to the core of her heart, and had always believed they felt the same way. But now everything she knew about them, about herself, was a lie. They had murdered the only human father she had ever known and stolen her from her mother and sister. Forbes had been right all along. Dragons were violent, cruel monsters. She had lived with them all those years not knowing the immense destruction they had wreaked on her life.

The scale was rough, its scallops jagged and sharp. The streak of blood across its convex side had tiny chips in it, perhaps flaked away in the boiling stew of the witches' cauldron. It looked dead and gray and far removed from any meaning it had once held. She reared back to throw it—her old life—to the wind.

I am daughter to the King. I am a princess.

But she couldn't bring herself to do it. Every second she held the scale, ripped from her dragon father's body as he saved her life, she broke apart even more. She hated her dragon family but she had loved them once, and she supposed she still loved them now, but she hated them just the same. Her arm fell. All strength left her, and she collapsed to the sill.

I hate them . . .

The blood on the scale shimmered once more. She held it to the moon and let the light sparkle across its surface. Then she lowered it to her eye and disappeared into a swirling void . . .

And a faint image spun out of the nothingness. It was the great clearing in the Dortchen Wild. Pennyroyal Academy stood atop its hill, but it had been devastated by war, an abandoned relic from a time when princesses still had hopes of defeating the wicked witches. Walls had crumbled, fires had charred the fields, and the Queen's Tower had been sawed in half, leaving only a broken stump. The ruins of the Academy slipped back into blackness. Before long, another image began to form. It was an octagonal tower of granite. A hard rain beat down against its roof. Remington was there, water streaming from his nose and chin. He was on his knees, sword in hand.

The image flickered wider and she saw another figure. It was a witch, though her face was obscured by the downpour. She floated three feet off the stone, her bony arms extended to the sky. A slow swirl of smoky magic wafted from her heart like the first warning of fire. Suddenly, a ribbon of black snaked toward Remington's chest. He threw back his head in agony as his doublet burned away and the skin above his heart faded to the dull gray of dead stone . . .

She tore the scale from her eye. She sat there a moment, trying to catch her breath. Then, with racing heart, she tucked Callahan's portrait into the scale's concave side and slipped them both into her knapsack. She sat in the windowsill staring at the night sky until it lightened to a dim yellow. If what she had seen could truly come to pass—and even Volf, despite his skepticism, admitted that dragon's blood did predict the possible—then Pennyroyal Academy, and the fate of all princesses, was in jeopardy.

And Remington, the first human she had known since the dragons took her, might end up a forgotten piece of stone in a crumbling tower, frozen until the end of time in a state of pure agony.

18

OVER THE NEXT few days, Evie did all she could to avoid Hard-castle and Wormwood. Her mother must have sensed her need to be alone because the days passed quietly, and there was always a hot meal waiting outside her bedchamber door. She would sneak out of the servants' entrance near the buttery and spend most of the sunlight hours away from the main house, off on one of Hardcastle's jennets, a brown one with black hooves and mane. If Evie's life had been a peaceful lake, her conversation with Hardcastle had troubled the waters, clouding what had previously been clear. Those long rides exploring the grounds of Callahan Manor, quiet and blue-skied and bursting with nature's best offerings, helped keep her mind occupied.

She expected more memories might emerge as she rode the grounds. None did, though she slowly began to fall in love. Each hill she crested held another stunning secret. Meadows of wildflowers of gold and purple and white. Cascading velvet streams. Unexpected cliff-top vistas of pine and spruce forests so dense they looked like swatches of blue moss carpeting the mountains before the summits turned white with snow. The air itself seemed a thing of beauty, so clean and fresh it held the light better than in other places. On one ride, she discovered a freshwater pool at the base of a cliff, and the crystal mist of its waterfall cast everything in a magical haze. The King lived on all through these beautiful grounds. She could imagine the days they would have passed here had he lived. Had the dragons not stolen her, too. She had only scattered memories of him to cling to, and one in particular she hoped never to remember again, but exploring the land that had been his—theirs—made her feel closer to him.

And one morning, before she rose and slipped out of the house into his world again, a bell rang. She followed the sound to a side room, where the grimy windows looked out onto the forest. Malora was there, frail and sickly and wrapped in a woolen blanket. Hardcastle stood near a fire, Wormwood behind her. She held a wax-sealed parchment in her hand.

"Sit, please," she said. Evie joined Malora on a bench beneath the window. Hardcastle held up the parchment and said, "It's from the Headmistress." She peeled the wax free and opened the message. Her features hardened as she read. Once she'd finished, she folded it and looked down at her girls. "Well . . . it seems the missing wand responsible for the breach has been recovered. They will institute more robust checks on fairies' wands and so on and so forth, but . . ." She paused and gathered herself. "It seems your training will resume in two days' time."

Evie sat expressionless, unsure how to act. After a moment

of thick silence, Malora pulled her blanket tight and left without a word.

"So, my darling daughter, the time for your choice has come. Will you stay or won't you?"

Evie had never felt so completely divided before. If she could only utter the words *I will*, she would live a peaceful life at the Manor, establishing a new relationship with her mother and starting to right the wrongs the dragons had inflicted upon them both. Instead, she said nothing. With each moment that ground by, her decision became clearer. Eventually, her gaze fell to the threadbare rug.

"I see," said Hardcastle. She dropped the parchment into the flames, then turned to Wormwood. "Collect the girls' things and take them away."

And Evie didn't see her mother again, not even as the carriage bounced down the gravel path and began its long descent into the forest.

Two days later, under a quiet rain, she found herself sitting with her company on the benches of the berfrois above the jousting lists, deep in the part of campus farthest from the princess barracks. And she was staring at the very thing that had brought her back to the Academy.

"Go on, Remington!" shouted a Thrushbeard knight. The black doublets sat at the far end of the berfrois, lustily cheering him on as he limped down the stairs into mud pocked with thousands of hoofprints.

Evie wanted to run to him and tell him what she had seen

in the dragon's blood, to implore him never to go near another tower as long as he lived. But beneath her anxiety, something else lurked. When she saw him smile, laughing at the rowdiness of his company-mates, the grim vision dimmed just a bit, and she was taken back to the moments before the wolves attacked. To what might have been when he put his arms around her, closed his eyes, and leaned in . . .

"Right, Cadet Remington," said the Fairy Drillsergeant, "and who shall be your opponent?"

Remington glanced at Captain Ramsbottom, standing at the edge of the mud, rain sluicing off his huge, folded arms, then scanned the Ironbone girls. His eyes passed right over Evie and landed on . . .

"You. Come join me, won't you?"

"Me?" said Basil.

"I'd rather not fight a girl. Mother would have my head."

"You will all fight girls," said the Fairy Drillsergeant, "and quite a few of you will end up with bruised egos for it. Cadet Basil, if you please . . ."

Basil reluctantly made his way off the berfrois and joined them in the jousting lists. The Thrushbeard cadets heckled Remington, who took it all with a confident smile.

"Ordinarily, close-quarters combat is a second-year discipline. But things have gone a bit away from plan, haven't they? Being able to defend yourself when you're in proximity to your enemy feels slightly more important after what's happened."

Rumpledshirtsleeves stepped onto the berfrois and took a

seat on one of the benches. Two of his assistants held a tasseled umbrella over him to keep the rain away.

"What's he doing here?" said Kelbra.

It is odd, thought Evie. With the exception of Captain Ramsbottom, other staff members never attended the Fairy Drillsergeant's sessions.

"Remember your training, Cadet!" he called to Basil. The girls looked at one another in confusion.

"Training? What's he on about?" whispered Demetra. Evie could only shake her head.

"Two falls to win. Ready?"

"No!" said Basil. Remington nodded and crouched into a grappling stance.

"Let's begin."

As rain fell gently as snow, Remington and Basil circled each other. The mud was slick and heavy, and neither wanted to give up footing. The knights began to shout for action.

"Come on, cadets! This isn't the Grand Ball!" said the Fairy Drillsergeant.

Remington lunged, throwing his shoulder into Basil's middle. They landed in a puddle with a splash, but Basil managed to scramble away. Remington hobbled to his feet. His leg was clearly bothering him. The Fairy Drillsergeant circled Basil, trying to spur him on.

"Twenty-one brothers and you never learned to fight?"

"No! I didn't! They all fought one another!"

The cheers from the knight cadets grew louder as they

sensed a victory for their side, while the princesses watched glumly. Evie glanced back at Rumpledshirtsleeves. He was as happy as she'd ever seen him, and it annoyed her. Of all the drills to observe, had he chosen this one just to witness their humiliation?

"A moment, Fairy Drillsergeant," called the tailor troll. He motioned to Basil, who trotted to the edge of the lists. "Tell me, Cadet, why does a princess spin?"

"To make clothes for the needy," said Basil, incredulous.

"Correct! That's kindness. And as you've been training your heart with kindness, you've been training your body all the while. Remember, don't fight the flax. Let the flax fight itself and you'll end up with a beautiful garment every time." He tapped the side of his nose knowingly.

"That's it? That's your advice?"

"Come on, before it starts to rain," said Remington, shaking his head like a wet dog. Basil sloshed back over and they began to circle each other again. Thunder rumbled in the distance.

"Steady, Cadet . . ." said Rumpledshirtsleeves. "Don't watch his eyes . . ."

Remington pounced, staying low to maintain leverage.

"Now! Break the flax!"

Basil reacted instinctively, jerking his arms down like he was working a flax break. His fists thumped Remington's head, plunging him face-first into the mud.

The girls erupted in cheers. Basil turned to them with a look of utter bafflement.

Remington pulled himself to his feet, wiping the muck from his eyes. He worked his sore knee back and forth, then charged Basil again.

"Spin the drive wheel, lad!" called Rumpledshirtsleeves.

Basil wound his fist and connected with Remington's chin, spiraling him to the ground.

"That's two falls! Princesses win!" shouted the Fairy Drillsergeant. Ironbone Company hailed Basil, who stood stunned, a puppet without a puppeteer. The Thrushbeard cadets rained jeers down on Remington, who gave a sarcastic bow and limped back up the berfrois.

"I'll have a go, Fairy Drillsergeant." It was Forbes, already stepping down to the rain-soaked weeds at the edge of the lists. "And I want to fight her." He pointed squarely at Evie.

"Brilliant," said the Fairy Drillsergeant. "Cadet, come forward, please."

Evie shot to her feet and charged down the stairs. She hadn't realized it until then, but she relished the opportunity to dirty his arrogant face. She glared at him, then scooped some mud and splashed it across the front of her dress, eliciting a roar of cheers from her company. He offered a cocksure smile and shook his head.

"Begin!" called the Fairy Drillsergeant.

She tried to emulate the crouch Remington had done, mirroring Forbes's every move. His arm shot toward her and she slapped it away. The girls howled with delight.

"Why are you so obsessed with me?" she said.

"Don't flatter yourself. I only brought you down here because I have something to tell you."

She saw a tightening in his jaw a fraction of a second before he lunged. It was the same thing her sister used to do when they would spar in the meadow. She sidestepped and grabbed his arm, using his own momentum to throw him to the mud. Jeers poured from one side of the berfrois, cheers from the other.

"That's how you comb the flax," she said with a smirk. He pushed himself up, rain streaming from his hair, and wiped the sludge from his face. He was not smiling.

He came at her straightaway, catching her around the shoulders. Her arms were pinned in his embrace. He began forcing her to the ground, and she wasn't strong enough to stop him.

"Are you going to listen or do you actually want to fight?" he asked.

She gritted her teeth and focused all her energy into breaking his grip, but to no avail.

"Work the treadle! Then hang the fibers!" called Rumpledshirtsleeves.

She drove her heel into Forbes's boot, which slackened his hold just enough for her to sweep her arms up and break free. Her elbow caught him square in the nose.

"*Gah!*" He staggered back, hands at his face, but didn't fall. She charged at him. He rooted himself like a tree and she slammed into him, bouncing away to the mud. It knocked her wind away. He grabbed her dress and hauled her to her feet, pinning her arms behind her back. Slowly, her lungs began to draw thin streams of breath. "Now listen to me and listen closely," he whispered, blood running from his nose. "It was Malora who let those wolves in. She wanted me to help her get some sort of revenge on you and Remington. I couldn't care less about either one of you, so I told her to bog off."

Her breathing slowly returned, but the fight was over. His words staggered her more than any attack could.

"Just thought you should know," he said. Then he threw her to the mud and stormed back to the berfrois, the knights cheering him along.

"Knights win!"

Evie struggled to her feet, battered and beaten. She trudged back to the benches where her eyes found Malora's, as cold and gray as the rain.

When they'd arrived back at the Academy from Callahan Manor, Evie had noticed that several things were different. The most obvious was that not everyone had returned. Ironbone was eight cadets fewer, and it had been lucky compared with some of the other companies. But other things had changed as well. Malora never seemed to get past whatever had been ailing her at home. Her silky confidence had withered into a constant cough and a permanent scowl. She and Evie hadn't spoken a word since discovering they were sisters. Even Kelbra and Sage afforded her a bit more distance. The Queen had proclaimed a foreshortened year because of the attack. Several weeks of training would need to be condensed into days. The Grand Ball would proceed as planned, but after only one more lesson. The end of term was now even closer than it had seemed, a thought that filled Evie with dread. The Helpless Maiden, for all its mystery, loomed.

Remington seemed different as well, like a veil of melancholy had fallen over him. She decided to try to find out why at Sir Osdorf's only remaining lesson before the Grand Ball. They sat together on a stone bench beneath a willow outside the Piper of Hamelin Ballroom. It had been a rough practice, with neither of them able to anticipate what the other would do. Remington's knee was clearly bothering him, and a constant barrage of Osdorf's fury only made matters worse.

"Is something the matter?" she said, finally breaking a heavy silence.

"How do you mean?" He leaned down to rub his knee.

"You just seem a bit distracted, is all."

"No. I'm perfectly fine."

She frowned in frustration. *Why can't humans just say what they mean?*

"Aside from the fact that I've dedicated my life to killing your family, of course."

She looked up at him, stunned.

"Do you understand that I'm going to be a knight, Evie? My sword will kill your kind or they'll kill me. Those are the only two outcomes."

"But they're not my kind." She felt like she was sliding down a muddy hill, desperately grasping at the weeds. "They're not."

"And you'll still say that when I've lopped off their heads?"

He pulled his leg back and let out a deep exhale. "I have some-thing to tell you. I should have been honest from the beginning, but, well, I wasn't."

"What is it?" she said warily.

"I have killed a dragon before."

The corners of her mouth quivered. Blood pulsed inside her head. "You lied."

"I did."

She looked away, to the white cobblestones beneath the steps to the ballroom.

"I was a boy of eleven. We'd gone to my uncle's palace at Fid-dlehead Downs for some business of my father's. My brother and I went off toward the seaside to explore with a pair of old swords my uncle's captain of the guard had given us. We ended up on a little trail through the forest and followed it along for quite some time, half a day or so. He wanted to turn back, but I . . . I don't know, really, I suppose I was asserting my status as elder brother and I made him continue on. Not long after that we found a strange black substance on the ground. It looked like tar or something, the kind you find bubbling up from the ground in Devil's Garden. I had to know more, naturally, so we followed its trail and found . . ." He took another deep breath and slowly let it out. ". . . a dragon. She'd been wounded some-how, and gone into the forest for protection. That's my theory, anyway. Regardless . . . she never heard us coming."

From the corner of Evie's eye, she saw his head drop. He paused, picking at a fingernail. "She nearly tore my brother in half. I'm sure it upsets you to hear that, but those are the facts."

She found herself at a complete loss. She didn't want to hear another word of the story, but couldn't find the words to stop him.

"To be honest, I don't really remember much beyond that. I drew my sword, and . . ." He raised his hands and let them fall as words failed him, too. "It's a bloody business, killing dragons. Bloody and awful."

Evie's stomach churned, and she thought she might be sick. She leaned forward, elbows on her thighs, and cupped her forehead in her hands.

"I *hate* that people see glory in what I did." His voice had taken on a hard edge. "There's no glory in it at all. I only wanted to keep her from killing my brother." An owl's call echoed from somewhere beyond the ballroom, one long hoot and two short. "I was born where I was born to the family I was born to. I was always going to be a knight. But it's never been something I relish. I thought I'd come here, put my head down, and do my duty, but . . . but now I know you, and nothing's what I thought it was."

The owl sang again. After a long silence, made heavy by the undeniable, unchangeable fact that he had not killed his last dragon, she finally spoke.

"Nothing is what I thought it was, either."

She roamed alone outside the barracks long after leaving him. Images of her dragon father after the crash, bloodied and injured, swirled through her head. Despite everything she had learned about her family, she didn't want to see her father in pain. Yet there he was and there was Remington, sword in hand, ready to slash the life out of him.

When the light from the barracks had dimmed to almost nothing, she finally ventured inside. She had gone numb. The only thing she wanted was a dreamless night. She passed Demetra, then Maggie, both sleeping peacefully, both handling their familial complications far better than she ever could. She slipped off her left shoe, then her right, and then she stopped dead.

Her Grand Ball gown, the piece she had built from whole cloth and had been honing and refining for months, was in tatters. It hung haphazardly, with seams torn out and panels ripped away. Colored dye had been splashed down the front.

Her nostrils flared as that old, buried dragon anger began to ignite. She looked across the barracks, and in the dim light of the few remaining torches, she found Malora staring back.

"Just because your mother married a king doesn't mean you're not trash."

Evie's anger pulsed through her lungs, then her jaw, and finally her eyes. She glared across the room with such force that Malora leapt from her bunk and sprinted for the exit. Evie bolted after her, and they burst into the night, their bare feet sending up cold sprays of mud and dewy grass as they streaked across Hansel's Green.

"Get away from me!"

Evie dove. Her fingertips slapped Malora's calf just enough to trip her up. She leapt onto her back and they writhed through the sodden grass, each fighting for leverage.

"Get off!" shrieked Malora, clawing at the turf to pull herself free. But Evie's anger had taken control. She grabbed a fistful of raven-black hair and drove Malora's face into the mud. Months of frustration and helplessness poured from her hands into the body struggling beneath her. The relief was overwhelming.

Finally, though, she heard Malora's choked gasps, and her anger evaporated. She threw the hair aside and let her stepsister up. As she sat there in the wet grass, her tears finally came out in sobs. "Why are you so horrible to me? I never did anything to you!"

Malora pushed herself onto her elbows. Between gasps, she spit out mud, then flipped onto her back and tried to catch her breath.

"We're meant to be sisters," said Evie, her fury turning to heartbreak. "Why would you ever do that to your sister?"

"I don't know, all right? I didn't mean to, I just—"

"Of course you meant to! That doesn't make any sense!"

"I didn't." She sat up and wiped the grass from her face. Her voice was soft, thoughtful in a way Evie hadn't heard before. "I don't know why I do half the things I do. It just . . . *happens* and I can't control it. I'm sorry."

Evie wiped away the last remaining tears. In the darkness, after a flurry of emotion, the numbness had started to settle in again.

"I know I'm meant to be a princess," continued Malora. "I've known it since the day I was born. But sometimes I just feel so *rotten* inside. And then I do rotten things."

Evie leapt to her feet and charged back to the barracks.

"I didn't mean to!" called Malora, but Evie was through listening.

The next day she sat on a hard wooden stool in Rumpledshirtsleeves's cottage, missing every word he said.

"A shallower curve in your sleeve pattern will generally provide you greater range of motion for hand-to-hand combat. Far more importantly, it will maintain the sleek, fitted look we all seek—"

The cottage door creaked open. The cadets, who sat at dress forms in a half circle around their instructor, turned to see who it was. Two people stepped inside, a man and a woman, wearing the muddied wool and leather of the peasantry. Their faces were haunted, their eyes ringed with purple exhaustion. Malora coughed, eyeing them with barely disguised contempt.

"Mother? Father?"

It was a girl called Cadet Amaryllis, the same girl who had returned the dragon scale necklace on the first day of term. Evie knew her only slightly, but had always felt gratitude toward her since that encounter. She could only imagine what might have happened had someone less kind found the scale that day.

"You'll pardon our interruption, sir," said the father, taking his hat in his hands. "Amaryllis . . ."

She hurried across the room to embrace him. Something about these people, the echo of death in their eyes, sent a chill through every cadet in the cottage.

"Our kingdom, Goldharbor, she was taken three nights ago by witches."

"Oh," said Demetra softly, her hands going to her mouth. Amaryllis collapsed into her mother's arms in despair.

"It's all gone." He didn't seem to be speaking to anyone in particular, just staring off at some unseen horror that existed only in his memory. "They took dozens of our people off into the forest . . . burned the rest to the ground . . ."

Amaryllis's mother shepherded her to the door. The father turned to follow.

"Where will you go?" asked Rumpledshirtsleeves.

"To the north. They say that's where Princess Middlemiss is, protecting the refugees."

And with that, he led his daughter into a world smothered beneath furious black clouds.

Amaryllis's wails echoed in the cottage as the cadets looked back to Rumpledshirtsleeves, but even he seemed a bit wobbly after what had just happened. Evie was the only one who hadn't yet turned away from the door. Someone she knew, someone who came here just as she had, an anonymous person of common birth, someone she had bled with on the training field, would now be wandering a witch-ravaged countryside looking for comfort and protection. It brought Princess Middlemiss right off the page. This was not a story. It was real. It was the thing she was working to become, and it had never felt so impossibly far away.

"Why don't we leave it there, shall we?"

The cadets gathered their things, and the whispers began.

"A word, please," said Rumpledshirtsleeves, his droopy eye fixed on Evie. Demetra gave her a grim smile and a squeeze on the shoulder as she and Maggie left. Once the door fell closed, Rumpledshirtsleeves put his hands on his hips and hung his head. "At times I feel such unbearable sadness . . . For a world with so much beauty, there is just *so much cruelty*."

She said nothing. Her supplies of sadness had run low. She felt mostly anger now.

"I heard about your gown."

Her eyes flicked up, but he waved away her concern.

"Keeping up with idle gossip is one of my more enjoyable pursuits. It used to be the hunt, but I've slowed and the deer haven't." He smiled. She didn't. "It is a pity about your gown. Your design showed sophistication and taste. Have you any idea what happened?"

Evie looked back to the floor.

"Yes. Such a pity we'll never know who was responsible, isn't it?"

She scoffed, but didn't look up.

"I've spoken to the Headmistress about *her* on more than one occasion. I inquired as to how a cadet with such a basic

261

lack of our four founding principles could still be among us. She told me to keep my warty nose out of Academy business."

"What?"

"Do you think people stop being cruel as they age?" He shook his head sadly. "I have great admiration for Princess Beatrice and all she's done for the Academy, but she has always disliked trolls. It is only my astonishing skill that has kept me in her employ for so long."

Evie had never felt any great affection toward the Headmistress, but it seemed unnecessarily cruel to treat such a wise, skilled member of staff so harshly.

"I've trained the best princesses ever to wear the crown," he continued, tottering toward her. "And all of them, to a woman, had horrible things happen in their lives. Truly awful things that made them doubt themselves." He rested a scratchy palm against her cheek. The gesture was so tender and paternal that she had to fight back tears. "You know, the staff talks here at the Academy. And many of them gamble, the degenerates. You were everyone's choice for first dismissal. Including me. I lost a week's pay on you." He patted her cheek and smiled down at her. "But you have fought and you have scraped and you have committed in a way that very few can. No one in any company has come as far as you have this year. No one. There's a princess in you, Evie, and a cracking good one. You've simply got to allow yourself the chance to be great."

He began to pack away sewing supplies into wooden tubs. "Surviving the Academy only becomes more difficult next year. If you're planning to be here through the end, there is one thing you must absolutely understand. No victim has ever graduated from this Academy."

She studied his bulbous back as he shuffled to the storeroom, letting his words linger.

"You are not a victim in this world unless you choose to be. And if that's your choice, then you'll never be more than a frightened girl lost in the woods."

He paused in the doorway, rubbing his back with the heel of his hand.

"But the nature of choices is that there is always another." And a great, mischievous smile crawled across his face.

19

EVIE SHIFTED from one foot to the other. The glimpses she caught inside the Piper of Hamelin Ballroom showed warm firelight and flashes of lustrous gowns. Music and happy chatter poured into the antechamber where she now waited. Only one couple stood before her, but the knight's shoulders were so broad, the princess's gown so billowing, she couldn't see much.

"Please," she said to the footman standing tall and stiff in the doorway. "I really don't need an introduction—"

"Never been to a proper ball, have you? Everyone gets introduced." He peered inside as a song ended to polite applause. With a nod to the couple in front of her, he lifted a silver trumpet and blasted a fanfare. "The daughter to King Pinzberg and Queen Fennels of the Kingdom of Stonearch Common, Her Royal Highness the Princess Elisabeth, escorted by the son to King Roland and Queen Schnoor of the Kingdom of Horn o' the Ram, the Most Honorable Sir Alten!"

What a bloody waste of time. No one's even listening. Why can't I just . . .

Her thoughts faded away when the couple stepped forward and she got her first real glimpse of the ballroom. It was magic. Showers of candlelit chandeliers hung from the ceiling, bathing everything in a warm glow. The song of strings wafted down from the minstrels' gallery. Girls in a stunning array of gowns swept across the floor, led by boys in full military regalia. As she watched the tapestry of elegance before her, she thought back to a day from her childhood. It hadn't been a particularly memorable day, but for some reason it was the one that came to mind. Her father and mother had flown away across the mountains to search for new hunting grounds. She and her sister were left alone for several weeks, and before long their stores of smoked fish and deer meat began to dwindle. One day, driven by intense hunger, Evie spent hours crouched in the mud, lifting rocks and looking for scupperworms or bits of lichen to eat. Now, as she waited to be presented to a room full of her peers and teachers, she finally understood what Rumpledshirtsleeves had meant. Perhaps she had come farther than she thought.

"Well, I don't know where your escort is, but it's a shame to him he ain't here," said the footman. "Between you and me, you're the prettiest one to come through yet."

It was dark in the antechamber, but she was sure he could still see her blush. "I think he's inside already. I'm a bit late."

"He ought to have waited," he said with a fatherly wink. "Give that lad a good cuffing when you see him, will you?"

The song seemed endless. All she wanted was to run inside

and find Maggie and Remington and be a part of it all. But she had to remind herself that there were bigger things at play. *The goal is to win,* she reminded herself. *Win here tonight, and there will be no Helpless Maiden.* The thought helped to calm her nerves, but not her excitement.

"It's Cadet Nicolina, is it?" He checked a small piece of parchment from his pocket.

"No," she said with pride. "It's Evie. Cadet Evie."

He blew a harmonic on his horn, and Evie's heart began to thump anew. "The daughter to the late King Callahan and the Queen Dowager Hardcastle of the Kingdom of Väterlich, Her Royal Highness the Princess Evie!"

She breathed in and held it, as though she were diving into the sea, then stepped inside. And now, all the people she had been watching and waiting to join turned to look at her.

She stood beneath the candles in Rumpledshirtsleeves's moonsilk gown, a shimmering star come down from the sky to make all the others look ordinary. It glimmered the blue-white glow of the moon, not bright like a torch, but softly, like a reflection in a still pond. She took a few more steps inside, and even the musicians stopped playing. The fluid fabric slid across her skin like heavy water. Her hair, courtesy of Rumpledshirtsleeves's assistants, rolled across her shoulders in soft waves, baby's breath flowers swirled throughout like a miniature galaxy. When she first put the gown on, she thought back to one of Rumpledshirtsleeves's earliest lessons, when he told the cadets that the design of a gown should highlight the girl inside. She couldn't be sure, but as the fabric fell over her shoulders and swept down her body, the fibers seemed to glow just a bit more brightly than they had on the dress form.

"Evie, you look bloody gorgeous!" said Maggie, dragging Stanischild behind.

"Thanks." She was smiling so much it started to make her self-conscious, but she couldn't stop. "So do you!"

Maggie's gown was dark emerald green, nearing black. Her auburn hair draped loosely over her ears, where it was pinned up in back. "I made Stanischild wait while I adjusted the hem. But it was worth it, wasn't it?"

Stanischild gave a slight nod, barely disguising his discomfort. The music began again, and the ball slowly resumed.

"You should have heard the ridiculous introduction they gave me. For him," said Maggie, jerking her head toward Stanischild, "it was titles and land and this and that, but for me they didn't even mention Mum or Dad." She glared at the footman, who didn't notice. "Bloody cretin."

"But that's absurd. Surely we're all the same in here."

"The curse of the common," she said with a shrug. "The musicians are brilliant, though, aren't they, Stanischild?"

He gave a prim smile, and nothing more.

"Is Remington here?"

"I think I saw him this way. Come on."

Maggie took her hand and led her through the ballroom, with Stanischild trailing behind. Hushed comments passed between the other competitors, but they weren't the vicious, needling remarks from the start of term; they were admiration and surprise.

"You'd better get started straightaway," said Maggie. "I think the judging has already begun."

Evie glanced up at the balcony that ringed the ballroom. Members of staff, princess and knight alike, sat at small tables observing the proceedings. She even saw Sir Osdorf shaking his head in disgust and making notes on a parchment.

"There he is," said Maggie, dragging Evie up the tiered floor.

He was chatting with another knight cadet. She didn't recognize him at first. He wore a black leather doublet with intricate embroidery and heavy silver braids. A sword hung in a gleaming scabbard from his hip, with matching buttons glinting from navel to neck. He looked sophisticated and rugged, a youthful version of the king he would one day become. He turned and their eyes met.

"Come on, we've got work to do if we're going to beat her in that gown," said Maggie as she led Stanischild onto the floor.

Evie stood alone, smiling, as Remington looked at her. He excused himself from the other knight and started toward her, but she couldn't judge his demeanor. Other than the initial surprise, he didn't seem to have much reaction at all.

"I'm sorry I took so long," she said. "Rumpledshirtsleeves wouldn't let me leave without alterations."

He smiled, then took her hand. "Let's get started, shall we?"

As he led her to the middle of the floor, she couldn't help noticing the deference the other dancers gave her. Complete strangers seemed to have more awareness of her than her own partner. She tried to shuffle the thought away, but there was no denying that his coolness stung.

He turned to face her with a curt smile. "Ready?"

"I suppose so." She inhaled deeply and reminded herself what really mattered about the Grand Ball: *win*.

He took her hand, then placed the other on her hip. As they moved across the floor, Evie's confidence began to slip. She heard the music, felt the pressure from his hand guiding her, but she couldn't concentrate on where she was stepping. His reaction had been so odd. She didn't know what she had expected him to do or say, but she had expected *something*—

"You're fighting my lead," he said. She glanced up at the evaluators, whose faces were as blank as his had been. "What are you doing?" He abruptly stopped just as they were about to bump another couple.

"I'm sorry." *Focus, Evie. Forget about him and win.*

They started off again, slipping into the rhythm of the music. She ignored the vacant look on his face and tried to focus only on the dance. Subtle pressure from his hands told her feet where to go. The music took over her thoughts, then trickled down through her body until it was the strings leading.

Evie and Remington glided across the floor, two bodies moving as one, swept along by music. She remembered back to the stories she had read in Volf's book about Cinderella. *This must be how she felt, dancing with her prince at the ball. She didn't belong there, either, yet she charmed him with her grace and elegance. She* didn't belong there, either, yet she somehow made it through. *She didn't belong there, either . . . She didn't belong there . . . She didn't belong—*

"Ah!" grunted Remington. He doubled over, clutching his knee.

"I'm sorry!" She looked up at the evaluators, mortified. Other dancers paused to gape.

"If you're going to tread on my foot, at least try to make it the one that wasn't savaged by wolves, all right?"

"I'm sorry, Remington, really."

"It's fine." He straightened his uniform, grimacing through the pain. "Let's keep going. But follow my lead, will you?"

He took her hand and they started off again. Her mind raced. Was he angry? Did the evaluators notice? Would it cost them the Grand Ball? Across the room, the footman announced the arrival of another pair of latecomers—

Steel clashed as Remington's scabbard hit another cadet's. "What's the matter with you?" he hissed as he pushed Evie back.

"I'm sorry, I think I'm just a bit nervous."

He offered an apologetic nod to the young man he had just bumped. "Any more mistakes like that and we've got no chance, do you understand?"

She nodded, though a small burst of anger flickered through her stomach. Every misstep so far had been hers, but she still didn't care for his condescending tone. *Perhaps he's just nervous, too.*

He stepped into the music and she stepped another way. He

270

tumbled across her leg and landed in a pile on the floor. The others cleared a circle around them.

"Right, I've not come here to be made a fool." He scrambled to his feet and limped off through the sea of cadets, leaving her alone in the middle of the floor. Gradually, the other couples started to dance again. She wanted to turn back time, to try to correct a night that had started so right and then gone so horribly wrong. But through her humiliation, that glimmer of anger returned. He had left her. Without any consideration of how she felt, he had left her. She pushed through the crowd, lifting the moonsilk from the floor as she descended the tiers.

"All right, Evie?" said Maggie, but she had no intention of stopping. She charged past the footman and through the antechamber, across the crimson silk rug that ran out the door, and down the stairs outside. Huge, luminous orbs hung from the willow trees, with torches flanking the doors. Crickets chirped and frogs croaked from somewhere in the darkness. Remington hobbled across the courtyard, then stopped when he heard her heels on the stone.

"What is it, do you want to throw me into a tree or something?"

"What's the matter with you? Are you still obsessing about that dragon you killed, because I've told you it doesn't matter!"

"I don't appreciate being made a fool. I would've quite liked to have won this Grand Ball, but you saw to that, didn't you?"

"You may have liked to win the Grand Ball, but I *needed* to,"

271

she said. "It doesn't matter to you, with your family influence and fame and all the rest, but this was my best chance to make it back next year."

"Well, perhaps you shouldn't have slung your partner to the ground, then."

She shook her head in disbelief. *How—when—did this all go so wrong?* Then, without another word, she turned away and started to walk toward the barracks.

"Did you kiss Forbes?"

She stopped at the edge of the courtyard, where the torch-light faded to night.

"Answer me."

"Did I *what*?"

"That girl, Malora's friend, she saw you kiss him. In the Infirmary."

"What, at the beginning of term? *He* kissed *me*! And just before that he had a snout and hooves!"

Remington opened his mouth to retort, but her response caught him completely off guard.

"He'd just gone from a pig to a human and he thought I had something to do with it, so he kissed me. And what bloody difference does it make if I did kiss him, and why in the world are you listening to Malora and her friends about anything?"

He took a step toward her, remorse in his eyes. "I . . . I didn't . . ."

"Is *that* what this is all about? Bloody hell, at least feeling guilty about killing a dragon made sense!" So Malora had failed to keep her from the ball by destroying her gown, but she had still kept her from winning with a stupid piece of gossip.

"I didn't believe her straightaway," he said, "but it just kept niggling at me. I suppose I . . . Well, I suppose I was jealous of Forbes." He sighed. "You have no idea how painful that is to say."

"Malora," she said, shaking her head ruefully. "Your best mate Malora was the one who tried to kill us that night, did you know that?"

"*What?*"

"She let the wolves into the bog. Your other best mate Forbes told me. She went to him because she wanted some sort of revenge against us." Her eyes met his. "Because she was *jealous.*"

Remington chuckled dryly. "So this is what it feels like to be a fool."

"Why couldn't you have just said something instead of acting like a buffoon?"

"I don't know." His voice, his entire demeanor, had softened now that he knew the truth. "I'm sorry."

He wrapped his arms around her, but it offered no comfort. She wanted more than a simple embrace. She wanted that moment of romantic magic that so many princesses of the past had experienced. The moment promised by the dragon's blood and that night in the bog. She wanted to be kissed, to be lifted up and away into the sky where nothing of the dark, cruel world existed.

"Let's go back inside. Perhaps it's not too late—"

"Yes it is," she said. A gust of wind blew up the hill from the Dortchen Wild, chilling them both. "Yes it is."

They did go back inside, and they tried their best to salvage the night, but the music had lost its mirth. They held each other closer than before, but nothing could warm the chill around Evie's heart, put there by her stepsister. All around them cadets laughed and smiled. Others sweated and focused intently, trying to earn final favor with the judges. It was almost as if Evie and Remington weren't there at all.

They separated in the rush of bodies when the footman announced that the results of the ball would be read. While everyone gathered around Princess Leonore to see who took the prize, Evie drifted off to the side. Her moonsilk gown seemed a bit dimmer now.

"The winners of this year's Grand Ball competition, and the very first members of next year's second class . . . *Princess Cadet Magdalena and Knight Cadet Stanischild!* Congratulations!"

For a moment, true joy broke through the melancholy. Cadets applauded and hooted as Maggie and Stanischild stepped forward from the crowd. Tears of disbelief streamed from Maggie's eyes. Evie smiled and applauded, knowing how happy her friend must have felt at that moment. The musicians started up once again, and everyone formed a circle to watch as Maggie got her fairy tale moment. On this night, at least, she really was a princess.

Evie glanced across the ballroom and found Remington. In his eyes she saw a stark reminder that this magical evening couldn't last forever, and that there were dark things waiting in the night that would still need to be faced.

The next few weeks sped past in a blur of inkwells, parchments, endurance tests, and intensive evaluations as the term wound to a close. More and more girls heard the dreaded news that they had been discharged. Evie felt profound sympathy for them. To have made it this far only to be sent away without even getting to attempt the final challenge . . . It must have been gutting. The Fairy Drillsergeant had made vague hints that the Helpless Maiden would take place beyond the wall, but other than that chilling piece of information, the cadets knew nothing more about what to expect.

At meals, Evie found the knotted bench even more uncomfortable than usual. Remington was always watching, but rather than provide solace, it only made her feel the danger of the unknown that much more acutely. Malora, on the other hand, seemed to have recovered nicely from whatever had ailed her. She laughed with Kelbra and scowled with Sage, her eyes periodically falling on Evie with empty coldness.

Finally, when written exams had been completed and final designs submitted for Rumpledshirtsleeves's evaluation, Princess Hazelbranch gathered the cadets together. Night had fallen early, it seemed, and the torches had already been lit. The remaining cadets of Ironbone Company were but a fraction of the number that had once filled the barracks. And after tomorrow, they would be even fewer.

"You must all try to get some sleep," she said. "I spent the night before my Helpless Maiden awake in the dark, running through every eventuality. By the time my fairy drillsergeant called us together, I was bone-weary and my mind was slush. It's a miracle I even finished."

Demetra glanced over at Evie. She looked as nervous as Evie felt.

"We've said farewell to many friends over the course of this year. The bunks next to you now go empty each night. But there's a reason yours does not. You have been tested and monitored this year, probably more closely than you might realize. And there is a reason each of you is still here." Her lips tightened as she looked over her cadets. "I've stood where you now stand. I know the unbearable torment of not knowing what to expect. But I also know, because I've done it, what it takes to survive. Courage. Compassion. Kindness. Discipline. So when you're lying in your bunks tonight, remember to let tomorrow happen tomorrow."

Evie climbed beneath her quilt and coverlet, worried that she wouldn't be able to heed Princess Hazelbranch's advice. Instead, she fell almost immediately into a deep sleep. And her dreams were filled with clouds and smoke.

"THE HOUR IS UPON US, LADIES!"

Evie leapt from her bunk at the sound of the Fairy Drill-sergeant's voice. She was wobbly, her mind not yet awake. An intense rumble thundered outside on Hansel's Green. *What in the world is that?*

Inside, girls scrambled into their uniforms, ran for the latrine, or snapped the blankets back over their bunks. The cold reality of the morning quickly set in, and it filled Evie with dread.

"TWO MINUTES! TWO MINUTES TO THE FIELD!"

Evie slipped her uniform over her head. *This could quite easily be the last time I wear it.* She tied the trimmed white belt loosely around her waist and straightened her sleeves, but it somehow felt unfinished. Running her hands down the deep blue linen, she couldn't think of anything she had forgotten. Malora, Kelbra, and Sage had already finished their preparations and were heading for the door. She had to move quickly. Inside her footlocker, she found the dragon scale necklace, and, pressed into that, the portrait of her stepfather. She put her lips to the canvas. *You'll come with me,* she thought, slipping it around her neck. In the corner of her footlocker, she noticed the Pennyroyal Academy compact she had gotten from Rumpledshirtsleeves on the first day of term. She picked up the cool silver clamshell and slid it inside her dress. *It's better than an empty pocket.*

"Ready, Demetra?" she said.

"Nearly."

Maggie stepped toward Evie. She looked like she wanted to say something, but didn't know how.

"All right, Maggie?"

She ran her hand absently across Evie's bunk. "I just . . . I have to say that what a princess does, it's important to me." She looked up and met her friend's eyes. "And it means a lot that it's important to you, too."

"Of course," said Evie, trying to understand what Maggie was really saying. "Are you all right?"

Her eyes went to the floor and her cheeks flushed red. "I just don't want you to leave me because you're a princess of the blood now."

"Are you mad?"

"I've got no one back home. Sevigny is so far removed from the rest of the world that nobody cares about anything but Sevigny. They all laugh at me because I read princess stories. They laughed when I came here as well. My dad, my own dad, asked why I would want to leave paradise to go fight someone else's poxy war."

"ONE MINUTE, CADETS!"

"Maggie . . ."

"I'm completely alone there, Evie. I can't be alone here, as well."

Evie took her hands. "As long as my blood flows, royal or not, you'll never be alone. I promise." She embraced Maggie, who smiled sheepishly. "See you at supper, all right? Save us some pudding."

"No," said Maggie. "No . . . I'm going with you."

"Why would you do that?"

"Because I came to the Academy to be a princess, not to sit round here all day like I'm better than everyone else." The resolve in her eyes told Evie there would be no talking her out of it.

"Are you sure?"

Maggie gave her a grim nod.

"All right, then. Let's go." Maggie quickly got herself together and they hustled for the exit with Demetra, the final three cadets to leave the barracks.

Outside, the sky was a symphony of swooping curves of black. The clouds seemed closer to the earth, fast-moving billows that looked like open mouths trying to howl a warning.

The girls followed another cadet around the final barracks and discovered the source of the incredible noise. There, in the middle of Hansel's Green, sat two enormous dragonflies, each as big as the Dining Hall. Their massive, transparent wings battered the air so fast it sounded like a thousand horses running at once. Each had a woven basket hanging from its middle.

Evie, Maggie, and Demetra joined the ranks of blue. All across the field, the rest of the third-class cadets stood in neat rows by company color. Evie felt a twinge of pride when she saw them all in formation. So many she had never met and likely never would, yet these were her sisters. Sisters of the Shield, just as the Fairy Drillsergeant had said when they left Marburg for the Academy all those months ago.

Now, as the Fairy Drillsergeant floated before them once more, her shimmering dust was blown nearly horizontal by the twin winds of the dragonflies' wings and the violent sky. She had to shout to be heard above the roar.

"One of the most common features of fairy tales is a girl lost in the woods. Today, you're that girl."

Evie flinched. The previous two times she had been lost in the woods, she was nearly killed by witches.

"These are giantsclub dragonflies. They will take us where we need to go."

Other companies began to fall out, running doubled over against the force of the wind as they boarded the baskets. The Fairy Drillsergeant floated down the line, casting a hard glare over her girls. *"All the great princesses have had to survive crossing through enchanted forests. Every single one. This is your chance to join them."*

Evie's stomach churned like the clouds above. She glanced at Demetra and saw her wipe sweat from her forehead. It was bitter cold, windy as a year of Marches, but the elements were powerless against fear.

"To complete the Helpless Maiden, you must do only one thing: make it back to the Academy by nightfall! Use your training, use your intuition, use your mother's third husband . . . I don't care, as long as you're here for supper. Do you understand?"

"Yes, Fairy Drillsergeant!" Evie could barely hear her own voice above the rumble.

"The only thing you may not do is work together. This is an individual challenge, and you must complete it as such. Now, we have staff positioned all throughout the forest for your protection, but make no mistake: these are live woods! There are witches and wolves and perhaps even the odd giant roaming about. You've got to trust your training!"

A blast of wind pounded the Green, scattering the Fairy Drillsergeant's dust into the black sky. She continued her slow patrol, looking each cadet in the eye.

"Today we find out who you really are. What you're really made of." Her voice had nearly gone, but somehow she rasped on. "You girls make me very proud to do what I do . . ."

She trailed off and turned her back to them. Evie and Maggie exchanged a confused look. When she finally faced them again, she wiped a tear from her eye.

"What are you made of, ladies?"

"Courage. Compassion. Kindness. Discipline," they shouted as one.

"Then get out there and BE PRINCESSES!"

The girls broke ranks and sprinted for the dragonfly baskets. As Evie glanced up at a translucent wing, she thought that the majestic creatures really did look like giants' clubs, with their long, ridged tails and bulbous black bodies. She piled into one of the baskets, already laden with princesses, and realized she had lost track of her friends. The girl next to her, a doe-eyed cadet in red, gave her a meaningful nod. She had never seen the girl before, but knew what it meant and gave her one in return. Someone tugged at her other arm; Basil, crouching next to her, held his ears against the thunder. She motioned for him to grab the edge of the basket next to her. As they waited to lift off, she scanned the faces onboard. One stared back. With an eyebrow slightly raised, Malora smiled. Her velvety confidence had returned.

Shrieks of panic from the other basket pierced the steady drum of wings as the giantsclub lifted off the Green. Evie watched, squinting from the dirt and grass flying through the air. The bottom of the basket sagged dangerously under the weight of its passengers. She clenched her jaw, certain it was about to break open and spill everyone to the ground. Higher and higher it rose until she could no longer see it behind the slick, black body of her own dragonfly.

Suddenly, the ground fell away beneath her as they began to lift off. She clutched the edge, her heart lodged in her throat. Cadets screamed and tumbled to the middle of the basket. The soaring spires of the Academy, the magnificent towers and imposing walls, all fell away as they lifted higher and higher into the sky. Wisps of frozen clouds began to lick at the giantsclub as it swooped over the plain, then across the wall and into the sea of trees. From above, the endless hills and valleys of the forest looked insurmountable. Evie turned away from the biting wind just in time to see the faint outline of the Queen's Tower disappear behind a wall of cold green pines.

No one spoke during the journey across the forest. Evie kept one eye on the clouds above and one on the relentless waves of green below. She snuck the occasional glance at the others in her basket. Some were familiar, either Ironbone girls or cadets she had noticed in the Dining Hall or around campus. Others she had never seen before. But in each of them, she recognized the depth of intensity behind the eyes. The grim pursing of the lips. The fear of the task ahead.

Finally, after an eternity in the air, the giantsclubs began to descend, skimming the canopy of pine spikes. They dipped into a clearing of dead stumps and marshland. The baskets smashed to the ground with a violent thud.

The girls filed off one after the other, running in a crouch from the deafening blast of the wings. Evie followed Basil, who had spotted Maggie and Demetra. They both looked terrified.

"PRINCESSES OF THE SHIELD!" called the Fairy Drillsergeant. Her voice had nearly gone, but everyone still heard her. *"MOVE OUT!"*

The two great insects began to rise, ferrying the commanding officers back to the Academy. As they disappeared across the treetops, an overwhelming silence settled in. The cadets were well and truly alone, lost in the woods, and had only until nightfall to find their way back. They began to disperse into the trees. Evie and her friends looked at one another, lingering as long as they could before they had to go their separate ways.

"You're all princesses," Evie said, "each of you. And I know we can do this." She grimaced and glanced at Basil. He raised a hand to cut her off.

"It's fine. I'm a princess."

She smiled. "Just remember, bravely ventured is half won. I'll see you back at the Academy."

Maggie nodded, set her jaw, and ran for the trees. Then Basil went, and then Demetra. Evie stood alone in the clearing as the final flashes of color disappeared into the endless murky green. She closed her emerald eyes and stilled her breathing, letting the icy breeze wash over her. And when she opened them again, she knew exactly which way to go.

She tromped through the marsh sludge until she reached solid ground, and by then the muscles in her thighs were already burning. With one deep breath, she stepped beneath the dark canopy of the Dortchen Wild.

The air felt colder under the trees, thinner and more claustrophobic. The winds were reduced to the shivering whisper of leaves and needles overhead. Everything else seemed unnaturally silent. She read the horizon, searched the shadows of every cracked red trunk for . . . *anything.* An hour passed this way, with unbearable tension each time a gust rattled the canopy. The terrain was unyielding, rising and falling over cliffs and streams and ancient rock slides. Trees groaned lethargically in the wind, but none attacked. Another hour passed, and the silences became nearly as frightening. She tried to remain vigilant, to take each step with as much caution as the last, but the endless pillars of wood gradually became hypnotic. She paused at a deadfall and realized she had been going for some time without thinking.

I am never safe until I'm back behind that wall, she tried to remind herself. *And if I'm still in this forest by nightfall—*

Something snapped in the distance. A broken branch. She wheeled, boring her eyes into the mist hanging just off the forest floor. There was nothing there, yet she stood still as a statue for half a minute. Then half a minute more. Nothing moved, not even a falling leaf. Still, she had the chilling sensation that there was *something there.*

Tap tap tap . . . Darts of rain began to pierce the canopy. She hadn't realized how distinctly her sapphire dress announced itself until she was in the drab gray of a forest shower.

Another snap. Then a run of them, like twenty big boughs breaking at once. Something moved in the corner of her eye, a fleeting glimpse, black and airy. She ran, vaulting a bulbous tree root, and sprinted through the forest. Even now, with something undoubtedly out there, Evie noticed that her flight was urgent, but not panicked.

I am not the same person I once was.

A cackle tore through the forest, sharp and cold, a laugh to chill the blood. It bounced off the hillside and the trees and the rocks until she couldn't tell where it had come from. She tore through a patch of bramble and raced up a hill of tightly packed larches. The higher she went, the slower it got. *Push, Evie, push!* As she finally struggled over the top, she noticed a faint patch of blue in one of the trees. She jumped behind a pine and peered out into the murk.

It was Maggie.

Maggie held up two fingers and pointed into the trees, there and there. Basil and Demetra each had vantage points of other parts of the hill. Basil pointed to his eyes, then a specific stand of larches. *She's in there*, thought Evie with a shudder.

She took a few quick breaths and broke for a mossy stump that would provide better cover. The ferns slashed at her, but she managed to leap the stump and duck down behind it. Within moments, Demetra and Basil joined her.

"She's about two hundred yards that way," whispered Basil.

"I saw her, too," said Demetra. "What do we do?"

"Right, let me think," said Evie. A ferocious crackling sound zippered through the trees.

"*LOOK OUT!*" Demetra threw Evie to the ground as a stream of spiraling liquid splattered against the stump. Some of it splashed onto Demetra, who yelped and fell back. Her entire body began to shudder.

"Demetra!" shouted Basil.

Maggie raced over, and her eyes went wide. "Come on, let's get out of here!" She grabbed Demetra's arms and Basil took her legs. They hauled her through the trees to a massive black stone jutting high into the sky. Evie trailed behind, keeping watch. They laid her down at the base of the stone. Her eyes were open, staring off at some unseen horror.

"Oh, Demetra . . ." said Evie.

"Where's the bloody staff?" shouted Basil. "This isn't supposed to happen!"

Maggie tore open the seam near the point of contact. Bright blue spots marred Demetra's skin, fading to gray around the edges.

"It's an iceflesh spell," said Maggie. Evie and Basil looked at her in confusion. "I read ahead for next year."

"Grab that branch. I'll not let her freeze to death," said Basil. He and Evie lashed together a crude stretcher from branches and vines while Maggie watched the shadows for the witch. Once they had loaded her on, he took the front and Maggie took the back.

"Good luck," said Evie.

"What do you mean? You can't—"

"We'll never make it back with a witch on us. I'll be all right."

Maggie's head shook slowly from side to side. Her mouth was open, but no words came out.

"Come on, we've got to go!" said Basil.

"Be careful," said Maggie. Evie nodded, and her friends moved out.

Once they were gone, she assessed her environment and her options. The witch had gone silent. She could still be lurking or she might have followed the others, which would be disastrous. There was no obvious cover anywhere, just an endless fortress of ancient wood. She needed some sort of advantage.

A demonic cackle rang out, and her options were instantly reduced to one: escape.

The jagged black stone loomed above. She scrambled up the side with the climbing techniques the dragons had taught her and moved swiftly to the top. The view wasn't as vast as she'd hoped, but there was something out there amidst the pale green spikes of the treetops. Something that at once gave her hope and made her blood run cold with fear. Something that was entirely out of place in the middle of the forest, and yet had been waiting there centuries for this moment to arrive.

A crumbling tower.

21

THE GRANITE TOWER sprouted from a muddy knoll, thick
and draped in star-leafed ivy. The battlement crowning the
octagonal walls, well over seventy feet above, was badly de-
teriorated. Great hunks of stone lay strewn across the forest
bed next to moss-filled craters. Twisted, leafy vines reached
through cracks in the mortar as the forest slowly reclaimed
what man had built.

Black magic crackled from the trees. Evie dove, rolling behind one of the broken stones. Behind her, the dark spell splattered against the earth. She sprinted through the tower's arch
and took the spiral stairs three at a time, nearly choking on the
moldy air in the shaft. At the top, dim daylight awaited. She
scanned the tower roof for somewhere to hide. Ivy curled over
the battlement like spider's legs. One entire corner of the roof
had fallen away, leaving a yawning hole where a rogue pine tree
poked out. Huge bricks of granite lay scattered across the roof,
green with moss and lichens. Everything was crumbling.

She spotted a section of wall that had tumbled into a natural arch and ran for it. But before she could climb inside, a voice came, soft and calm.

"Hello, Nicolina."

She wheeled to find Countess Hardcastle standing near the top of the stairs. "Mother! We've got to hide, there's a witch out there—"

"This tower is all that remains of Pinewall." She looked out over a forest being swallowed by fog. "The keeps, the castle . . . all gone, returned to the earth."

"What?"

"A once mighty kingdom reduced to a single heap of stone."

Evie didn't move. Her eyes tracked Hardcastle as she ran an elegant hand along the ruins of the battlement.

"Things crumble when witches come. It's nicer this way, don't you think? Peaceful . . . quiet . . . lifeless."

And you're not what you seemed to be, either. "The staff are out there. They're watching."

"Are they? Or is it, perhaps, a Pennyroyal benefactor, a trusted friend of Princess Beatrice herself, who is looking after this part of the forest?"

Evie's heart began to race. No help would be coming. Her eyes darted across the roof looking for any sort of advantage.

"I must say, Nicolina, I never expected this. I offered you land, title, family, all the gold you could ever want. And you threw it right back in my face. We could have avoided all of this so easily."

"My name is Evie."

Hardcastle studied her, incredulous. "You really don't know who you are. And that bloody pie was my first attempt at a memory curse. It seems I have a gift."

The wind howled, throwing rain like darts of ice.

"How did you manage to stay alive that day? I watched you both eat the pie. Sent you off to such an active hunting ground, where your father died just as he was meant to. And yet . . . here you are."

"*Why?*" Nausea and panic swirled inside her, the same uncoiling sensation in her stomach that she had had on Hardcastle's terrace when she learned the truth about her family. And now that truth seemed to be crumbling as well.

"Malora needed royal blood to get into the Academy. Your royal blood."

Evie blinked away the rain, struggling to understand. "King Callahan was . . . *my* father?"

Hardcastle paced, edging ever so slightly toward Evie, like a snake approaching a frog. Something about her had changed. The features that had always seemed so rigid and smooth, the subtle smile that contained so many secrets, had begun to slacken. She looked haggard, as though her body itself were deteriorating.

"And everything I had so carefully planned was rendered meaningless when the Queen decided to throw out centuries of tradition and allow the lowborn to enlist."

"Malora is *your* daughter. You married my father so you

could pass her off as me. As the daughter of the king. It was the only way to get her into the Academy—"

"Mother?" Malora stepped onto the rooftop, her slate eyes sharp and edgy. "What's going on?"

"Malora! What are you doing here?"

"I don't know . . . Something told me to come . . ." Her graceful features curled into a mask of fear. *"What's going on?"*

"She's a witch—"

"*SHUT UP!*" roared Hardcastle. Her pale skin mottled gray, a flash of the horror that lay beneath her facade. Evie dove behind a stone and slowly peered out.

"What's she talking about?" howled Malora. "Mother, why would she say that?"

She doesn't know, Evie realized. *She doesn't know what she is.*

"I WANT TO KNOW WHAT'S GOING ON!"

"Malora, please—"

"*ARE YOU A WITCH?*"

"Yes, of course, and so are you!"

Malora let out a forlorn wail. It echoed through the rain like the last howl of a dog, alone and dying.

"This was to be our year, my darling! All our careful planning come to bloom . . . but then *she* turned up. And even my wolves couldn't kill her."

Evie clutched the dragon scale so tightly her knuckles went white. It was Hardcastle, not Malora, who had tried to kill her and Remington that night. Malora was guilty of nothing more than being born badly.

"The Sisters . . . Calivigne . . . all of us have been watching you since you first crawled out of the cauldron. Don't you see? You are our great hope! It's been inside you all along, waiting to come out!"

Malora reeled in agony. She couldn't catch her breath, and her skin had gone ghostly white.

"You will be the ultimate warrior of fear trained as the ultimate warrior of love! A hero with a heart as black as night! *A Princess-Witch!*"

Malora's devastation was so pure and raw that Evie's heart burned for her. Nothing that had happened—not the fight with Anisette, not the destruction of the gown, not even the wolf attack—was Malora's fault. She was a witch who had been tricked into thinking she would be a princess, and the result was a girl who never felt comfortable in her own skin. Where she knew she should have felt kindness and compassion, she found only anger and confusion and turmoil.

She lurched free of her mother's hands and staggered back against the battlement. Evie saw what was happening and bolted from her cover. She threw a shoulder into Hardcastle, knocking her over a pile of stones, then lunged for Malora just as she pitched back over the wall.

Her fingers locked around her sister's hand, and the weight jerked her into the stone. She tried to reach down with her other hand, but if she let go of the wall they would both fall. Under the relentless rain, Malora was only moments away from plummeting to her death.

"Please . . . just let me go . . ." She dangled limply from Evie's hand, the rind left rotting after the fruit has been eaten. There was nothing left in her eyes. No fight, no life, no hope.

"Malora, listen . . . I spent my whole life believing I was something I'm not. Never feeling good enough. Never understanding why. I know what you're going through because that's exactly what she did to you."

Malora's delicate hand slipped another inch, down to the knuckles. Tears streamed from her eyes. "It's not fair . . ."

Evie reached for a tangle of vine growing up from a crack in the stone. She tore some loose and dropped it over the side.

"Take the ivy! TAKE IT NOW—"

And her hand was empty. Malora flailed for the vine as she plunged down the tower. She grabbed a fistful and slammed into the stone, then began to swing wildly. The tender green vine sawed against the granite.

"Hold on!" Evie pulled the ivy up hand over hand, carefully, before it could snap. Something moved at the edge of her vision. She turned to see . . .

A witch. It was Hardcastle, but with none of her cold elegance. The witch's bones were sharper, and covered in a fine film of pale, blistered skin. Her yellow eyes were scribbled with blood vessels. A small bloom of black smoke swirled in front of her chest.

"If you do this, you'll kill her, too. Not just me," said Evie.

"I have my orders as well. Calivigne suspects you to be the Warrior Princess. And you are to die."

Evie looked down at Malora, dangling like prey in a net. Her heart ached for the girl who had once been both her enemy and her sister. Tears began to fall, not for her own death, but for the death of the girl hanging from the wall, so alone and shattered apart inside.

"Then do it. I won't let her go."

Hardcastle's arms, bone-thin and streaked with veins, rose. Her lips cracked open into a sinister grin as her black magic began to billow and churn. Suddenly, the spell blasted forth, tearing the air apart with a deafening ripple . . .

But nothing happened. Evie opened her eyes and saw tendrils of smoky black magic splashing away, as though a wall stood between them that neither could see. *It's like a shield protecting me . . . but not only me—Malora as well. It is compassion.*

"*I won't let you hurt her anymore!*" shouted Evie. She pulled up the vine until Malora's hand appeared in the crenel. Hardcastle shrieked in frustration as her stream of black magic suddenly splattered to the floor.

"How dare you use my own daughter against me!"

Evie hauled Malora onto the roof and they both collapsed against the wall. She pushed the long black hair out of her stepsister's face. "Malora . . ."

"Don't touch me!" She shoved Evie away and sprang to her feet, then raced into the mouth of the staircase and disappeared down the tower.

"So," said Hardcastle, "found our compassion, have we? No matter. You're still the same coward you were as a child . . ."

She trailed off as a long creak sounded deep in the forest, followed by the sudden snap of wood. Ancient trees slammed to the earth with dull explosions, each louder and closer than the last. Evie scrambled behind a block of stone just as a colossal talonwood pine pounded into the tower, knocking Hardcastle onto her back. She clung to her stone, worried that the impact of the falling tree might finally topple the last remnant of Pinewall. As the talonwood crashed to the ground, something out there among the treetops caught her eye. The white-green head of a dragon.

"Father . . ." He was alive. After all this time, alive.

Hardcastle didn't move. Her yellow eyes darted between the dragon's head looming over the battlement and Evie, who had emerged from behind the stone.

"Father . . ." She stepped toward him. "But you're dead . . ."

"How can I explain what's happened?" growled the dragon. "What I've done?" Even as rain streamed down his scales, his voice remained a scorched rumble. "It was I who killed the king that day, but only to protect my daughter from his blade. As he sought to protect you from me."

Evie's knees quaked as she neared the wall. This was her father, of that there could be no doubt. Still, something wasn't right. *I don't care,* she thought. *I don't care, because he's here and I thought I'd never see him again.*

"When your sister brought you back to the cave . . . I've never felt such guilt. I made a vow to your father, the man who loved his daughter as much as I loved mine, that I'd look after you as best I could."

Go to him, she thought, but still she didn't move. *Go to your father.* Her hands began to tremble uncontrollably. Her mind and heart knew what they wanted, but some mysterious instinct kept her away.

"Come, my daughter. Come back to your home."

Ghostly words trickled up from the hidden recesses of Evie's memory in the soft voice of Princess Hazelbranch: *"Mirrors show what our eyes can't see. Mirrors reveal the truth."*

Her hand shot to her waist, to the small lump in the pocket of her dress. She fished out the Pennyroyal compact and clicked open the lid. With shaking fingers, she angled the mirror toward her father . . .

And he wasn't there. Nor was the stone floor stretching out to meet him. She began to sob, crushed by the awful truth of her father's return. He was nothing more than a witch's trick. One step more and she would plunge off the side of the tower to her death.

"I'm sorry, Father . . . I know you're not real, but I believe your words are."

His eyes softened with heartache and love, only for a moment, and then he disintegrated into the roiling sky like volcanic ash.

"You've been studying," came Hardcastle's silky voice. Evie wheeled to see her floating above the stone, black smoke wafting once again. "But a student is not a princess. Nor a warrior."

Evie staggered against the wall as panic shot up from her stomach. She stared into the depths of Hardcastle's fluttering black spell. Without Malora there, her fear choked away her compassion like weeds in a garden. And with nothing else to protect her, no courage to be found, she had only the paralyzing knowledge that she would now die.

"Evie!" Remington emerged onto the roof, his steel drawn. He had come to save her. But a moment after having that thought, the horrible dragon's blood vision flashed into her mind. The crumbling tower. The rain. The witch floating just off the ground. The anguish on his face as he was turned to stone . . .

"GO BACK! GO BACK!" she screamed.

He charged at Hardcastle, sword raised. The air cleaved with a horrendous crackle as a black lance of liquid magic slammed into Remington's chest.

"NO!"

His doublet bubbled away where the magic struck him, and his face broke into a silent scream. Every muscle in his body clenched as tight as stone. At his chest, the magic began to create a patch of slate gray on his skin.

"REMINGTON!"

"And after I've done him, I'll have your heart," said Hardcastle with a sneer.

A cackle rose from the sodden forest below. Hardcastle stopped her attack, and Remington dropped to the floor. The laughter came again, a haunted sound filled with anguish and malice.

"Who's there?" called Hardcastle. And an image of perfect horror floated gently across the battlement. It was Malora, eyes glowing yellow, a ghoulish shell of what she had once been. Her flawless ivory skin now shriveled tight against her skull, and her lustrous black hair flapped in the wind like a raven's wing.

"My darling . . . you're beautiful!"

Malora fixed her eyes, the bloody yellow of a fertilized yolk, squarely on her stepsister, and the sensation took Evie's breath away. Fear iced over her heart as Malora peered inside of her.

"This is what has been in you all along!" said Hardcastle. "This is who you were always meant to be!"

Malora still didn't speak. Her lips spread into a smile so terrifying it drove Evie to her knees.

"Go ahead, my sweet daughter. Let them be your first."

The tattered blue linen of an Ironbone Company uniform thrashed against Malora's body as a gust of wind swept across the tower. Black smoke began to billow and churn before her chest. She held her arms out as though commanding the furious clouds to do her bidding, and she launched a magic of purest evil.

It slammed into Hardcastle's chest. She soared across the roof and crashed into the battlement.

Evie looked up at Malora, stunned.

"That's the *one time* I'll help you," said the witch. "And it's only because you were kind to me."

Her feet touched the stone and she went to Remington's

motionless body. She knelt next to him, studying the agony on his face, and her lips began to tremble.

"You should have been mine . . ." She glared at Evie with anger and pain. *"He should have been mine!"* She ran her bony fingers tenderly down his cheek. Then, with the devastating realization that her life as she knew it was over, now and forever, she rose and walked calmly to the wall.

Evie ran to Remington. She pressed a finger to his neck and felt the sweet bounce of life. *Still alive . . . He's still alive . . .*

"Thank you, Malora," she called. "Thank you."

Malora stood atop the battlement, a muddle of fury and hatred and sympathy and love. She was beautiful, even in her torment. Even as a witch. "She made me forget everything, but I remember it now. I wasn't ill on your birthday. I was upstairs crying in my bed because she'd locked me in. I wanted to go with you on that picnic and she wouldn't let me." The sisters stared at each other for a moment, neither sure what to say. Then Malora dove from the wall and vanished into the desolation of the enchanted forest.

Evie turned to Hardcastle, who leered back with yellow eyes. The woman she had thought was her mother looked small, a figure to be pitied. When she had left the cave that night, she had known nothing of the world. Now, atop this crumbling tower, she understood the true essence of a witch. A witch was the absence of everything that made a princess special. A witch could create penetrating fear with a glance, could summon darkest magic, could even turn the living flesh of the innocent to stone, but she could never muster what Evie felt building inside her at that very moment.

A witch had no courage.

Flares of light began to pulse from Evie's chest, just as they had when her father's scale sank into the cauldron. She glared at Hardcastle with fierce righteousness, and found that she was no longer alone on that black tower. She stood in a vast, sunwashed meadow of flowing grass and tiny yellow flowers. A figure materialized from the crisp, clear air behind her, a woman in an ethereal violet gown with a lily in her hair. The same princess she had seen the first time she looked into the dragon's blood.

"You are not alone," she said.

"Who are you?"

"I am Princess Middlemiss. And I am always with you. We are all always with you."

A sheet of air glistened behind her, and dozens of others appeared. They were princesses of all ages, all shapes and shades and types. She saw a woman with black hair and sharp blue eyes and knew her instantly as Princess Snow White. There were others she recognized from Volf's books: Blackstone and Rose-Red and Chambéry. The great princesses of the past and present, all standing with her now.

"As long as there is goodness in your heart, you are never alone."

Evie turned back to Hardcastle, and the gray rain fell again. The witch hovered in the air, eyes rolled back into her head, black magic boiling before her. Her arms and legs began to elongate grotesquely, her tattered cloak flapping in the wind.

This was the full nightmare of one of the most wicked of witches, a member of Calivigne's Council of Sisters.

And Evie stood alone beneath her.

"I'm not afraid," she said, her eyes never leaving the witch.

The air erupted and black magic spewed toward her, but shimmering strands of courage flared up to block it. As the magic of a witch battled the magic of a princess, Evie knew that no evil could hurt her.

"*In Calivigne's name, you shall not leave this tower alive!*"

Evie's courage pulsed from her chest like the sun itself. "I am not afraid!"

A ribbon of white lit up Hardcastle's eyes, and that was when Evie saw it, and knew she had won. *Fear.*

Hooves slapped through mud in the distance. A voice came, far off, yet nearing. "Up there! The tower!"

Hardcastle's magic trickled to a stop, her face a mask of rage. "You shall answer to Calivigne for this! She will not allow the Warrior Princess to be born from this place! The Sisters shall have their victory!" With a furious snarl, she leapt over the side and swooped into the fog.

"*Ungh . . .*"

"Remington!" She ran to him, lifting him into her lap. "She's gone. The witch is gone."

He grimaced in pain, then forced a smile. "So I've saved you again."

22

A FOOT DUG into Evie's neck. It pulled on her skin and stabbed into her shoulder, but the desire to win blotted out the pain. She pushed with all she had, shoving the pile of cadets higher.

"Come on, Ironbone!" came a shout from somewhere in the mass.

Her foot slipped, but she held position. Bodies upon bodies pressed down on her, each straining to reach the silver crown resting atop a thin marble column.

"Come on, girls! Surely you can do better than this!" shouted the Fairy Drillsergeant. She circled the pile of muddy cadets with a smile. "You lot on the bottom, is that all you've got left?"

"Almost there!" called Demetra's voice from above.

"None of you are second-class cadets until you've secured that crown!"

"Everyone, on three!" shouted Maggie. "One . . . two . . . THREE!"

Evie closed her eyes and pushed as hard as she could. Her feet slipped away an inch at a time until finally her whole body slammed to the mud and the tower of girls collapsed on top of her. They pulled themselves from the slop, groaning that they'd have to do it all over again.

"I got it!" said Demetra, pulling her arm from the sludge. The crown was clutched in her fingers, mud dripping off of it. The entire company roared with triumph, pulling her to her feet. They danced as one sloppy, stomping, triumphant mess.

"Congratulations, girls!" said the Fairy Drillsergeant, applauding.

At some point, though the cadets were celebrating too much to notice, the thick blanket of clouds broke, and a ray of sunshine shot through.

Later that day, after congratulations and farewells from their individual instructors, the girls of Ironbone Company donned their sapphire dresses and began the long march through campus to the Queen's Tower.

Great arched holes had appeared at the base of the crystal walls, the Imperial Gates opened wide. They passed beneath a colonnade carved with strange, mythical beasts and into the Throne Room. Sunlight flooded the hall through forty massive, dagger-shaped windows, and even more light entered through the walls that supported them. The limestone was partially transparent, somewhere between stone and glass. From the outside, the walls were opaque, but from the inside, Evie could look out at the blue sky stretching off in all directions. Applause rained down from friends and family packed into the double galleries flanking the hall; a second colonnade sat atop each gallery, lined with even more people.

Companies stood in formation across the wide marble floor, princesses on the left and knights on the right. Ironbone filed in behind the copper uniforms of Schlauraffen Company. Evie took her place next to Sage and stood tall. As she waited for the rest of her company to fall in line, she found Anisette waving from the first-tier gallery and couldn't stop herself from smiling. Of all the different things she had experienced since leaving the cave, pride might well have been her favorite.

At the front of the hall, the Pennyroyal staff sat atop tiers of ancient thrones, their wood aged and bare. These were the original furnishings from Princess Pennyroyal's own Throne Room at the Academy's founding. *That's where the great witch fighters sat,* thought Evie, and the sudden moment of perspective sent chills down her arms. And there were her leaders, Hazelbranch and Volf and all the rest. Even Rumpledshirtsleeves, though a troll, was honored with a throne on the dais. He winked at Evie, one velvet-clad leg draped over the other.

The cheers from the galleries began to die away as Corporal Liverwort rose from her throne and crossed to a lectern carved with scenes from fairy stories. She read from a parchment in a stiff, uncomfortable voice.

"Headmistress General, Princess Beatrice, distinguished faculty and staff of Pennyroyal Academy, and honored guests." She glanced at Beatrice, sitting in pride of place atop a huge cherrywood throne, then back to her parchment. "Cadets of the third class, you lot have accomplished something many others could not. You should be quite proud of yourselves, as are the whole of us."

Evie studied the Headmistress, who seemed more interested in a loose thread in the hem of her gown than the proceedings at hand. Something about her demeanor was troubling. "Shouldn't Princess Beatrice be saying this?" she whispered to Sage.

As Liverwort continued with her remarks, Evie tried to force those thoughts from her head. *Beatrice may have trusted Hardcastle, and even been a friend, but she couldn't possibly doubt what happened on that tower . . . could she?* She looked around at her company-mates to try to refocus on the joyousness of the event. But even that led to dark speculation. What might have happened had Malora still been with them? Or worse, if she had made it through all three years and become the Princess-Witch? Had the old hag's prophecy really been referring to Malora all along, or did the Warrior Princess still stand among them?

"In closing, we look forward to seeing you all back here next year. That is all." She folded her parchment and walked back to her throne. All through the hall, including the galleries, people looked at one another in confusion.

"That's it?" said Sage.

The Fairy Drillsergeant's voice rang through the hall. "WELL DONE, CADETS! GO HOME AND GET SOME REST. YOU'LL NEED IT FOR NEXT YEAR!"

Someone in a knight company cheered, and it quickly spread to the entire third class. The ranks dissolved as cadets embraced and congratulated one another. Evie kept her eyes on Beatrice, who remained rooted in her seat. She had no expression, not joy or pride or anything else. She was completely inscrutable.

Eventually, the cadets began to file out, merging with their families in the great sloped courtyard outside the Queen's Tower.

"They put the ceremony in *her* bloody tower and she can't be asked to come down and say hullo?" Evie recognized the voice immediately.

"Anisette!" she said, pulling her into an embrace.

"Well done, Eves. Can't wait to be able to say I knew all these great princesses when."

They walked together back to the Ironbone barracks. Anisette told her all about her life since dismissal. She had been assisting Demetra's sister, Princess Camilla, back at the Blackmarsh, meeting with villagers and country folk to gather information about witch activity in the area.

"It's great fun," she said. "This whole training palaver was never for me, but who knows, maybe someday I can assist Princess Basil."

With Evie's meager possessions stuffed into her knapsack, she and Anisette joined Demetra and Maggie in the arrival area outside Pennyroyal Castle. All around them, cadets and siblings and parents and instructors buzzed about, while horse teams pulled coaches and carriages around the fountain to be loaded.

Demetra gently stroked a white draught horse as it passed by, then she and Evie shared a smile.

"So, back to the cave then, Eves?" said Anisette.

"That's right. I can't wait to sleep on solid rock again!"

"Hiya, girls!" Basil trotted over, twenty-one churlish boys mocking his every move. When he noticed Anisette stifling her laughter, he said, "The brothers. Ignore them."

"Can you handle a whole summer with that lot?" said Evie.

"Reckon so, I've done it before. Somehow." He shook his head, taking it all in one last time. "I still can't bloody well believe we made it." He embraced each of them, enduring a hail of hoots from his brothers. "Listen, I just want to say . . . clearly I never intended to be a princess, right? But as I am, it does me proud to serve alongside you lot."

"Bassie Bassie and his lassies!" shouted one of the brothers, and the rest roared with laughter. He shrugged, then ran off to join them as they moved in a great herd toward their coach.

As the girls chuckled, Evie noticed a peasant couple approaching from Hansel's Green. The man fiddled with his folded, ratty hat.

"Ah, here's Mum and Da. Ready, Demetra?" asked Anisette.

"Whenever you are."

The four friends exchanged hugs and farewells and promises to visit one another in the months before second year began. As Demetra and Anisette turned to go, Evie heard the father say, "It's our sincere honor to welcome you in our humble carriage, Your Serene and Exalted Highness—"

"Oh, shut it, Da, you're so embarrassing."

Evie and Maggie laughed. The joyousness of the day was tinged bittersweet as the group splintered back into the world.

"Is your dad here?" asked Evie.

"You having a laugh? He'd never come this far just to see me home."

Though she said it with a smile, Evie could hear the pain underneath. "Good, then we can ride together." Maggie hugged her once more, and Evie could feel tears on her neck. They were two girls who had both lost their mothers, but in ways that could not have been more different. "Your mum would be so proud, Maggie. I know she would."

Maggie broke the embrace and wiped away her tears. "So would your dad." She sniffled and composed herself, then said, "Oh, I've forgotten that bloody riding hood. Grandmother will kill me. I'll just collect it from the barracks and we're off."

Maggie ran across the Green, leaving Evie to watch her fellow cadets reunite with their loved ones. In the shadow of Castle Marburg, she had stood alone amidst these same people and nearly crumbled under the fear of them. But now she felt a powerful love for humanity, for all the complexity and heartache and joy that being one of its members brought. It was more exhausting than being a dragon, but in many ways more rewarding as well.

Her eyes swept the crowd, taking as much of it as she could into her memory to hold her through the months to come. She found Forbes standing away from the rest, dressed in a shining silver breastplate over a black tunic. He was talking to a man laden in armor and furs. The man had a bushy silver beard curled at the corners of his mouth. Several heavily armored men on horseback waited behind them. She sighed, then started across the courtyard.

"I beg your pardon."

"Ah, it's you," said Forbes with a sneer. "One last fight before you go?"

"I wanted to thank you, actually."

An arrogant smile crept across his face. "In that case, Father, this is Cadet Evie of Ironbone Company. Evie, my father, King Hossenbuhr."

"Ah," said the King with haughty disdain. "The girl from the portrait. *The Princess of Saudade.*" A sudden wave of faintness washed over her. She couldn't move, even as Hossenbuhr said, "I see no one has taught you to bow to a king. Come, boy. We're away."

"I'd like to get my thanks," said Forbes.

The King mounted his destrier, a behemoth of a horse, its face obscured beneath a spiked black faceplate. His glare cut his son dead.

"Perhaps next year," said Forbes, all his confidence suddenly gone. He mounted his horse and the party rode off, leaving Evie staggered.

"I thought he'd never leave."

"Remington!" she said, wheeling around. "Are you all right? I looked everywhere for you!"

"Well, they've had me locked away in the Infirmary. I've been poked and prodded and tested and studied . . ." He untied the laces of his doublet and pulled it apart to reveal a small patch of coarse gray stone in the middle of his chest. He rapped it with his fist to show it was solid. "Built-in shield, I suppose."

Evie ran a finger over the rough stone. *How close you were to death.* "How did you ever find me out there?"

"After the Grand Ball and what you told me about the wolves, I had the most awful feeling about Malora. I couldn't let you go out there alone. Didn't you notice the extra frog in that dragonfly's basket?" Her eyes went wide. "I would have found that tower sooner, but you're much faster than I am."

"Well . . . thank you. I really do owe you my life."

He bowed his head. One of the coaches pulled away from the courtyard with a clopping of hooves. "Well, I suppose I'd best be off." He tightened his doublet and smiled, but it wasn't the easy half grin she was used to. There was an awkward pause, neither of them sure what to say next. "Until next year, I suppose."

He glanced around, but too many people had noticed them together and stopped to watch. *Do it anyway,* she thought. *Do what the vision said you would.* He smiled once more, lips pursed tight, then turned to go. Her heart sank.

"Remington . . ." He faced her and she threw her body into his, clutching him around the neck and pressing her lips to his. His arms slid around her hips and he held her tight. Other cadets stopped and stared and laughed and clapped, but neither of them paid it any mind. They kissed the way a knight and a princess always should.

After many carriages had come and gone, and the crowds had thinned to only a handful of stragglers, Evie and Maggie boarded the final coach, which was nearly empty. They took seats on two benches near the back. Maggie almost immediately started chatting to the few cadets and parents also on the coach, leaving Evie alone with her thoughts. They bounced across the cobblestones and back onto the dirt ruts leading to the edge of the hill. As they passed the towering sculptures of knight and princess, courageous and triumphant, Evie realized that was exactly how she felt at that moment.

Rumpledshirtsleeves stood with Hazelbranch, waving farewells. Evie smiled and waved back as the coach began its descent down the hill. The sun painted the trees at the border of the Dortchen Wild a deep orange. Evie was quite sure she had never seen that particular shade ever before.

As the horse team pulled the coach through the wall and into the trees, she reached into her dress and pulled out the dragon scale. She pried her father's portrait from the concave side and ran a finger, scarred smooth by a witch's brew, across his laughing face. She kissed the rough hatching of the canvas, then kissed the coarse ridges of the scale itself. With a smile, she slipped the portrait back inside the scale and let them both fall gently over her heart.

Acknowledgments

SO MUCH GRATITUDE:

To Mom for taking me to the library.

To Dad for taking me to the movies.

To Brooks for taking me everywhere else.

To Anthony Minghella for giving me an ideal to strive for.

To Yvonne Millar, an excellent psychologist, for helping me with the adolescent mind.

To my exceptional editor, Jennifer Besser, and everyone at G. P. Putnam's Sons.

To Rowan Stocks-Moore for the stunning cover art, and to Ian Wasseluk for many hours spent plotting this world on a map.

To my wonderful literary agent, Alexandra Machinist, and to Mark James for helping me find her.

To my wise and incredibly tasteful film agent, Sally Willcox, and to Bryan Lourd for helping me find her.

To Reese Witherspoon and Bruna Papandrea for being fierce and passionate and the perfect match for this book.

To Kimberly Jaime and Deborah Klein for navigating me through treacherous legal seas.

To Dr. Allan Thexton, a limitless resource for information on castles and medieval arcana and pretty much everything else.

To Tracey Becker, Denise Stewart, Kim Ohanneson, Gemini Adams, Robert Braudt, and the Ron Book Team, the earliest readers.

To all the assistants and editors whom I have not yet met who helped along the way.

And to Lilah, who I hope will approach the world the same way as Evie: with wonder, with strength, and with the knowledge that she is never alone.

ORBIS
TERRARUM
NOTARUM

DRAGONLANDS

GRISELDA'S TEARS

Old Castle Farm

Goldharbor

Fiddlehead
Downs

Callahan
Manor

Western
Kingdoms

Brentano

THE TWO BROTHERS

THORNY RIVER

Dornröschen
Castle

Marburg

Waldeck

Ölenberg

Hundschloss

Pennyroyal Academy

Darmancourt

Ruins of
Pinewall

DORTCHEN WILD

GLASS MOUNTAINS

VALLEY OF GIANTS